About the Author

Following six years in teaching, Colin Croft joined the Royal Ulster Constabulary. In a police career of twenty-five years, he served in some of Northern Ireland's most challenging places, from the cruel sectarian streets in North Belfast to the terrifying, yet beautiful, hills and drum-lins of South Armagh. On leaving the police in 2006, he undertook a number of international policing projects; in the Balkans, training witness protection officers; in Lebanon, working with government and non-government bodies working on police reform; and in Bulgaria, embedding human rights into police structures and processes, to name but a few.

In 2008, he rediscovered his zeal for writing when his mother fell ill, and he composed short stories of family events and holidays to read to her at night.

Dead Man Calling is the fulfillment of a promise that he made to his mother and of a long held desire to write his own crime thriller.

DEAD MAN CALLING

Colin Croft

DEAD MAN CALLING

Vanguard Press

A CIP catalogue record for this title is
available from the British Library.

ISBN 978 178 465 174 9

Vanguard Press is an imprint of
Pegasus Elliot MacKenzie Publishers Ltd.
www.pegasuspublishers.com

First Published in 2016

Vanguard Press
Sheraton House Castle Park
Cambridge England

Printed & Bound in Great Britain

This book is dedicated to my late mother, Mary, who inspired in me the desire to write, and to my wife, Jayne, for her constant love and enduring support.

It is further dedicated to the courageous police colleagues with whom I served in Northern Ireland, especially those who made the ultimate sacrifice.

Acknowledgments

I owe a very special thanks to:

Former police officers Alan Mains and George Millar of the Police Service of Northern Ireland, Mick Larkin of An Garda Siochana. And to Doctor Peter Farling, for their technical assistance.

John Green, Helen Graham and Niall McLean for the helpful feedback on the first draft.

My editor Rachel Neely, for her intelligent guidance and advice.

I should also like to thank Hugh Jordan, investigative journalist, author and friend for his steadfast guidance and continuing support.

Finally to my beloved wife Jayne for her gentle encouragement and constant belief in me.

I will come silently in the night and rob you of your joy.
Turn your life into one of grim sorrow and recrimination.
Then you will share my pain and desolation.

Chapter 1

The stranger stepped out to greet another July morning. It was eight a.m. The sky was blue. Sunlight was spilling across the bay. Waves lapped lazily on the shore. He savoured the moment. A beaker of hot coffee rested easily in his right hand. He supped it thoughtfully, memories of the past came easily to mind. As he drained the remnants of the Columbian dark roast, he turned towards the cottage door, having allowed himself one final peek, lest he forgot the bay's vivid beauty. He would not see it again.

He took a last reflective wander inside the cottage walls. Each room had its own echoes of the past. At the door to the little back bedroom he stopped. His head told him to go inside but his heart did not allow it. The echoes here were loud and piercing, painful. A tear crept down his cheek as he turned towards the kitchen. There he dumped the empty beaker in the sink and picked up his Berghaus rucksack. He locked the front door behind him. His footsteps crunched on the gravel driveway as he crossed to the waiting VW camper van. A surge of adrenaline mingled with the caffeine hit. He felt almost euphoric. He tossed the half-filled rucksack onto the back seat alongside his meagre box of provisions. Three syringe drivers and a number of cannulas sat neatly packed beside the box.

A metal container lay in the foot well. It was one of three which had been perfectly crafted. Each was light and manageable and well capable of housing the little girls for whom they had been fashioned. The other two were located elsewhere. But the one on the camper floor was special. Unlike the others it was lined with billowing red velvet. It was for a very special little girl indeed. He wanted the final minutes of her short life to be terrifying but comfortable at the same time.

The engine burst into life and he adjusted the wing mirror. As he entered the main road, he stole a final fleeting glance at the little house where he had encountered pleasure and pain in almost equal measure. How cruel it was that one dreadful episode could outweigh the sum of all the happy ones he had enjoyed there. He needed to restore the equilibrium. The time was almost right.

The stranger felt excited by what lay ahead. He had planned for every eventuality. Once more the country North and South would wince at the horror of the events which were about to unfold. They would seem like gruesome repetitions of the past. The name of Peter James Ramsey would again be central to the police investigations. It was seven years since Ramsey was Ireland's most wanted. Seven years since little girls were taken in the night, brutalised and murdered. Six years since he had taken his own life, robbing anguished parents of the satisfaction of his imprisonment and a life sentence without parole.

Again, little girls were about to disappear in the night. Talk would be of a copycat criminal. Few if any would figure out the real motive behind the crimes, not gratification or admiration, but a burning desire, a need even, for justice. The stranger settled into the journey. Donegal was just three hours away. His route bypassed industrial Belfast with its fine harbour and towering cranes. In another hour he was toppling down the Glenshane Pass, heading for Dungiven. On the outskirts of the town, ten bright-eyed young republicans looked down on visitors from a fresh poster. The hunger strike of '81' had taken them; their names and the dates of each departure embedded in the country's conscience.

Along the road in Claudy, a kneeling girl is set in bronze. Her innocence honours those wiped out in July 1972, with no warning, no compassion and no chance. Young and old sent hurtling skyward; flesh, blood and bone falling to ground in a grotesque amalgamation, children known only by a bright shoe or knitted sweater covering a dismembered limb. A bloodied cross and crucifix laid together amidst the human rubble, the blast unable to tell Catholic from Protestant.

It was just past eleven o'clock when he crossed the border. The journey had taken longer than he had imagined. The camper's aging engine had struggled for much of the way. Soon it would be pensioned off, its purpose fully served.

In another hour he reached his destination. He parked the camper to the rear of the derelict house, stepped out and stretched his legs. There were still some hours to kill. He made his way along the twisting narrow road towards the harbour.

He turned into the holiday park on the headland. In the midst of the mobile homes all was quiet. It was the annual sports day on the ample grassy stretch overlooking the bay. The loud hailer was calling a group of children to the 'On your mark' position as he unlocked the door to the mobile home. The starter's gun cracked as he stole inside. In the kitchen he opened the fridge. The half-filled bottle of wine lay on its side beside a wedge of Cheddar cheese which was approaching its 'best before' date. He rummaged in his pocket, extracted the tiny bottle and relieved both the wine bottle and his own of their screw caps. He poured in the potion and gave the bottle a shake. He replaced the screw cap and set the wine bottle precisely on the refrigerator's shelf. He placed his own bottle in his pocket. As the starter invited competitors for the father's race, he locked the door. Then he took a discreet route between the other holiday homes, stole past the security hut and onto the road.

He headed for the Stores bar which sits proudly above Portsalon quay. It had just past one o'clock, when he settled into a window seat. The stunning view across the lough was matched by the succulent plate of prawns and Marie Rose sauce, which he washed down with a cooling pint of cider.

By two thirty p.m., the stranger was on the road again heading for Downings on the adjoining peninsula. He would take his time getting there. Idle along the Atlantic Drive, freewheeling when the undulating terrain allowed. Call in at the Singing Pub for a pint of Guinness or two, kill time until the Baillie family's annual memorial down on the beach at eight p.m.

Chapter 2

The years had been kind to Portsalon, a harbour village on the shores of Lough Swilly, in north Donegal. As other resorts lost out to the lure of sunshine abroad, its appeal continued to attract holidaymakers. The sweep of Ballymastocker Strand forms a golden arc from the neat little harbour to the townland of Drumanny and is worthy of its place among the top beaches in the world.

Extended families of three or more generations enjoyed simple pleasures. The young nervously clung to parents' hands. Teenagers skimmed the broken surface on windsurfing boards or tested their skills zigzagging across wakes cut by speedboats, the opposite sex watching wishfully from the beach. Older folk seemed content sipping tea relaxing on tartan rugs or ambling hand in hand along a beach, rich with memories.

The harbour is the beating heart of the town. Safe and secluded, it provides a haven for the very young. They build sand castles and wet their feet for the first time in the gently lapping tide. Older siblings whoop and laugh from the harbour's end. They jump and plunge from the old granite wall, trying to outdo each other for distance gained or tumbles completed. Only a hardy few now brave the cool Atlantic without the comfort of a wetsuit.

The village plays host to a range of holiday homes. They congregate in small communities around the lovely bay. Just the right number, not too crowded, rather each added tastefully to protect the character of their beautiful surroundings. All in full holiday mode as July ratchets up the numbers and the warm and welcome summer tries to atone for the harsh burst of late Easter snow.

Bayview Heights lays claim to be the best site in the region. The two hundred or so mobile homes take pride of place to the northeast of the village. The prime sites look out on the bustle at the harbour, the sweep of the bay and the twinkling lights at Rathmullan to the south when the sun goes down.

A party was in full swing at site A42. A strong puff of air extinguished seven candles and Megan Reilly blushed and smiled at the applause of her guests. The hot summer's day had left many wishing that they had been more generous with their 'factor 30'. A star flecked sky and full moon provided just enough light to pick out the darkened shapes of fellow holidaymakers, before a vale of cloud passed over. John and Sheila Reilly watched proudly as their daughter prised open wrapping paper and thanked each guest for their generosity.

Some miles west, Paul and Linda Baillie stood distraught, unaware of the stranger's presence behind a huge granite outcrop at the furthest reach of the outgoing tide. He watched with sadness as they clung tightly to one another. They had done so for the last seven years on that evening in July. He imagined how they must be thinking of their flaxen-haired Emma. Were they united in their thoughts? Perhaps they pictured her skipping lightly along the beach at Downings, watching her beaming smile and hearing her shrieks as waves lapped over her? Or were they on the shore at low tide, scouring rock pools for common and spotted Goby and the occasional Hermit crab to be teased into a fishing net on a calloused bamboo cane and dropped into a bucket? Then they would be recalling the cruel way she was taken from them in the night. The potion that left them lying powerless to protect her and oblivious to what was happening in Emma's bedroom. There was the horror of the morning, the empty bed, the fruitless search, the surge of revulsion and desolation when her violated corpse was discovered a day later, some sixty miles away, in the North.

The flowery wreath floated out on the ebbing tide and they turned to face another lonely night without her. Year after year, their hatred for Peter James Ramsey still burns as fiercely. The stranger disappeared into the shadows, harbouring his own hate and wishing he could go to them. Give them a hug and tell them he had not forgotten. But that would reveal his identity. For he was someone he felt sure they would recognise from the past.

In ten minutes more he was heading back to Portsalon. As he reached the quiet laneway beside the holiday park the sun was disappearing behind Horne Head. The camper van trod carefully as it made its way along the narrowing track. It stopped just passed a gap in the hedge and he reversed into the space. The stranger moved stealthily from the van along the cover of the hedge and up the steep incline. Then he settled into the grassy hide and waited.

Chapter 3

"Almost time for bed now, Megan," Sheila Reilly said, as the last of the guests disappeared into the dark.

"Oh, please, Daddy, just one more walk out to the headland and back. After all, it is my birthday!" Megan pleaded. In an instant, she was on her father's shoulders and heading for the headland as Sheila muttered something about how fathers love to spoil their daughters.

She took the half full bottle of Pinot Grigio from the fridge and poured two generous glasses. There would be just enough left for a little top up she thought. Who said that twist caps do not have their advantages?

"You're getting too heavy for this, Megan. Growing older has its disadvantages too you know," John jibed, as they watched the last stragglers leaving the Stores bar. The moonlight spilled across the lough as father and daughter headed back to site A42, oblivious to the pair of eyes that had watched their every move from a grassy slope overlooking the site. The stranger had decided weeks before that John would wake in fear, afraid that his shoulders would never feel his loving daughter's weight again.

"Hurry along you two, it's way past your bedtime young lady," Sheila exclaimed, trying to sound more irritated than she was. In minutes, Megan was tucked up snugly.

"That was a lovely day. Imagine the fun we will have for three whole weeks. What's on for tomorrow, Daddy? Can we go out on the banana boat and play rounders on the beach? What about lunch at the Stores bar and can Melissa come for tea?"

"Perhaps we should let tomorrow take care of itself, Megan. Good night, my little princess, sweet dreams," John replied as he turned out the light.

In minutes, the excitement of the day had lulled the little girl to sleep. John and Sheila curled up together to enjoy their wine, oblivious to the tasteless potion that laced their nightcap and of the terror that the morning would bring.

The stranger lay unnoticed in the hide behind high tufts of grass, unmoved by all the happiness he had watched the Reilly's enjoy together over the last number of years. He considered how easily one could take advantage of this sort of situation, how parents dropped their guards so readily in such innocent surroundings.

People's selfishness was intolerable to him. How quickly most had forgotten the violent events of seven years ago, he thought. Did any of them stop to think of the grieving family's annual tribute to little Emma Baillie just a few hours ago? Had he alone witnessed their despair, as another garland floated out to sea? Did any of them consider that the horror of the past could repeat itself? But that this time it might occur in their own midst, even to one of them.

The stranger checked his watch. It was one thirty a.m.; in another hour, all would be quiet.

He considered how Peter James Ramsey had ruined so many lives. He knew so much about him and his passion for young blonde six or seven-year-old girls. In the early days, his apprenticeship as he had called it, he would find them at local children's parks on the edges of large city housing estates. Parents there would drop their guards more readily and community police officers were almost extinct. He would follow a familiar pattern, befriending young girls of single parents. He gained their trust buying cuddly toys and other gifts. He would pay the occasional outstanding bill for the 'cash strapped' young mothers and indulged them on shopping sprees and trips to the cinema to see the latest releases. Each young mum was encouraged to go out with friends, to relax and have some well-earned fun. Why he might have even put a few pounds in their pockets to pay for a round or two of drinks and a taxi home. His deceitful charm left them convinced that their little daughters would be safe with 'Uncle Peter'.

Ramsey would rent the children's favourite DVDs and sit beside them munching popcorn and placing a reassuring arm around them when their heart's leapt with excitement or when something made them stir. A reassuring cuddle would be welcome. An inappropriate touch seemed accidental. But the touching became intimate and unwanted. He wondered how Ramsey could be so convinced that each child's innocence was his to do with as he pleased. The stranger considered how Ramsey's sexual gratification became more difficult to satisfy, how the abuse grew more persistent and obscene.

He took advantage of children's fears and feelings of shame. Many felt soaked with guilt when they considered what they had let him to do to them. Parents, alerted to the abuse were reluctant to report it in case it was 'the worse for them' with 'The Social'.

It was brave, young Kelly Freeman who exposed his dark side. She had stood in Belfast Crown Court, her frail finger of accusation pointed at him, as her lip quivered. The nature of his abuse told in tearful tone. The jury left doubtless whom to believe. The verdict returned in two hours. The judge's carefully chosen words must have rung in Ramsey's ears, as he sent him down for five years.

The stranger pondered how Ramsey must have spent his twenty-three hour lock up with the other perverts at Magilligan Prison; the endless planning for his release, his clever duplicity that beguiled the doctors and shrinks. How taken in were those idealistic 'do-gooders'. Lulled by his honeyed word, they recommended his parole just three years into his sentence. A contrite character, as he led them to believe; the system was working, or so they chose to accept.

He contemplated Ramsey's callous consciousness and the decision never to leave a victim alive again. He knew, by the time of his release, Ramsey's dangerous appetite for young girls had become insatiable, that no Sex Offenders' Register, reporting restrictions or police and social worker home visits would discourage or deflect him from his dark obsession.

The stranger considered Ramsey's mother's wealth, which had helped to create his dangerous anonymity. This led to the deaths of three young girls in July, seven years before. The first was Emma Baillie, so cruelly taken from her holiday retreat in Donegal and left to die in a cottage overlooking Magilligan Strand. The second was Hannah Graham, snatched again in the middle of the night from the family holiday home in Portstewart in the North. Discovered the following day off the Planting Road near Newcastle. The third was Holly Oran, taken from a cottage close to the same seaside town in County Down, found barely alive off a mountain road near Rostrevor, only to die in her father's arms in hospital two hours later.

The stranger reflected on Ramsey's attention to detail in each abduction. How he had described them in colourful and impassive terms during police interviews. He taunted his interrogators and reminded them of the opportunities missed to catch him. He told them they might have saved the last child had they only found her earlier. He thought it was rich that the investigators took credit for his capture and finding the fourth little girl alive. A chance road stop on a lonely mountain road in South Down had been his downfall and the girl's greatest fortune.

He pondered the days Ramsey must have spent watching Emma Baillie skipping and playing with her friends in school at break and lunch times. How had he escaped the notice and attention of so many teachers and parents? Why had no one been alert to his predatory instinct?

Ramsey came to know all he needed to about Emma and her family: the daily collection at the front gate of St Thomas's Primary School by her mother Linda. On Thursdays, they would go for tea at her granny's house on the outskirts of town. Tuesday nights were Irish dance nights. Saturday mornings were spent in the park with dad and Beckett, their friendly Irish setter. On Sunday, they attended St Nicolas's church and weekend breaks were taken in Portrush or on the shores of Lough Erne. Summer holidays were always spent in their mobile home in their beloved Donegal.

Chapter 4

He checked his watch. It was two thirty a.m.

"It's time," he thought. He struggled briefly with his conscience and then considered the years of pain and planning. He was certain that what he was about to do was just. After all, he was not the same type of pervert as Ramsey. He was reassured that his motive was never to serve a craving lust for children. He was driven solely by a thirst for justice.

The security guard had just completed his hourly patrol, the familiar indifferent circuit of an overweight middle-aged man on the minimum wage.

The stranger left his cover, slid down the grassy bank and moved stealthily towards the surrounding fence. His black attire and ski mask concealed him. He cut the wire and slipped silently inside the compound. He moved effortlessly between darkened tents and mobile homes, towards site A42. His senses were acutely aware of the slightest noise or movement. Apart from the rhythmic rush of the waves, and the pounding of the blood in his veins, everything was still.

He unlocked the door and slipped inside. There was just enough moonlight to pick out the slumbering forms of John and Sheila Reilly, huddled together on the sofa. Still dressed as they had been for the party. The potion had done its work well. He moved to the mantelpiece under the mirror and lifted a photograph. Megan was on her daddy's shoulders, beaming from ear to ear. John was peering up at her open mouthed. It reminded him of a shot he had seen in a local tourist summer brochure. He set it down quietly and gently lifted another. A family snap this time, parents and grandparents beaming as Megan extinguished the six candles on the cake. Last year's party. The picture taken from just about where he was standing just then. He replaced it and moved through the kitchen to the back bedrooms.

Megan was asleep on the divan in the bedroom to the left. She clutched a pink comfort blanket under her chin. The embroidery near the right corner said 'Megan's Blankey.' Her long blonde hair lay like flax on the pillow. Her breathing was light and rhythmic. He pocketed her iPhone, which lay beside her on a pillow. He took the tiny vessel from his pocket, unfastened the lid and emptied the ethylene onto the gauze pad in his left hand. Then he casually discarded the bottle, which landed softly on the duvet cover.

As he bent over her, she stirred drowsily. "Is that you, Da?"

In an instant his hand was cupped around her nose and mouth. Her eye lids closed and she was silent. He wrapped her in a dark blanket. In seconds he had carried her through the caravan and passed her sleeping parents. He locked the door behind him and made his way towards the hole in the fence. He passed her gently through the gap, snagging his Merino wool top as he did so. He cursed and looked frustrated at the hole which had been created on his left sleeve. He recovered the fibres from the mesh and placed it in his pocket. This was not part of the plan. He made his way the sixty metres or so to where his vehicle was parked out of sight. He placed her sedated form in the concealed compartment to the rear of the van and inserted a cannula into her right arm. The syringe drive released the Dexmedetomidine. He was content that it would keep her asleep and her airway would remain clear. John and Sheila Reilly did not stir, unaware of what the morning held in store.

The camper stole quietly from the laneway onto the road. He turned left towards the village. An approaching driver sounded his horn and swerved to avoid him. He imagined the irate motorist must have cursed him. The tyres skidded slightly as the rubber met the road.

The van was a work of art. He had bought it several months ago in Dundalk, from a man well used to shady deals, who asked few questions as he pocketed the asking price and handed over the keys. Its tasteful restoration had taken hours of patience in a garage on a 'long term' rental just outside Hackballs Cross, along the border. The classic light blue was a mirror image of the model used by Ramsey seven years before.

But there was something unique to its construction, something that Ramsey had overlooked. Two lads from South Armagh had added the final touch. Men well used to creating concealed compartments in vehicles, for republican snipers along the border in the Nineties. He remembered hearing as a teenager, the ghastly reports of another soldier or police officer gunned down from long range by one of the sniper teams operating in what became known as 'bandit country'. He recalled television footage of the 'Highway Code' style triangular sign, mounted on a telegraph pole outside Crossmaglen. It bore the image of a darkened gunman with rifle raised in revel. 'Sniper at Work' was the chilling post-script. He read in later years that nine police or army staff had been killed by gunmen secreted in the backs of 'built for purpose' vehicles. The last was Bombardier Stephen Restorick, gunned down most brutally, on a narrow country road, outside quaint Bessbrooke village. He had been exchanging pleasantries with a local Catholic woman on a sunny day. It was 12 February, 1997. He was the last soldier to be killed during 'the Troubles'.

The men had listened with little care for his tale of trips to Calais and his line in contraband booze and cigarettes.

He was certain that the van was truly fit for purpose. In the makeshift cubicle beneath the floor lay, heavily sedated, Megan Reilly.

In an hour he would be in Letterkenny, another would see him well past Londonderry. The route would be anonymous, beyond the scope of prying cameras' lenses, except as and when he intended. By the time of Megan's discovery, she would be secreted in a rental cottage in Binevenagh Forest near Castlerock. When she woke she would be frightened and confused. She would look agonisingly in the mirror, wishing her flaxen hair had not been taken. She may even need some child counselling. But she would be alive and her parents would be thankful.

Chapter 5

There was hardly a vehicle to be seen on the R245 to Ramelton. As he crossed the stone bridge over Lough Swilly, he yawned, rubbed his eyes and thought of his childhood.

He recalled the squalid hovel that he bitterly had called home. His mum, Leah, did more tricks than a show pony, to feed her addiction to heroin and crack. The endless hours spent listening to the rattle of the rusty bed frame as mother ground out her miserable existence. He had watched television in front of two bars of the electric fire, if the meter was full, and tried to block out the noise.

There was no father to act as a role model or to praise and chastise, just a string of junkie losers, who sponged off his mother and beat him regularly when the horrors of withdrawal took hold. She had sent him on errands with small packages to be collected or delivered. He was six years old when the runs started. They took him into the grimmest parts of the town. Sometimes the money was short, so the dealer would take it out on him.

He still imagined the frenzied shouts of the police in dark suits and helmets and the barking of a sniffer dog, as they broke down the door and ran amok on the last morning that he would see his mother. He remembered lying petrified beneath the putrid bedclothes as the officers stormed inside. The dog was quickly on him, snuffling and whining with excitement, making for the pillow beneath his head where his mum kept her stash.

"Well I suppose that's mothers for you," he thought.

He remembered sitting in the police station in the early hours of the morning. The hands of the clock barely moving as he took comfort from the blanket wrapped tightly round his shoulders and waited for a social worker. He had just turned seven. He was alone and frightened. As a kindly middle-aged woman led him to a waiting car he wondered what the next few years held in store.

Children's homes can be insensitive places and not for the faint-hearted. Older boys picked up quickly on the issues that teased and tormented new arrivals. The stranger was no different. He recalled how his mother's hopeless existence came back to haunt him. Explicit drawings of her money making practices appeared on walls and notice boards. Exaggerated heavy breathing would greet him in the morning when he woke and at bedtime. In the first six months, his sleep was often broken by bitter memories and nightmares

Mickey McIvor was the ringleader, a cruel and callous youth. The stranger imagined that the mocking would be turned on the next poor novice with a sorry history. But maybe he was wrong, maybe McIvor would continue to pick on him. Make his life more intolerable than it was already. There was no point bringing it to the supervisors. It would only make it worse; no proof you see and snitchers were despised by the other residents. He was on his own.

The taunting stopped three nights before Christmas. At tea time the stranger relieved the kitchen drawer of its paring knife. Smuggled it out with its blade turned up along the curve of his spine, held in place by his trousers waist band.

It was two a.m. when the keen knife edge settled on McIvor's jugular vein. He wakened with a stir. He dared not move. The young stranger's warning had caused the home bully to wet himself and whimper. The caution was re-enforced by the subtle slice of the knife along the skin line above the vein and the promise to make a much deeper cut if the taunting did not stop. McIvor got the message. The jibing stopped for good, not just for him but for little Billy Purvis who had just arrived, in circumstances similar to his own. For the next two years he took him under his wing.

A hint of a smile stole across his face as he thought of the first time he met Bob and Sally Heron, in the clean but spartan sitting room at the home. He had just turned nine and was angry and mistrusting. For the first few weeks, he struggled to come to terms with people who really wanted to get to know and love him. He had never known a mother's or father's love before and as hard as they tried at the home, he knew that true love had to be something more. He had sensed that Bob and Sally could show just how much more it could be.

At the start he talked little about himself, suspicious of their motives and cautious of every question. But bit-by-bit as his trust in them grew, the once closed book began to reveal the colourful chapters of his pitiful young life. Within a couple of months, he had told them most of the terrible truths of his short existence and had shared with Bob the brighter aspects of his childhood: his love of Manchester United and of sport in general, his interest in all things scientific, in wild life programmes and outer space especially, his pride in being top of his class, and, above all, his love of art.

He recalled the first outing on a bright spring day in April. He had sat anxiously, staring out the window down the long leafy driveway, for what seemed an age. He recalled the terrible fleeting doubt that they would take cold feet and leave him tearful and disheartened. In a second his uncertainty vanished, as the black BMW moved sedately up the driveway and stopped just outside the front door.

"Make sure you are on your best behaviour," a carer had shouted, as he ran to meet Bob and Sally, who had just made it through the front door. He could not resist the urge to accept Sally's embrace. In minutes he was in the luxurious front seat of Bob's top of the range 7 Series.

"You're the navigator for today," Bob had jested, as the car sped along the Sydenham by-pass, towards Belfast and then to Newcastle.

The journey took the best part of an hour, before the car turned onto Tullybrannigan Road. The stony driveway wound its way to a beautiful country cottage overlooking the grandeur of the Mourne Mountains and the sweep of Dundrum Bay. Trips of this kind became more frequent as the bonds grew between them. He remembered the first visit to their beautiful home, on a leafy avenue off My Lady's Mile in Holywood. Was it too much to imagine a bedroom overlooking Belfast Lough, bedecked with all things Manchester United, he had wondered? Perhaps it was.

The memories were still fresh of the endless interviews with social workers, concerned that Bob and Sally were at the upper age for fostering. He had so wanted to be with them and he knew that they shared this desire. As time passed, his hopes began to fade, until one day in June he was summoned to Mrs Crombie's office where Bob and Sally threw their arms around him and said he was going home for good. It was the happiest day of his life.

He remembered the tears in his eyes as he opened his bedroom door and saw Bryan Robson, Paul Magrath and

Norman Whiteside standing proudly over his Manchester United duvet cover. It was 1985 and United had won the cup. Whiteside had scored a wonder goal in extra time. He peered through the window across Belfast Lough to Carrickfergus and watched a plane descend into Belfast Harbour airport, as the Fast Speed Ferry cruised up the Lough, heading for Stranraer.

The move had created little disruption to school life. He still attended Holywood Primary, where his rivalry with Gemma Davis continued. She would top him in English and all things musical. He would squeeze home at maths, sciences and art. It was nip and tuck who would win the 75-metre-sprint each year on sport's day. Their healthy competition would continue for many years into their secondary school days at Sullivan Upper College and well beyond.

Saturday mornings were spent with Bob at Kerr Park and along the Esplanade, playing football and learning to swim in Belfast Lough. The wonderful summer holidays they enjoyed together at the holiday retreat near Newcastle. They would fish for spotted goby in rock pools when the tide was out. Nights were spent enjoying shows at the bandstand, or at the fun fair, where Bob fancied himself at the coconut shy or knocking over ducks on the rifle range.

As a special treat on Saturday nights they would have fish and chips at Nardini's. The three-ringed circus in Donard Park was the highlight of the summer break. Crowds of excited holidaymakers sat spellbound at the sight of lion tamers, clowns on stilts and trapeze artists.

In his early teens he learnt to surf at Tyrella beach. Trips would usually end at the Smugglers Inn, where conversations turned to waves and winds and wet suits. Just like the angler's fish that got away, so the waves grew more impressive. He recalled the first time he rode one nearly four feet high, the exhilaration of standing up and acceleration, the feeling of imbalance as he tumbled into the cooling breakers.

He thought of Sally's wonderful home cooking. Her smiling face, as she handed him the laden beating spoon to lick. On occasions when he misbehaved she scolded him. Could ever a woman have ticked him off more mildly?

He still could picture the countless shoeboxes full of photographs of every event and occasion. His face crumpled as he remembered Bob and Sally at sports days and prize givings, just as proud as any adoring parents.

He never noticed the decline in her some years later, the growing frailty and unsteadiness, the pained expression on her face, the ashen pallor and the yellowing of her eyes. She never complained as the levels of morphine increased to combat the incessant pain. He recalled her last moments as she joined his hand to her beloved Bob's. He could almost hear her final words, as she thanked him for being the son she had always wanted. Then she smiled one more time and fell asleep forever.

He considered how quickly Bob had followed her, as he simply let go of life. The solemn scene at the grave side, where he was laid to rest six months to the day after the passing of his beloved wife. He reflected on his return to care for another two years. How quickly had the previous seven slipped by? A tear dripped down his cheek.

Chapter 6

The stranger dipped his lights and swerved to avoid an approaching vehicle, as he turned left onto the Culmore road just outside Londonderry. The sun was rising, as he approached the Foyle Bridge. The road signs gave fair warning of the speed limit and the speed camera ahead. The stranger dropped down a gear and pressed the accelerator. There was no immediate jolt. Just a sluggish surge that found the vehicle running out of puff when it topped 60mph and the camera flashed. Then he shifted back into top gear and headed through Campsey towards Greysteel.

The Foyle View Bar and Lounge just outside the town was once called The Rising Sun Bar. A name that those of a certain age would never forget. He thought of its violent history: the brutal murders during Halloween 1993, the loyalist gunmen bursting through the doors, hate coursing through their veins, the shout of "Trick or Treat," as 'volunteer' Stephen Irwin sprayed the bar with lethal consequences. He imagined the smoke that must have belched from the muzzle of his AK47, as nine customers lay dead or dying and friends fought frantically to save them.

It was three days after the bombing of Frizzle's Fish and Chip shop on a busy Saturday afternoon on the staunchly Protestant Shankill Road in Belfast. An IRA device had exploded prematurely, killing ten people and injuring another fifty. The bomber was one of the victims of his unstable

Improvised Explosive Device, a device common enough in Belfast to be widely known by its acronym 'IED'. What a pity it had not gone off in the anonymous garage where it had been primed, the stranger thought. Detonators could be quite unpredictable he supposed.

The UDA had needed their revenge. Once more, the silent majority hung its head in shame as the world's press flocked to another war torn rural town in Northern Ireland.

Chapter 7

The traffic was just as he had imagined: the occasional long distance lorry driver, hard pressed to catch the six thirty a.m. ferry from Larne Harbour, the late night reveller or errant husband heading home to a stony reception, the early morning milkman, carrying on the family tradition in an ever decreasing market.

It was 4:20 a.m. when he turned onto Bishop's Road. It was barely wide enough for his van. The road narrowed even more as he continued into Binevenagh forest. A fox darted in front of him, swerving elegantly to avoid the front bumper, and disappeared into a hedge as the sun peeped through the trees. One hundred metres along a narrow lane stood the little cottage and outhouse that would be his and Megan's hideaway for a short while. It was ideal.

He parked the van to the back of the outhouse, opened the boot and carried the sedated child inside. He laid her gently on the bed in the back room and checked the syringe drive. He tethered her hands and feet with silk scarlet ribbons. For a second or two he thought of Emma Baillie, Ramsey's first victim. He was elated by the ease with which he had carried out his first capture. He returned to the camper and recovered his provisions from the back seat. He left them on the kitchen table.

There was just one more thing to do before he took a well-earned snooze.

He locked the door, climbed back into the van and turned the key, in minutes the camper was heading across the River Bann just outside Coleraine. He knew the police would be reporting for duty around six a.m. He wanted to avoid the danger posed by straggling constables hurtling down the road intent on being seated when the duty sergeant called the role. He followed the Portstewart Road until he reached the roundabout in the heart of the town. He turned right onto Church Street and came to a halt beside the garage of 2 Springtide Gardens. He quietly reversed inside and switched off the engine. There was no one about as he unloaded the 1979 Vespa 75 Primavera from the back of the van. He locked the garage door and placed the key in his pocket. Then he kick-started the scooter's engine and fastened his helmet. The route back to the cottage was more obscure.

A strong cup of coffee was top of his agenda. Within minutes he was collapsed on the sofa, a cup of Columbian dark roast in hand, contemplating how quickly time had passed. It was seven a.m. and he needed to grab a few hours' sleep. As his head hit the pillow, the morning lights were starting to flicker at Bayview Heights. John and Sheila Reilly had woken to their worst nightmare.

Chapter 8

Chief Superintendent Eamon Lynch was a punctual man, always at his desk by seven forty-five a.m. In his late teens, he had toyed with the idea of following his dad into the Irish Army, of United Nations duties and seeing the world. But a chance encounter with Katy O'Callaghan at a dance in Letterkenny, on his nineteenth birthday, put an end to such fancies. Two years later they were engaged. The following day, with his hair cropped tight, he paraded for the first time on the square at An Garda Siochana Training Depot in Templemore. Katy and he married a year later.

As he sat gazing at his ever mounting in-tray, he reflected on thirty great years of service, and how good fortune had allowed him to finish his police career in his beloved Donegal.

He recalled the early days spent on beat patrol on some of Dublin's most hostile streets, in Ballymun and Finglas. His later promotion to sergeant and the almost obligatory transfer out of the capital. In his case to Limerick City, where Gaelic games give way to Rugby Union and Thomond Park, the home of Munster rugby, is the city's most revered shrine.

He picked up one of two treasured photographs on his desk. He looked along the rows of smiling faces of young policemen from North and South. It was the annual match between the Garda Siochana and the Royal Ulster Constabulary. In many ways the score line was incidental to the occasion. The fixture had been abandoned for some years, at the height of the Troubles. It cheered him to think that on 23 March 1993, he had proudly hoisted the trophy above his head, before the celebrations began. He focused on the RUC lads on either side. He thought of Constable John Stanfield, so brutally taken by a car bomb on a bright Sunday morning on his way to collect his mother and take her to church. She never recovered and passed away in a nursing home a year later, unable to accept her great loss and convinced that John would come bursting through the door, tuck the rug more tightly round her and kiss her forehead tenderly. To his left was Mike Thornton, the RUC captain, larger than life and a timeless friend.

They had each been past their best when an All-Ireland Police team played its first game at the Garda Club just outside Dublin, in March 2003. How the dream of two of the 'old guard' of 1965 was realised when they walked tearfully through the player's guard of honour. Triumphs came at the annual Royal Air Force tournament in Cyprus in 2003 and 2004. Servicemen found it trying to accept defeat by one of the other services. But to be beaten by a police team was quite intolerable. This led to sponsorship and to fixtures against the Scottish, French and Welsh police, to coincide with the annual International Six Nations Championships.

Mike and he had worked together on a number of cross-border operations over the years as each of them had soared up through the ranks. When the firework displays and the popping champagne corks heralded the new Millennium, they were dealing with organised crime along the border. The Republican godfathers had moved with the times. For them, 'the conflict' was no longer 'romantic', thirty years on. Instead it was an opportunity, there was money to be made, and plenty of it. Meanwhile dead and wounded foot soldiers were patriots with a legitimate cause, so they thought, as they unwittingly shed blood for the wealthy few at the top of the pile, who had seen their stashes expand exponentially. He recalled the last time they had worked together. It was seven years ago. Emma Baillie had been taken in the night from a caravan park outside Downings, Donegal. She was seven years old. Her violated body was found two days later in a holiday let in a Forest Park in the North, overlooking Magilligan beach in County Londonderry.

He reflected on the terrible events that followed, the kidnap and murder of two more seven-year-old girls in the North. He had been the senior investigating officer in the South, Mike Thornton his counterpart on the other side of the border. It had been the blackest time of his career.

He opened his bottom desk drawer. It contained a number of personal letters, some other memorabilia and his Scott Gold medal for bravery. He had rescued two children from a burning terraced house in Limerick over twenty years ago. He could still sense the mother's anguish and hear her woeful plea as he charged up the staircase towards the children's cries, the feeling of relief as he hoisted them from beneath the bed, his eyeballs red and screaming as his lungs felt ready to burst. His faltering steps as the wall crashed down behind them, as he and the children were catapulted through the open front door and returned to their mother's arms.

Beneath the medal was a burnished metal box. He paused briefly before picking it up, and paused again. It was like exposing the darkest recess of the mind, the place where terrible memories reside. Like sleeping dogs, they lie undisturbed, until sentimental moments such as these. He eyed the tragic note from the mother of a heroin addict. It thanked him for his efforts to save her beloved son. The lad overdosed in a rancid bedsit in Galway city, where Lynch had served as an inspector in the late nineties. The syringe hung limply from his right arm as Lynch broke down the door. There was the photograph of his nephew hanging pitifully from a tree. A victim of juvenile depression, the pain of his short life had been too much for his vulnerable young mind to bear. Then there were the printouts of the photographs sent by Peter James Ramsey. 08843 59462 was the grid reference, typed out underneath which told of the whereabouts of Emma Baillie's violated body. It was precise to a point beyond which orientation rarely goes, even for hikers and hill walkers, leaving Lynch's team guessing at its significance. It was signed 'Scarlet Ribbons'.

He picked up his most treasured snap of his darling Katy and his twin children Sarah and Michael. Both now doing their parents proud, studying medicine and economics respectively, at University College Dublin. His retirement in two weeks' time could not come soon enough. It would give the time he needed to write that book he had always wanted to and to reduce his cholesterol to a level that would keep Doctor O'Hare off his back.

Chapter 9

It was eight thirty a.m. when the phone rang.

"Good morning, sir. It's Inspector Brenda Hughes. We have a major incident at Portsalon. A seven-year-old girl is missing. I believe she may have been abducted."

Lynch felt the cold chill of déjà vu, as he sat gathering his thoughts and looking at Ramsey's cruel correspondence.

"Where are you at the moment?" he said.

"I'm at Milford Station with Detective Sergeant Gorman. He has already informed the Senior Investigating Officer, Detective Superintendent Keenan, who has just arrived. I have been in touch with the press office and our divisional scenes of crime examiners. They have requested two photographers. A search team is just about to be deployed. There are three officers securing the scene at the moment. The parents are here at the station, sir. They are in a terrible state," she replied.

"Great work, Brenda. I'll be there in half an hour. Have you ensured that all the residents at the campsite remain in their mobile homes? "

"I have, sir. It would appear that the family has only informed one other family and the site warden, so we are currently in control of the flow of social media."

"That's great, Brenda. I take it the arterial routes have been sealed off?"

"They have, sir. The local beat and patrol cars are being assisted by traffic branch and mutual assistance has been requested from Letterkenny."

"Excellent, Brenda," Lynch said, reassured by her competence.

Brenda Hughes was a Donegal lass, one of the rising stars of the force. She was a young woman whose ability outweighed her considerable ambition, something not always evident in many aspiring young officers today. Most were studiously risk-averse and it seemed regrettably to be paying off. Single-minded high flyers now soared well above the limits of their capacities.

He rebuked himself for his cynicism, put on his best uniform and summoned his driver. He replaced the items in the tin box and the box in the drawer. He contacted the commissioner's office to advise her of the situation. He wished his retirement had come two weeks sooner. He feared that he might be adding to the box's sad contents before his time was up.

Chapter 10

Inspector Hughes greeted him at Milford Station. The hubbub of the briefing room calmed as he entered. He passed the usual pleasantries before getting down to business.

"Can you fill us in with what we have so far please, Superintendent Keenan?"

"Certainly, sir. Please bear with me. At present the parents are being interviewed. I am strongly of the opinion that they are completely innocent. However, we are doing all that is necessary to eliminate them from our list of suspects.

"They say that they sat down to enjoy a nightcap together shortly after midnight and woke up on the couch at 6:55a.m., feeling groggy, very thirsty and wearing the same clothes as they had done for their daughter's party. It was Megan's seventh birthday yesterday. We have already seized a nearly empty bottle of wine for examination. I have tasked our search teams and two forensic scientists to commence the search of the holiday park. Another forensic team and a photographer are examining the mobile home.

"We have spoken to the park warden. A number of duplicate keys had been misplaced two weeks ago, only to reappear the following day. At the time they put it down to an administrative error or to one of the part-time summer staff having mislaid them. It may have some bearing on this case. There was no forced entry and the door was locked this morning when the parents discovered Megan was missing."

Detective Superintendent Keenan held the floor for a few more minutes.

"Thank you, Frank, that has been most helpful. Ladies and gentlemen, we have a great deal to do in a very short space of time. First of all may I remind you that anything said from this point on is treated in the strictest confidence? At this stage I am hesitant to compare this with the abduction of Emma Baillie seven years ago but there are some persuasive similarities. They were both seven-years-old and only children. They were taken on the same date and from similar types of holiday parks. Each child was seized in the night, when both sets of parents appear to have been sedated," Lynch explained.

There was a knock at the door and a young Garda officer stepped inside.

"Excuse me sir, I'm Inspector Finn O'Grady, the officer in charge of the search. I believe we have found evidence of considerable importance. May I brief you?"

The inspector replaced Lynch at the lectern and turned to a projected image.

"You can see that the projection shows the extent of the site. Here is pitch site A42 from where we believe Megan was taken. I am now pointing to the compound fence, which is some forty metres to the rear of the mobile home. You can see from the configuration of the other mobile homes, that there would be almost perfect cover for someone wishing to remain undetected from the Reilly's mobile to this entry and exit point along the fence. One of our dogs picked up a scent immediately and followed it from A42 to a hole in the fence that we believe to have been recently cut. The gap in the fence leads to a laneway. It runs to a T-junction, which is about one hundred metres to the left. I am now pointing to the headland to the right. It is a similar distance away from the breach in the fence. The dog made its way through the fence to a piece of open ground some sixty metres in this direction.

"It was here that we found a fresh set of tyre tracks. Both the scene of crime examiners and the photographer are confident that the tracks are good enough to identify the make of the tyre as long as time and distance do not remove the unique characteristics. I am now pointing to a raised area above the lane from where there is a clear view of the site. One of the teams found what looks like a makeshift observation point. It has been roughly but proficiently put together with ferns and grass and there is evidence that the grass has been compressed. It appears to have been used on a number of occasions. It was difficult to spot. If this was the vantage point, the person would have been able to see every coming and going from the Reilly's holiday home."

The inspector pointed at another spot on the map. "This is the only exit onto the main road. There is a tyre mark just as the laneway meets the road. It strongly indicates that the vehicle turned left towards Portsalon and not right to Fannad Head. All of these sites have been preserved for further examination, sir."

"Many thanks, Inspector. Please thank your teams for me. Well, ladies and gentlemen, that serves to confirm our worst suspicions. Frank, are you happy enough to run the enquiry from Milford or would you prefer to be based in Letterkenny?" Lynch requested.

"Letterkenny would be better, sir. It has superior facilities, with enhanced communications and better access to the internet. We also have a video conferencing facility. This one is likely to attract huge press interest, sir, so we will need a briefing room large enough to accommodate a considerable number of people."

"Fine, Frank. I'll inform Assistant Commissioner Larkin of your decision."

He turned his attention to an attractive young lady in the front row. Grainne Burrows had been the press officer for the region for the last three years and was excellent at her job. A first-class-honours graduate of Trinity College, she had been snapped up by *The Sunday Times* in Dublin and had excelled in an often begrudging profession, where the weak were hastily cast aside and friendships could never be taken for granted.

By 2000 she was working on high profile cases involving smuggling, red diesel conversion and cattle scams around the border regions. It was where Lynch had first met her. She had mustered a number of well-placed sources and won the trust and respect of investigators, spies and spooks, north and south of the border. But a turn of bad fortune changed all of this and she joined An Garda Siochana press office two weeks after her mother passed away.

"Grainne could you please join Detective Superintendent Keenan and I, we need to discuss our media strategy?"

The three retired to the empty station sergeant's office and closed the door.

Keenan broke an uneasy silence.

"I think we need to have a joint appeal. One from the parents to tell the public what happened and display the sense of trauma and loss they are experiencing; then one from us to provide as much information as we can. We must encourage potential witnesses to come forward."

"I'll look after the family," Grainne replied. "Garda Sarah McGivern is the family liaison officer. She and I will talk to them immediately after this meeting. I know already that there are a number of excellent photographs of Megan on the parents' iPhones. I will make sure that the best of these are available for the press conference."

"Thank you, Grainne. I am sure you will do the best you can," he said reassuringly.

"It's so important that we get this right first time. We must broadcast our appeal to as many media outlets as possible, before it goes viral on social networks. We all know how essential they can be to an enquiry. But we must keep them reigned in, no ill-advised speculations or overblown headlines. No amateur sleuths and no access to the family, or to those in whom the family have confided. A number of the press will have been around when Emma Baillie was taken seven years ago. We must be prepared to field any questions that try to make a connection.

"You make whatever arrangements necessary. I would like to hold a press conference at twelve thirty p.m. Does that give you and Grainne enough time?"

"It does, sir. I have already advised my office in Letterkenny to start preparing the briefing room. I have taken the heat off Grainne and informed the press office to contact all press and media outlets. The video conferencing facility will allow the commissioner to be tuned in. I'm sure the politicians will be all over this one, putting in their penny's worth and ready to deploy 20:20 hindsight if things go wrong. It's the election next year. They will all wish to express their hollow commitments to public and community safety.

"We can also link up to the outlets unable to attend. I'm thinking especially of those in the North. Everything there at the moment will be concentrating on the 'Orange' parades. After all it is the twelfth of July."

"That's great, Frank. I'm going to put out a Child Rescue Alert, so I need to inform Assistant Commissioner Larkin. As well as the media outlets, it will include all port and airport terminals as well as hospitals. I am reluctant to get in touch with Interpol at the moment. We need to ensure that the information is broadcast on road signs throughout the country. Whatever vehicle was used had to be on the road early. Someone is bound to have seen it and we need them to come forward."

The three of them left the office to be about their own business, confident in each other that all would be in place for the briefing at Letterkenny in two hours' time.

Chapter 11

Lynch sat in quiet reflection as his car sped towards Ramelton. He thought with discomfort that some eight or so hours ago a young girl was being taken, against her will, along that very stretch of road.

He hoped that somehow she was oblivious to the terror of her ordeal. But he doubted it. He picked up his phone and scrolled to the number that he needed. Assistant Commissioner Larkin had been awaiting his call.

"Good morning, sir. It's Chief Superintendent Lynch. I know that you are already aware of the situation at Portsalon. I have authorised a Child Rescue Alert. The SIO is Frank Keenan. He worked with me on the abduction of Emma Baillie seven years ago. Frank will be running the enquiry from Letterkenny. There's to be a press conference at twelve thirty p.m."

"I know something of the detail, Eamon and you will have my full support. Is there much in the way of evidence of an abduction and are you certain we can eliminate the parents from the enquiry as suspects?"

"There is considerable evidence of an abduction and I am confident that the parents are not involved, sir. I have to tell you that this case has many similarities to the abduction of Emma Baillie. It is my opinion that the person who took Megan Reilly has a precise knowledge of Emma Baillie's kidnapping. I only hope that the outcome for this little girl is not the same," Lynch said, in a less than confident manner.

"Please keep me updated, Eamon. Is there anyone you would like me to call?"

"If you could keep the commissioner informed. Please advise her of the press conference at twelve thirty p.m. at Letterkenny station. I am hopeful that the parents will make an appeal and that it will make the national and international news outlets by one p.m. I will ensure that the rest is seen to. Best to keep it all under the one roof sir," Lynch said diplomatically.

Chapter 12

It was just past eleven a.m. when he poured himself a cup of coffee and picked up the phone on his desk. The reply came from a woman with an engaging Belfast accent.

"Good morning, Police Service of Northern Ireland, may I help you?"

"Could you put me through to Detective Chief Superintendent Mike Thornton please?"

The dialling tone had barely sounded when Lynch heard the familiar voice.

"Hello. Mike Thornton speaking. May I help you?"

Detective Chief Superintendent Mike Thornton was a 'dyed in the wool' police officer. An outstanding student at Methodist College, Belfast, his size had dictated a place in the back row for three years on the 1st XV rugby team. To many it seemed as if rugby was the raison d'être of young sportsmen with promise. His good looks and irresistible charm had left him rarely short of female company as he walked through the 'windy gap' linking the original building to the science labs.

Long had it been his intention to follow his dad into the legal profession, be a successful criminal lawyer, make it to Queens Council before his fortieth birthday and end up one step up from his father on to the Northern Ireland Appeal Court bench. But a day in June more than thirty years ago changed all of that.

It was his last exam. He was driving along considering the relevance to his day of Newton's second law of motion, (F = ma). Most of the rush hour traffic into Belfast had already made its way down the Oldpark Road. As he approached Cliftonville Circus, he stopped to give way to a stream of traffic approaching from his right and to some elderly pedestrians, making their way to the Post Office to collect their pensions. A red Honda Accord was in a short queue of traffic to his left on Westland Road. The driver seemed engrossed by the young boy in the front passenger seat, struggling with his seat belt. He was oblivious to the blue Kawasaki motorbike, approaching along the tree-lined footpath to his left and the outstretched right arm of the pillion passenger, which reached its full extension as the bike pulled alongside the passenger's door.

The driver's personal protection weapon lay beneath his seat, just out of reach. Startled pigeons rose swiftly from a tree when the stillness of the morning gave way to chilling noises. The handgun's muzzle lit up six times. Two in quick succession, then another four at the gunman's leisure, the second volley irrelevant to the dreadful outcome. The first round pierced the driver's right eye and exited through the back of his head, with just enough energy to shatter the off-side window and fall like a stone to the road. It bounced twice and turned full circle before settling. The second passed through his forehead. It made light of the skull and turned the frontal and parietal lobes to mush. It ran out of steam when it reached the cerebellum. The bike sped through the roundabout and down Alliance Avenue. The gunman appeared ecstatic at his day's work. His uncontainable whoops audible through the helmet's open visor.

In a flash Thornton was at the door wrestling with the locking mechanism. Then he realised the driver was dead. The little boy, whom he lifted from the passenger seat, was screaming, saturated in his father's blood. His cherished belief in his daddy's infallibility most cruelly and finally shattered.

The following morning he contacted his local police station and the recruitment sergeant had called with him within the week. Thornton could not let go of the violent death of Detective Constable John Harbinson.

In April, he reported for the early shift at Oldpark Station in North Belfast, or Fort Apache as it was known locally. It was the start of a wonderful career that took him the length and breadth of the province and on many occasions to the outer limits of his endurance. Thirty years of hard graft, a huge talent and considerable family sacrifice had brought him to his current high position. He was the head of Serious and Organised Crime and responsible for investigations into child abductions.

Chapter 13

The stranger awoke to the sound of a belligerent rooster staking its claim to territory some distance away. He checked his watch. It was 11.05 a.m. The few hours' sleep had been just what he needed. He checked on Megan, the sedative was working well. She looked so peaceful. He entered the kitchen and filled the kettle. He set it on a heated ring beside a pan that was soon playing host to two sizzling eggs, three rashers of bacon and a couple of potato farls. In minutes he was sitting down to a hearty breakfast with smug satisfaction. He contemplated the scene at Portsalon: the parents' horror, the hollow endeavours of the police trying to piece together what had happened the night before and deciding how they were going to respond.

There would most certainly be a Child Rescue Alert and an attempt to have the parents make an appeal to catch the one o'clock news. Detectives would be toiling to discover why Megan was the victim. How had she been singled out? They would be testing their theories about social networks, about Facebook and Twitter and the internet. They would seize phones and iPads and send the Police Service of Northern Ireland (PSNI) to the family home to recover their desktop computer. Techies with shaggy beards and poorly fitting clothes would be swarming over the devices like locusts, confident that a clue lay within and they would make a breakthrough. They would be sorely disappointed.

He wondered when they would spot the clear similarities between this abduction and that of Emma Baillie seven years ago. He did not consider CS Eamon Lynch to be the 'sharpest tool in the box', but surely even he would recognise the parallels between the two cases. He wondered if and when Lynch would be in touch with Mike Thornton and how Thornton would respond.

Would he be cautious at this point, concerned at there being too much speculation, or would he be drawn uneasily to the uncanny similarities of the events separated by seven years? Then even if he did respond, what could he do? It was the twelfth of July. Every officer capable of pulling on a uniform would be on duty, policing the annual parades over the length and breadth of Northern Ireland. Thousands of officers would have paraded at five or six a.m. The order to 'stand down' would be given when the last Orangemen returned home from the march and the air was no longer filled with the blare of flutes or the clatter of Lambeg drums.

The stranger threw the dishes into the sink and pulled on a change of clothes. He checked in on Megan and walked out and locked the doors. He mounted the Vespa scooter and pulled on his helmet. There was one more place he had to visit before he headed for Portstewart to put the final touches to the second part of his plan. Then he would retire to a quiet pub for a bite of lunch and to catch the one o'clock news.

He assumed that the BBC and UTV would have scheduled the usual annual diet: aging Orangemen in suits and bowler hats marching proudly behind colourful flute bands and vivid banners, through the towns and cities of the province. Spectators, recognising the odd guy on parade, would holler, "What about ye, Billy, or Sammy or Jimmy." It was never Fergal, or Eugene or Padraig, nor would it ever be.

For this was the Protestant celebration of King William of Orange's victory over the Catholic James I at the Battle of the Boyne in 1690. The annual coat trailing had given oxygen to sectarianism for more years than anyone would care to imagine.

The bands would be loud and raucous, the followers well oiled and fuelled with fervour. He wondered if the timely phone calls from Garda press officers would change the stale programming for lunchtime viewers, replacing the tribal songs and speeches with something that really mattered.

The stranger kick-started the bike and headed for Bishop's Road. A mile along, he turned right into Downhill forest and proceeded slowly up a narrow lane. In the space of fifty metres the track became impassable, overgrown by brambles and ivy, heavy with weeds and lichen under foot.

There was an eerie silence as he brushed aside the thicket and caught his first sight of the deserted stone cottage. The once happy holiday retreat, so often filled with fun and laughter, he imagined, condemned to decay and seclusion seven years ago. The door opened with a gentle push. He found himself in a compact sitting room. He tried to imagine the horror that Peter James Ramsey had created here. He hesitated before entering the back bedroom, disgusted by the vile depravity to which he knew Emma Baillie had been exposed, the torturous sexual violation, the shaving of her flaxen hair, the perverse clothing in a red party frock, the little girl's slow, inevitable death, tethered with scarlet ribbons and left to suffocate in a cold narrow metal chamber, the air supply insufficient to give any likely chance of rescue.

He stayed for a minute or two before carrying on through the cottage to the back door. Its rotted frame put up little resistance. He picked his way through the tangled green canopy and stood overlooking Downhill strand. To his right he saw Mussenden temple, built as a summer library by the wealthy Bishop of Londonderry in 1785. To his left he could see Magilligan Point and the ample port of Greencastle, Donegal.

A restricted area of beach was just about visible to the naked eye. It was the stretch adjacent to Her Majesty's Prison at Magilligan. The institution where Peter James Ramsey had served his time for abusing Holly Freeman some years before he went on his sadistic spree. It was there in that prison that he had chosen never to leave a victim alive again. Suddenly, with sharpened clarity, he understood why Ramsey had chosen this location for his first murder.

A minute later he was making his way back through the tangle of branches. He fired up the scooter again and headed for Portstewart to prepare for the night ahead. He had an hour before the news bulletin and he did not intend to miss it.

Chapter 14

"Hi, Mike, it's Eamon Lynch. I wish it was a social call. We've had an abduction of a seven-year-old girl. She was taken from a mobile home in Portsalon early this morning. Mike, there are so many similarities with the Emma Baillie case seven years ago. We are holding a press conference at twelve thirty p.m. to catch the one o'clock news. We expect the BBC and UTV to run with it. Are you in a position to do anything at this point bearing in mind how things panned out seven years ago?" Lynch asked.

Thornton bit down heavily on his bottom lip as his mind scrolled back through the years. He considered the ghastly events of the past, which from time to time would still wake him at night.

"Eamon, I'll do what I can, but we are stretched to the limit today. Only the walking wounded are off the streets. We expect major trouble in North Belfast as the parade returns at around seven thirty p.m. tonight. The Parades Commission has refused to allow the Orangemen to march past the Ardoyne shopfronts on their return. The paramilitaries on both sides are well tooled up and the Loyalists have threatened to force the march through. If it starts there, it could spark a spate of attacks along other interfaces throughout the region. I'm looking after affairs in Londonderry from Maydown Station. Things will be pretty slack here from about one p.m., until the parade returns tonight. If there is something more compelling to suggest that the vehicle has headed this way we can put up a number of vehicle checks.

"At the moment the best I can do is make sure the road traffic signs carry the details of the abduction. I will have someone start viewing CCTV from cameras in Londonderry and Limavady. There are a number of speed cameras that might help. Between what times would you like us to search between Eamon?"

"We believe that the child was taken some time after one a.m. It would be at least two a.m. before a vehicle would be in the North so if you have the examinations start at two a.m."

"Not a problem, but send me a tasking request by email please. We don't want any hiccups with our procedures. Detective Constable Jean Harrison is in the office. You will remember her from the enquiry seven years ago. I'll put her onto it.

"I'll inform my boss what we are doing, just in case your commissioner gets in touch with my chief. Keep me informed, Eamon. Good luck with this one and let's hope and pray for a good result to herald your well-earned retirement."

"Thanks, Mike, much appreciated," Lynch replied, rubbing his furrowed brow.

Thornton phoned his boss. Assistant Chief Constable Barnett was a high flier. He had been an inspector at headquarters when Ramsey ran amok seven years ago. Thornton had always thought of him as an officer with a smidgeon of ability, but with a great capacity for arse licking. Barnett gave his usual guarded keep-my-ass-covered approval and hung up.

Thornton called the general office.

"Hi, sir, it's Jean here. How can I help you?"

How he had wished that his boss could have asked that same question. But it appeared he was already heading for cover, just in case things went tits up.

"Could you come in for a minute, Jean? I have an enquiry that needs your undivided attention. Bring your notebook, a tasking sheet and a decision log please."

Chapter 15

It was midday when Eamon Lynch and Frank Keenan sat down together in Lynch's office in Letterkenny.

"Is everything in place, Frank?" Lynch enquired.

"It is, Eamon. The press are assembling in the canteen while we add the final touches to the briefing room. There is huge interest in this one. International networks are trying feverishly to get linked up. The techies are sorting out the video links and we have a good, clear photograph of Megan to show them. The mother has agreed to make a short plea. Grainne is working on it with her. If you don't mind, I'll make the Garda appeal."

Lynch was quietly grateful to Frank for stepping up to the mark. He remembered his own appeal seven years before. He recalled the tragic outcome for the missing girl on whose behalf he had made it. He did not consider himself to be a superstitious man, but neither did he wish to tempt fate.

The crowded briefing room fell silent as the small party took their seats behind a table on the temporary podium. The atmosphere tightened as Frank Keenan rose to speak and tested the microphone.

"Good morning, ladies and gentlemen, thank you very much for coming and for being so punctual. My name is Frank Keenan and I am the Senior Investigating Officer. This appeal is also being video linked to those who can't be with us today.

"An incident occurred last night and we need your help."

A photograph with Megan Reilly's name under it appeared on the screen to his right. There was a natural pause as the journalists scribbled in their notebooks, anticipating what they would hear next. First he pointed to the little girl and then at her tearful parents sitting to his right.

"This is Megan Reilly and these are her parents, John and Sheila. Sheila has an appeal to make."

The booze beaten thirty-year hacks and the fresh faced novices sat in solemn silence as Sheila Reilly took the microphone handed to her, remaining seated, as though she feared her legs might not hold her up.

"This is our lovely daughter, Megan," she sobbed, motioning to the smiling face looking down at the crowd from the photograph. She fought to regain her composure.

"Megan is our only child and we love her so much. It was Megan's seventh birthday yesterday and she was so happy. Megan's daddy tucked her into bed just after midnight. When we woke this morning Megan was gone. We cannot bear to be without her. If the person who took Megan is listening please don't hurt her. She is our only child. Please give Megan back to us. Please."

Sheila set down the microphone and turned to be comforted by John.

The press officers had clearly worked hard with the distraught parent, evident in the constant references to the child's name, their attempt to humanise Megan, to prevent her remaining impersonal in the mind of the abductor.

Frank Keenan stood up. He did not hold back on most of the detail: the hole in the fence, the door locked from the outside, the makeshift vantage point and the fresh tyre track.

He continued, "I am now making an appeal to the public on both sides of the border for help. I believe that Megan was taken in a vehicle sometime after one a.m. and no later than six a.m. You may have been on the road between these times. You could have been coming home late for some reason or perhaps your work requires you to be on the road at that time of the morning. Did you see a vehicle on the road that seemed odd, out of place or unusual? Did anything seem out of the ordinary to you? We really do need your help.

"Please be assured that anything you tell us will be treated in strict confidence. Please help us find Megan and return her to John and Sheila. Now I will take a few questions."

"Detective Superintendent Keenan, its Damien McIlroy from *The Irish Times*. You will remember the young girl who was taken from Downings seven years ago. Would you agree that this case bears some resemblance?"

"I must admit it does, but I am reluctant to speculate too much at this point in time. However, that will be one of a number of lines of enquiry."

"Detective Superintendent Keenan, Wendy Muldoon, RTE. What message do you have for the parents of young children, who may be watching this appeal?"

"I would say to them that incidents of this nature are extremely rare. I would say that it is always important to know where their children are and whom they are with. I would tell them to try as far as possible not to disrupt their daily lives because of this. However, they must be vigilant and report anything they think is out of place.

"Finally, I would ask them to report anything that may have happened during the last twenty-four hours or even before that. We believe that this abduction was carefully planned over a number of weeks, months or even longer.

"Ladies and gentlemen, thank you very much for attending. Please be thoughtful about what you choose to write. Let it reflect precisely what you have been told and please do not speculate or assume. We do not want anything to interfere with our endeavours to return Megan to her parents. Grainne Burrows is the press officer for this investigation. Please refer all your enquiries to her. Thank you again."

In a couple of minutes the briefing room was clear except for the five still seated at the podium. Keenan put a comforting arm around Sheila Reilly as she broke down and burst into tears. He wished he could give them more than a glimmer of hope. He feared the worst.

Chapter 16

The stranger sat by a window in the Poacher's Arms, a couple of miles outside Portstewart. Everything was in place for tonight. The plea had been just what he had anticipated. But the delivery was superior to Eamon Lynch's faltering effort seven years ago. Keenan had revealed most of the clues which he had left for them. But no mention of the parents' suspected sedation or of Megan's missing phone.

He downed the last inch of his pint of Guinness, paid his bill and left a handsome tip. The battered cod and triple fried chips had been excellent. But mushy peas were not a favourite of his.

Chapter 17

Mike Thornton watched the appeal with a growing sense that the vehicle may have crossed the border and that Megan Reilly may already be struggling for air entombed in a metal chamber, beaten and violated somewhere on his 'turf'.

He phoned his boss again.

"Hello, sir. I take it you've been watching the appeal. Everything is quiet here, so I'm heading for Letterkenny. It is less than an hour from Maydown. I want to find out first-hand exactly what they've got. I'll be on my mobile."

Chapter 18

Eamon Lynch extended his hand and threw a welcoming arm round Mike Thornton. Lynch's cheeks were ruddier than when last they met and he was a pound or two heavier. A taste for fine malt whiskey and a pint or two of stout may have had something to do with that, Mike thought.

"Glad you made the trip, Mike, I've a gut feeling about this one. There are too many similarities to the last time." He led Thornton to his office at the top of the stairs thinking that a problem shared was a problem halved, though this did not dispel Lynch's sense of anxiety.

In a minute they were joined by Frank Keenan and Grainne Burrows, both looking remarkably fresh in spite of all that was happening.

"Good to see you again, Frank," Thornton said as he readied himself for the Kerry man's vice-like grip. He was not disappointed.

Grainne Burrows beat Thornton to the punch with a conspicuously warm embrace and a lingering kiss on his right cheek just below the earlobe by way of greeting.

"Hi, Mike. It's great to see you again. How long has it been?"

Thornton thought back to his days as a detective inspector in Newry. To the joint police operations that straddled the border and the elegant young reporter who had exposed a local republican as a leader of the Provisional IRA. It had been headline news. The article had involved a considerable amount of enquiry and a huge set of balls. They were difficult times in more ways than one and he had come to know her very well indeed.

"Good to see you, Grainne. It's been a long time." Thornton knew precisely how long it had been and so did she. Their eyes met from a distance as Frank Keenan began to speak.

"There are a number of interesting developments. The forensic department has done a great job with the turnaround of the samples we sent them. The kidnapper had laced the wine with Zolpidem. It took some time to identify. It is more commonly used in the States. The tyre track was made by a Continental Vanco Camper tyre, model 190/55/R17 and designed specifically for older vans. The forensic team think that it was recently fitted.

"Ten minutes after the appeal, we received a call from Peter O'Hara. He had just passed through Portsalon at about 2.40 a.m. As he approached the entrance to Bayview Holiday Park a vehicle pulled out from a laneway causing him to swerve and blast his horn. It turned left towards the town. He gave a scant description of a flat fronted light coloured vehicle which he believes to be some sort of camper van. He was unable to see how many were in the cab or give any useful description of the driver. That was all he was able to tell us. A detective is calling with him to take a statement.

"We received another call from a Declan Henry, a local baker in Ramelton. He starts every morning at three a.m. He had just fired up the ovens and gone out for a smoke. A small light coloured camper van crossed the bridge, headed past his shop and turned right towards Letterkenny. It was about 3:10 a.m. He believes there was only one person in the front of the vehicle. I have sent a detective to take a statement and to let the witness have a look at some camper models.

"The team is currently trying to eliminate all local sex offenders from our investigation. At this point we do not believe that any of them have the knowledge of Ramsey's Modus Operandi to be involved. The parents are still being interviewed. We need to find out how Megan became the victim. And one last thing, sir; Megan's phone appears to be missing."

"That's good work, Frank. Have you put out another appeal to see if we have any other sightings of a similar vehicle?" Lynch asked. "We need make or model ASAP."

"I have considered it, sir, but I am reluctant at the moment. We don't want to be swamped with crank calls from everyone who knows a family with a small light coloured camper van, or from some guy with an axe to grind. You know how the 'well-meaning public' react to these things."

It was three p.m. when Mike Thornton answered his phone and put it on to loudspeaker.

"Hi, sir, it's Jean here. I'm afraid there is nothing on CCTV but we do have a partial registration of a vehicle caught speeding on the Foyle Bridge at 3:56 a.m. this morning. For some reason the last two figures are obscured. Traffic branch tell me that this is quite common when an early morning mist is settled and the sun is rising. What we have got is Y110H followed by two unclear letters. It has the appearance of a personalised number plate. The chief constable's office has been in touch with the Vehicle Licensing Office. There is nothing they can do for us today but they will deal with it first thing in the morning. It may be that the vehicle isn't even registered."

"Great work, Jean. I'll get the team up here to make similar enquiries. It's likely that I'll be here overnight and I've cleared it with the boss. Thanks for all your hard work, I only hope we're not too late. Would you mind phoning Tony Rogers and see what he's doing at the moment? If this enquiry comes our way, I will want the best investigative team I can get. He's the best serious crime co-ordinator I know."

Chapter 19

Jayne Thornton was reclining on a sunbed taking advantage of the uncommon heat wave. She was aware of the disarming sea breeze that could often catch you out. She and Mike had always wanted a summer retreat, somewhere within easy reach of their home just outside Bangor. A place they could go to at a moment's notice. She recalled the haggling, with a hardnosed farmer to get the prime site overlooking Glenarm. 23 Tully Road had become their sanctuary from life's tiresome realities.

She never wearied of the view of Scotland on a clear day or of the summer ferry steaming past Ailsa Craig on its way to Troon. As she lowered her eyes, she saw a queue of vehicles making its way past the salmon fisheries with all the time in the world and nothing at stake. Beneath her, Glenarm Castle stood. Its immaculate walled garden, once home to the Earls of Antrim, now playing host to seminars and social gatherings.

In a moment Rachel Thornton was beside her, phone in hand.

"Mummy, Daddy wants a word with you," she whispered as if it was some kind of secret.

"Hi, sweetheart, it's me. I trust you are enjoying the sunshine. I'm afraid you will have to put the Pinot Grigio on ice. Did you catch the one o'clock news?"

"I did, Mike. What a terrible thing to happen. The parents must be in bits. Where are you at the moment?"

"I'm in Letterkenny with Eamon Lynch and his team. Things are starting to pick up pace, so I'm staying over to keep ahead of the game. I'm afraid it is either a local hotel or a roll out mattress back at Maydown."

"What do you mean by keep ahead of the game, Mike? Do you mean it's the same as the Ramsey case? Please tell me I'm wrong," Jayne pleaded anxiously.

"It's too soon to say, pet, but I don't have a good feeling. Who's with you?"

"Just me and Rachel at the moment. My sister Patsy and her two boys are coming down on the fifteenth. They are staying until the sixteenth. Rachel has her friend Barbara coming to stay tomorrow. Will you be here by then?"

"I wish I could tell you for certain. It depends on what happens here. But one thing is certain. I'll definitely be back on the fifteenth, I promise. I must go now, love, there's a conference at four p.m. Tell Rachel I'll see her soon. Love you, sweetheart. Bye."

She stood up from the lounger, threw a wrap around her waist and ambled into the kitchen. There was little you could tell her about the unpredictability of police work. She had been a policewoman for ten years and a policeman's wife for what seemed like an eternity.

She remembered their first meeting in the superintendent's office at Oldpark Station. It was 1989 and she was fresh from the training centre. Mike was to be her mentor. She recalled his wonderful way with the locals. With older ladies, faltering under the weight of heavy shopping bags, and with boisterous kids, who wore his cap and were curious about the new Heckler and Koch sub-machine guns. He would lift them into armoured vehicles and always responded with an approving nod when they asked, "Hey mister, mister, mister can I sound the two tones?" In Belfast it seemed that one mister was never quite enough.

He even earned a guarded nod from the hardest cases on the mean streets of Ardoyne and 'The Bone'.

She recalled the day in September, when the coded call came in. It was two forty-five p.m. on a sunny afternoon and they were on patrol in Rosapenna Street. The memory still made her shiver.

"Uniform, uniform to all call signs, wait out. We have a coded message from a loyalist terror group of a car bomb in Alliance Avenue near the junction with Berwick Road. The vehicle is described as a red Ford Orion VRM SER7509. All call signs please radio in on your arrival. Start evacuation procedures immediately, the caller said we have fifteen minutes."

In a few seconds he was on Ardoyne Avenue with horns blaring. A right, left, right took him along Etna Drive. At the end of the street he turned left and stopped. Two hundred yards ahead the car sat empty. Local school children and their mothers walked passed it oblivious to the danger. School was out for five and six-year-olds.

"Uniform, uniform from Delta Oscar 8-0," she replied. "We are at the junction of Etna Drive and Alliance Avenue. I am setting up a cordon here. My partner has gone to assist with the evacuation. Delta Tango call signs are giving a hand. They have a cordon at the top of the avenue. Could you have a call sign go to the junction of Oldpark Road and Alliance Avenue and create a diversion? Could you also send one to Deerpark Road and divert traffic away from this location?" Her instructions were clear and precise. They invited confidence in her as if she was a seasoned officer and not one in her second month on the job.

She switched on the hazard lights and stepped out of the car.

She watched Mike race from house to house, evacuating those closest to the suspect car first and telling the elderly and infirm to go to the rear of their houses and stay away from the windows. There were a couple of minutes of pandemonium as other cordons were set up. In ten minutes the area was presumed clear and Mike went back to help Jayne.

To his right was a staunch Protestant who had been evacuated from Alliance Crescent on the other side of the peace line. To his left stood Tommy McConville. He seemed agitated. The usual jaunty swagger had abandoned him. Tommy was a long-time republican and a genuine hard case, the fabric of his thoughts influenced by many events. His father, Finbar, had fought along the border in the previous campaign in the fifties and early sixties. As a boy he had witnessed young nationalists being bludgeoned and torn from their mothers' or wives' clutches by British soldiers at dawn on 9 August 1971. Three hundred and fifty men were interned in Long Kesh that day. None of them were Protestants, so much for the even-handedness of the Unionist government.

He had shared the common anguish of many republicans as one volunteer after another died painfully on hunger strike in 1981.

That same year Christopher Black was arrested for a number of terrorist offences. Within months detectives and spooks had made him an offer he could not refuse. Black became a 'tout'. He had set aside a republican warning: 'Whatever you say, say nothing when you talk about you-know-what'.

He recalled the days in August 1983, when Black gave evidence against thirty-eight republicans. Many were his long-time friends. Some would say you could not have written the script. The Crumlin Road courthouse was a fortress. Armed police patrolled the perimeter, checking potential mortar sites. Mobile Support Units set up checkpoints around the network of roads leading to and from the courthouse. Judges arrived speedily in armoured cars, escorted by close protection officers. They swept through the hastily raised barrier and passed to the rear of the building. Each morning, sniffer dogs swept judges' chambers and public courtrooms. Some seasoned lawyers took umbrage at having brief cases rummaged each time they wished to enter the impressive chamber. Lowly constables gained great delight in searching the most pompous thoroughly.

Courtroom one looked like a scene from some exaggerated Sicilian mafia movie, armed officers standing rigidly to the rear of the courtroom throughout the proceedings. Their arms wearied by the weight of M1 carbines. Their brows sweated by the burden of NATO sweaters and heavy woollen trousers. The clamour abated and the assembly rose as the judge entered. He bowed before sitting behind the cover of the bulletproof glass; his already portly shape further puffed-up by the armour plate beneath his crimson robes.

The cocky republicans rose one by one to answer the charges. The evidence was never tested by a jury. The latest raft of Northern Ireland Emergency Provisions had seen to that. These were the days of the Diplock courts. Judges sitting alone, deciding on the guilt or innocence of the accused, writing endlessly to justify each decision, open to ridicule and accusations of political interference. Most were given long sentences by Justice Basil Kelly. To most the system seemed terribly flawed. As quickly as suspected republican and loyalist terrorists were imprisoned under the system, their appeals against these convictions were upheld.

Of the twenty-two sent down that day, eighteen were released on appeal in 1986.

Tommy lived in a cul-de-sac off Ardoyne Avenue. The memory of 2 April 1987 and the succeeding days would never leave him. He had been playing darts in the Glenpark Social Club. A grudge match against The Shamrock Club at the bottom of the avenue. It was just after nine when he heard the shots, two bursts of rapid fire and a couple of single shots. He raced to the door as the getaway car sped by.

"We got the bastard," he heard the rear passenger shout through the half-closed window.

A crowd had gathered in Havana Gardens. Larry Marley lay dead on his porch. On that night a wife became a widow, six children lost their father and the republican movement lost one of its most dedicated volunteers. Of the previous fifteen years Larry had spent only two at home.

The funeral was attempted on three occasions. The RUC refused to allow any military trappings. As quickly as the coffin was carried from the house on the first and second days, so it returned. Flanks of police officers blocked the way. Most couldn't care less whether a coffin bore a pair of gloves, a beret and a tricolour on top. But the politicians' sensitivities had to be satisfied.

On the morning of 6 April, here were two or three hundred police and a similar number of mourners. The day after, the numbers of each had more than doubled, as the standoff hardened. He had heard one senior officer say to the family,

"If you don't bury him tomorrow, we will bury him the next day."

On the eighth, the police had more than one thousand officers close to the house and along the funeral route to Holy Cross chapel. Their number more than matched by the republican followers.

Police armoured vehicles stretched endlessly along the Cavehill and Oldpark Roads.

In the end Larry received his military send off, though not the one the RUC had tried to prevent. It happened in the early morning beside the memorial to dead comrades at the corner of Berwick Road. Three gunmen fired three volleys and paid their respects.

At dawn on the last day a compromise was reached. It was the largest display of republican solidarity since the hunger strike. By the time the cortege came to the Falls Road in West Belfast, the police were hopelessly outnumbered. Only God knew why there was not carnage that day.

It made Tommy think of the compelling words of Terence MacSwiney, a hunger striker from the twenties; "It is not those who inflict the most, but those that endure the most, that shall prevail."

The PIRA avenged Larry's murder some days later. William 'Frenchie' Marchent was in his usual company outside the Progressive Unionist Party office on the Shankill Road. He never had the chance to run away or dart inside. He barely had time to face his nemesis. Three shots rang out from a passing car and Frenchie lay dead. Tommy had been party to the planning, but he was not the triggerman. He was never the triggerman.

Chapter 20

"What's the matter, Tommy?" Thornton enquired.

"I've one missing," he gasped. He turned to his wife. "Mary, where's Nancy?" There was a collective gasp as the six-year-old appeared beside the suspect car, petrified and crying, her fists clasped pitifully under her chin as if she had done something terribly wrong.

In an instant Thornton's cap and body armour were on the ground. He charged down the street, eating up the distance, like a sprinter. The gathering looked on in tense and shocked silence. Was this really a Proddy peeler giving everything he had to rescue the republican's daughter? Reaching the car, he scooped up the screaming child and turned to head back. He had taken some thirty strides, when his instinct told him to hit the ground. The little girl lay in his shelter as debris flew over them and the terrible noise made his ears ring. They lay for a minute covered in dust, shaken by the might of the bomb. Then he carried the little girl to the safety of the cordon and handed her to a tearful father.

Tommy McConville hugged and kissed his daughter as tears welled up and spilled down his cheeks.

He turned to Thornton, thanked him and cupped his hand in both of his. It was the first time he had ever shaken hands with a policeman. Four hours later he was telling the high command that his days of military action were over. Sinn Fein welcomed a talented political activist.

Jayne thought of the welcome on their return to the station, the slaps on the back and the congratulations. Bravery was a commodity that never lost its value. The black humour that fed the morale at the barracks raised its voice.

"What do you do for an encore, Mike?"

"Next time can you leave me your Gore-Tex insoles and mag light?"

"Glad you ducked in time, Mike. It's your round at Fealty's tonight."

The requisite glass of whiskey pushed into each shaking hand by a boss who knew little of such ordeals. It was his way of saying thanks. His way of showing the respect which rank alone can never earn. His days at headquarters seemed so irrelevant, a stepping-stone from the lower orders. But not one that carried any cache with those who really mattered, the guys and girls on the street.

She recalled the moment when Mike considered the reality of what he had done, as they sat together over a drink in a quiet corner of the Kitchen Bar. The tears in his eyes exposed his vulnerability. Her comforting hug put them together for the first time.

Thornton kissed her on the cheek and gazed deeply into her hazel eyes.

"I don't want to be alone tonight, Jayne. I need to be with you."

She recalled his tasteful apartment. They showered separately, each in silent reflection, wishing the powerful jets could wash away the grim day.

The minutes turned to hours as they cuddled up in matching bathrobes, in front of the fire, sipping an elegant Sauvignon Blanc. Neither wished to let go of the other, each of them convinced that the events they had shared that day had bound them forever.

He kissed her, with affection at first and then with the sort of passion that only soul mates can experience. The bathrobes tumbled from their naked bodies and he laid her tenderly on the bed to the then unfamiliar sound of Madame Butterfly and Lieutenant Pinkerton. His fingers and lips found the sensual zones that made her moan. She writhed as his tongue touched her swollen clitoris, feeling an instant need to take him inside of her.

"Make love to me, Mike. Make love to me."

She remembered his movement along the length of her body. His taught, muscular chest grazing her raised nipples as his piercing blue eyes looked deeply into hers. She felt his powerful back arch and his pelvis lower as she guided him inside her, just a brief resistance as her body opened to receive him. She raised her hips to accommodate the rest of him and gasped with pleasure as he pushed deeper.

They moved in perfect harmony, rising and falling together to the rhythm of the beautiful music in the background. She could not tell where her body ended and his began, so intense was the sensation. It was then that she knew she was with the man she loved, the man who made love to her like no other had before, the man whom she would marry.

"Don't stop, Mike, don't stop!" she pleaded.

But he could resist no longer. His head jolted back as he exploded inside her. For a second or two he was in his own world of pleasure, unreachable, a million miles from the deadly streets where he walked the beat. His orgasm triggered her own, which started deep inside, causing her pelvic muscles to contract tightly around him. The thrill raced through her like an electric current, setting her nerve endings tingling and leaving her longing for more. They were now as one in body and mind as the lovers' duet hit its own hot-blooded crescendo. She remembered thinking it was like some sort of exorcism that left them decontaminated, washing away the taint of the day's violence, an emotional cleansing that would prepare them for whatever came their way in the weeks ahead. They were a team, a very good team. Even stronger now, they were a team to be reckoned with.

Their bodies rolled apart and they lay satisfied and silent for a moment. Then they were in each other's arms again, her head resting comfortably on his shoulder. They talked and laughed and learnt a little more about each other. They fell asleep together. In the morning they awoke ready to face the day, and ready to enjoy the rest of their lives together.

Mike Thornton knew that his days in Oldpark were numbered. There was no place for soft sentiment and much less for RUC heroes, on the bitter republican streets in Ardoyne. He knew that and so did the PIRA.

Chapter 21

The incident room was a clamour of activity as Keenan, Lynch and Thornton arrived. It had just past four p.m.

Keenan made his way to the front of the room. He introduced Thornton before reviewing the information that had already come to light: the sighting of a vehicle leaving the laneway beside the holiday home at 2.40 a.m., the spotting of a camper van in Ramelton at 3:10 a.m., the on-going enquiry into the partial number plate, the identification of the tyre track and the now conclusive evidence that the parents had been sedated.

Oliver Maher was the team's crime co-ordinater and Keenan's right hand man.

"Ollie, can you fill us in with the current lines of enquiry, please?"

"Certainly, sir. I'll start with the additional information we got from the appeal. We've received two more significant calls. John Eddie is a milkman in Limavady. He phoned in about an hour ago. He said he was on his morning delivery when a light-coloured camper van drove past. It was heading towards Coleraine. He thinks it was an older Volkswagen model. There was only one person on board. He puts the time at about four a.m. He is coming to Letterkenny to make a statement.

We have a lorry driver appearing to confirm this sighting. He was in a hurry heading for Larne harbour to catch the ferry when he passed a small, pale camper van a mile or so further down the road. He phoned from a diner outside Glasgow an hour ago. He'll be back tomorrow and will call in to make a statement.

Turning now to our suspects. We have eliminated all local sex offenders. None had the unique knowledge required to imitate Ramsey in this way. We are interested in two men from the North. Each would have the knowledge needed, the stuff that was not released to the public during the Ramsey enquiry. They will be very familiar to you, DCS Thornton."

He pointed at an enlarged photograph on the wall.

"This is James Elliot. He's forty-six years old. He shared a cell with Ramsey at Magilligan whilst they were both on remand seven years ago. He served six years for a series of perverted attacks on young girls. He targeted them at parks and playgrounds on the outskirts of Belfast.

"He was very calculating in the way he singled them out. They were always on their own. Ones with further to walk to reach home. He chose the most secluded section of the route and pretended that his car had broken down. As the child approached, he forced them into the sheltered area to the side of the car, pinned them down and removed their pants.

He was caught after his sixth attack. The police had mounted a number of surveillance operations at some of the local parks and schools. Something clearly spooked him or perhaps he realised he was being watched. Anyway, he reversed up a one-way street and crashed into an oncoming vehicle.

"When they searched his car, they found four sets of number plates in the boot. The search of his house led to the recovery of the girls' pants from a box under the floorboards in his sitting room. There were a number of obscene photographs of these girls as well as those of other girls whom it was believed he was targeting. He was not going to stop until he was caught.

"Elliot was released last year and is currently living in Whiteabbey. Local police believe that he has reacquainted himself with his old friends. His Sex Offender's Probation Order prohibits any inappropriate use of social networks and there is no indication of such abuses. Anyway, the regular examination of his computer and other devices was one of the terms of his licence. But even this is not watertight. Elliot is a particularly resilient and intelligent paedophile.

"He is regular in his attendance at social service meetings and with the weekly signing requirements at the local police station. He is currently on holiday somewhere in the South. There are no reciprocal arrangements for him to sign in at a station in the South when on holiday. He told his probation officer he was heading for a week to a cottage in Donegal. We are trying to locate him. We have the make and registration number of his car and the authority to carry out surveillance on him, north and south. We are attempting to intercept his telephone communications. That will give us a good idea where he is staying. We can't rule out his existence as an accomplice, or that he might be our culprit.

"I believe that it was you who put him away, Mr Thornton? If he's our man and we follow the current information, he may already be back in the North.

"The second will be even more familiar to you, sir. Perhaps you would like to tell us about him?"

Thornton stood up and moved to the front of the room just beside the enlarged image.

"This is former Detective Inspector William James McCluskey. Jimmy was on my original investigation team seven years ago. He and I go back a long way. We were in the same squad at the Training Centre. We both turned out for the RUC rugby team and did the CID initial course together.

"He was a university graduate in chemistry. At one time he was seen as a high flyer. He had been accepted onto the Graduate Entry Scheme but had tumbled from it in the nineties. He had a real chip on his shoulder. When he was overlooked for promotion to DCI some years later, he became very disillusioned. Jimmy had made real progress since his days in care as a boy. He never talked about his past, although it was rumoured that he had been fostered or adopted for a number of years.

"This was confirmed during our investigation into his history, as part of the criminal enquiry. His pre-sentence probation report revealed that he was taken into care when he was seven and fostered by an aging couple for a number of years. He attended Holywood Primary School and then Sullivan Upper. From there he went on to Queen's University.

"His upbringing had left him with an unfortunate victim complex. He blamed everything, except himself, for his lack of progress, if it wasn't his poor start in life, it was the authorities or the new system of selection.

"His unhealthy interest in the details of the abuses and murders of the three girls only became apparent towards the end of the enquiry. He never viewed Ramsey with the same contempt as the rest of the team. He was very quick to point the finger at what he felt was going wrong with the enquiry. It's fair to say that mistakes were made. But he was reluctant to take responsibility for his own shortcomings. I removed him from the investigation just after Ramsey was charged. He was furious. In hindsight I should have put him off sooner.

"Some months later, I arrested him for possessing over twenty thousand pornographic images of young girls, all had blonde hair and were six or seven years old.

"He was released just over four years ago. He would certainly know everything about Ramsey's MO. Like Elliot he adheres to all monitoring arrangements. I have received authority for the full package of surveillance on him. A team is trying to locate him as we speak.

"At the time of his arrest we also recovered photographs of the three murdered girls. It appeared that he was perversely obsessed by the terrible way they lost their lives. He fought the case tooth and nail, saying that the photographs and downloaded images were part of his research into a thesis he was writing for a degree in Criminology. He showed no remorse or contrition at any time during the trial, or at any time thereafter. He appeared to me as a man who was only heading in one direction."

Ollie Maher thanked Thornton and then continued, "It seems that the parents have been unable to give us very much. They are not on Facebook or twitter and would rarely exchange or send photographs by phone or internet. There is nothing suspicious on their personal computer and Megan's use of the internet and her mobile phone is closely monitored by the mother.

"There was, however, something that they both independently referred to. It happened two years ago when Megan was in primary one. A number of parents and teachers had noticed a taxi, parked regularly across the road from the front gate when the kids were on their morning and lunch breaks and again when they were getting out of school. It appeared never to pick anyone up. It just hung around until the children left. When a teacher approached the vehicle it made off at speed.

There was a vague description of a man in his mid-forties with long dark hair and a beard. The car was a blue Skoda Octavia with a 'Low Cost' taxi sign mounted on the roof. The police ran a check on the number plate and it confirmed the model. The owner was investigated and found to be out of the country for most of the time when the sightings were made. It was seemingly a 'ringer' vehicle. The taxi firm confirmed that they had no blue Octavias working for them at that time."

It was seven thirty p.m. when Frank Keenan addressed his team.

"I can't thank you all enough, for your hard work today. I don't see that we are going to achieve much more tonight. I want to ask DCS Thornton to talk to you about how Ramsey targeted the girls seven years ago. You need to know the type of person we may be up against."

Thornton stepped behind the lectern.

"Peter James Ramsey was an intelligent and meticulous predator. There was no unique science to the pursuit of his quarries. No use of social networks or paedophile sites. Instead he undertook long, painstaking research. He targeted the places where children would regularly be, the local primary schools in Belfast, Lisburn, Holywood and Carrickfergus. It was usually girls' schools, simply because it increased the number of targets to choose from.

"Once he had identified the children, he got to know everything about them, their habits, their hobbies, even their birthdays. Did they have brothers or sisters? If they did then they were immediately discounted. He followed them home, to shops, to clubs and to relatives' houses. He knew how they celebrated special occasions and where they went on holidays.

If there was any hint of him being exposed, he moved on to another child. At all times he adhered to his reporting restrictions, never allowing any suspicion to fall on him. There were a number of sightings near St Thomas's, of a man fitting his description around two months before the abduction of Emma Baillie. You may recall that this was where Emma attended school. He was questioned about it and denied culpability. He stated that he was in Galway at the time.

"His mother backed up his story that he had been on holiday at her cottage in Connemara. We were not in a position to disprove this. Locals vaguely recalled a man staying at the cottage around the time of the sightings near St Thomas's but could not be sure about the dates. In any event, there was insufficient evidence of an offence to allow for an identity parade. It is doubtful if any of the witnesses could have picked him from a line-up.

"At the time of the abductions, he had arranged a holiday in agreement with his probation officer so that everything seemed completely above board. But he had stated that it was difficult to be specific as he was intending touring in a camper van.

"He was a suspect but we did not know where he was and there was no pattern to the abductions except for the ages of the girls who were taken.

"It was a genuine stroke of pure luck when we caught him in the early hours of 15 July. He had left Holly Oran in the bedroom of a holiday let on a mountain road some miles from Rostrevor, County Down. His latest victim was tied up and gagged on the rear seat of the camper van. I think it's fair to say that Lucy Henry had someone looking out for her that night. It is likely that he was heading south of the border again.

During one of his interviews he referred to the police having interfered with his 'grand tour' of the Island.

"It was about 3:05 a.m. on the fifteenth when the police got word of a failed gun attack on a local businessman in Warrenpoint. They were directed to set up checkpoints on the network of roads close to the town. Some minutes later Ramsey was stopped at a checkpoint on the Burren Road, near St Mark's School. He didn't try to reverse away or run. He just smiled at the officer and asked, 'What took you incompetent bastards so long?' Heaven knows how many more he may have taken but for that stroke of luck. The officers found photographs of Holly Oran, and a grid reference telling them where she would be found, on his phone, stashed in the glove compartment. The shaved locks of the girls' hair were discovered in the rear of the camper van. You may recall that Holly Oran was recovered alive from a cottage nearby but died in hospital a few hours later.

"I've only one more thing to say to you all. I believe our culprit has applied the same degree of meticulous planning, over a considerable period of time. He will think that he has left nothing to chance. We must find a way to interrupt his plans, to knock him off kilter. He may not deal quite so well if his plan is disturbed.

"There are already several things that are bugging me. Why did he allow his vehicle to be caught on camera, when there was simply no need? Did he do it intentionally? If he did, what was his purpose? The camera does not recognise vehicles. It had to be the vehicle registration mark. Was it the weather that obscured the last two letters or has he done this himself?"

He looked at the partial registration number pinned to the wall, Y110H, feeling that he was missing something. Then he turned towards the team, "We need to find the link. My instinct tells me that he is somewhere in the North, along the north coast. A young girl is in serious peril and he is ready to strike again."

Chapter 22

The stranger downloaded the app onto Megan Reilly's phone. It was eight thirty p.m. and time to be moving on. He recalled how Ramsey had revealed the location of the children through taunting notes, photographs and a grid reference, all posted to the investigator. But technology was now so much more sophisticated and instant.

He sat at Megan's side. She was very much his first project, one that had started on the first day of the autumn term two years ago. She had just turned five. He recalled the endless hours of watching and following, the time consuming singling out. At first, there were four potential victims. One by one they tumbled from the shortlist. Francis Telford had an elder brother, Patricia Slevan a younger sister. Pauline Goodall took continental summer holidays. This left Megan.

Mrs Thompson was her first teacher. Then it was Mrs Jeffers. She ought to be going into Miss Spier's class this coming year. Melissa Parks was her very best friend. They went horse riding together on Saturday mornings. Melissa had been at Megan's birthday party the night she was taken. In April that year Megan took a tumble from her favourite pony, Rhubarb. She suffered mild concussion. He had called at the hospital just to see that she was all right. When questioned about whom he had come to visit, he told the nurse he was lost. She gave him directions to the geriatric ward.

Harry Potter was her chosen reading. Piano lessons were given by Miss Travis, a bespectacled spinster with a love of Alfred Brendle's 1978 recital of Beethoven's Fifth. She had a hidden passion for the married Mr Dale, a senior teacher.

Then there were her parents, the lovely John and Sheila. Daddy worked for the Water Service, mummy for Giles Estate Agents. On Tuesday nights they played tennis at the Boat Club tennis courts. It was a regular mixed doubles match with the Glennings, normally a fierce fought encounter with little to decide between them.

They all attended St Mark's parish church on Sunday and visited her grandparents every other Saturday. Most importantly, they had a mobile home in Portsalon that they visited every July.

Chapter 23

He checked the syringe drive was working and applauded himself for the quality of the little girl's sedation. The trimmer moved easily near her scalp. Its tedious hum accompanied the fall of her long flowing locks, which came away like a golden fleece. He untied the scarlet ribbons and undressed her, careful not to displace the syringe drive. In minutes she lay serenely clothed in a crimson party frock. He tethered her again and retired to the precise focal point. He raised the little girl's iPhone and clicked three times. He was pleased to see that her naïve form was right in the centre. He studied the screen and pressing message, he attached the photographs and typed a chilling memo. He set the timer to seven a.m. He made sure that the syringe drive was amply filled. Then he gathered up a few provisions, taking no care whatsoever to wipe down shelves or shiny surfaces or rinse his coffee cup. He felt obliged to leave them something, a smudged fingerprint or two and potential DNA opportunities. What would it matter? By the time they had the results his mission would be complete.

The Vespa's engine whined as he headed for Portstewart, satisfied that the search party would arrive just as the little girl was waking up and that she would remember nothing of her ordeal. By the end of the week she might even be back on her daddy's shoulders, on a stroll to the headland before turning in for the night. But somehow he doubted it. He had a feeling that a 'For Sale' sign would appear in the not too distant future at site A42.

Thornton, Lynch and Keenan were joined by Grainne Burrows in Lynch's office. Lynch lifted four glasses from his cabinet.

"I take it you're all fine without water?" he asked rhetorically, as he poured four generous measures of Jameson. "Sorry I'm out of Black Bush Mike, but I've always preferred Jameson's anyway."

Thornton smiled absently and took a healthy swig.

"I've booked rooms for you at The Bailiff's Arms," he said turning to Thornton and Burrows. "They are small but comfortable. The food is excellent and it's just five minutes up the road. Before we break up for the night I want to thank you all. It means a lot to me to have such a good team around me to share the load. Let's hope for the best."

Thornton kept his own counsel. From previous investigation, he still retained the terrible image of Emma Baillie's tortured body. He could hardly bear to contemplate that Megan Reilly could end her life in a similar fashion.

He thought also of the taking of Hannah Graham and Ramsey's violent change of mood, the casing of the house, the silent entry through an open rear window, and Ramsey's sheer gall to have rented the property next door. The disbelief of the parents wakened at knifepoint. His heartless taunting and deceitful promise that Hannah's life would be spared if they did what he demanded. Their final plea left no impression on the cold-hearted killer.

He did not need to inform or remind the others of these thoughts. They too were preoccupied by such ideas.

Chapter 24

Eamon Lynch pulled up outside an imposing red-bricked house, overlooking the golf course just outside Letterkenny. It had been wife Katy's dream home for many years. The collapse of the market in 2009 had brought the asking price to within their reach.

She threw her arms around him as he struggled inside and onto his chair in the front room by the window. The weight of the day's grim events lay heavily on him. There was a look in his eyes that she had seen but once before. It was of fear and of fading hope. She saw it last seven years ago when Emma Baillie's body was found. She knew how close it had brought him to the edge. She was still haunted by the unbearable vision of her nearly broken husband, who hit the drink and cried when he thought he was alone. The pills that seemed unable to replace the nightmares and the dark moods that woke him regularly or caused him to sit in silence when in company. Months of cognitive behavioural therapy had allowed him to live with himself once more. His recovery to good health had been slow and precarious. She knew he could not face this again; that the loss of another child on his watch would be devastating.

"I'm tired, Katy," he said. "So very tired."

There was little she could say at that moment. She hugged him tightly. There had been many occasions in the past when the same show of affection was necessary. She thought how cruel a turn of events it would be if her husband's last investigation ended in the death of another child. He did not deserve that.

Chapter 25

It was nine p.m. when Thornton and Burrows sat down for dinner. They had taken advantage of some hefty towels and an endless supply of hot water to wash away the stench of a thoroughly horrible day.

Grainne was looking impeccable as always, her nails beautifully manicured, her hair in a frisky bob and the alluring hint of Chanel N°5, almost undetectable but not forgotten.

He surrendered fleetingly to the thought of the elegant lingerie, worn on the nights they spent together all those years ago: the furtive encounters in less well known hotels and country houses in the Cooley Mountains or sleepy seaside villages to the north of Dublin.

They had been hard times for both of them. Each sought comfort and intimacy from the other. Grainne had lost her long-time partner to cancer. Thornton's marriage was on a knife-edge.

For the Thorntons, the future had seemed so bright. Everything appeared to fall into place for them. Both were enjoying successful careers, when Jayne retired as an inspector in 1999. She was twenty-nine and feeling maternal. But pregnancy and full-term carriage did not come as easily as had professional competence and promotions. A cruel stillbirth followed three miscarriages.

She struggled to come to terms with the terrible misfortune. For a while they were like strangers in their own home, neither knowing what to say for the best, each wishing to express their love for the other but never finding the right words or moment for intimate contact. It became easier for Thornton to be longer at work, to come up with ready excuses for staying away another night, as he fell into the arms of the warm and receptive Grainne.

"A penny for your thoughts, Mike?" Grainne asked.

"Oh, just thinking of old times," he replied. Their eyes met across the table but not as they had done all those years ago. Then there had been searing passion in them. The type of desire that comes with long hours spent together in dangerous places and having an eye for each other in the first place. Their lust spilled out like a torrent when they came together for the first time. They made love like athletes, powerful and pulsating and leaving nothing to the imagination.

He recalled how the affair had ended one wintery night in December. They were cuddling between lavish Egyptian cotton sheets in a beautiful bedroom in Ghan House, just outside Carlingford, when his phone rang. It was his sister-in-law, Laura.

"Oh, Mike, thank God I found you. It's Jayne, Mike. She's taken an overdose. She's in the City Hospital. They've already had to resuscitate her once. We thought she was gone."

"I'm on my way, Laura."

Thornton recalled tumbling out of bed, suffering the keen first pangs of guilt. Why had he not been there for her? How could they have become so distant? Would she make it through this? Would their marriage?

"How have you been, Mike?" Grainne enquired.

"I've been well thanks. I celebrated thirty years on the job last month. I can hardly believe it."

"How's Jayne, Mike?"

"She's good and we're doing well. My transfer to Belfast helped a lot. It took a long time for us to get over everything, between the lost babies and the overdose, but we did it.

"Counselling helped, everything came out amidst the floods of tears. It was painful. Facing your guilt is not an easy thing to do. But she forgave me and we came through. We renewed our marriage vows some years ago."

He considered the things less appropriate to be spoken of just then. The renewal of their bond, the tender tentative moments in the Maria Cristina hotel in San Sebastian; so little had it changed since those honeymoon nights of years before. The view from the window of their corner room remained unsurpassed for him: the surge of the Urumea River as it met the Atlantic, the Zurriola beach stretching like golden braid up to the headland to the east (enjoyed by devoted residents, young and old, and a few discerning tourists), the bustle and clamour at the countless Pinxto bars along the cobbled streets of the Old Town, and retired fishermen eating heartily in quaint mariners' clubs down by the harbour. The dinner at A Fuego Negra that brought the conversation back to when first they met as mentor and student.

Jayne's desire for life was returning. The struggle within was fading fast. As they lay naked in each other's arms just after midnight they reclaimed the passion that had been taken from them and made love till early morning. Once again the dulcet tones of Butterfly and Pinkerton soared in perfect pitch and brought them back to the place that only true love can find.

"Mike, you seemed miles away there," Grainne said, not wishing to pry.

"Sorry, Grainne. I was miles away. They occur more frequently the older I get. As I was saying, eight years ago we saw a specialist in London.

"A year later, our lovely Rachel was born. The following years were not without their worries. She was three when we discovered she had asthma. The doctors said it was not to cause too much concern but she would be on medication until she reached her teens at least." Thornton took a photograph from his wallet and gave it to Grainne.

"She's pretty, Mike, Jayne's good looks and your long legs. I'm happy for you, Mike."

They sat talking through their first and second courses and shared a cheeseboard, before sinking into a comfy sofa by the fire and ordering two Irish coffees.

Until then, Mike had done most of the talking.

Then it was Grainne's turn. The turf fire glowed and offered up an earthy scent as she poured out her heart: the loss of her mother and the devastation that had caused. Her resignation from *The Times* and the challenge of her new role as a police press officer in Dublin, and the breakup of their relationship, for she had fallen in love with the charming man who now sat with her next to the fire.

More than a hint of a smile appeared when she spoke of the new man in her life, whom she had grown to love dearly.

"I am in a great relationship, with a Gard. I met him three years ago in Bar 51 on Haddington Road in Dublin. You probably know it. It is where a lot of the cops go before a big match. I was there on my own on the off chance of getting a ticket for the Ireland v Australia, autumn international. I had heard there was a friendly Gard with a ready supply of tickets. A bartender with a square jaw told me his name and pointed him out to me. He was at the back bar supping a pint of Guinness and watching Wales against South Africa on the wide screen. He was commenting on the scrum as if he knew something about it. He was sounding off about loose and tight head props. He scorned the referee for his scant knowledge of the difference between the two positions. I thought I would save the big Northern lad beside him from a further ear bashing. I was quite shameless.

"'Hi there, Brian, you don't know me. I'm Grainne and I work for the Garda press office. Would you happen to have a spare ticket?'

"'I may have one if you'll have a drink with me,' he said, half turning towards me. As he caught his first glimpse, his blue eyes widened and he smiled. "'Och, to heck with that. There's one for you whether you have a drink or not. I'm Brian O'Grady.'

"It was quarter to when he checked his watch, so we drank up and almost cantered past the Beggar's Bush pub and onto Shelbourne Road. His pace getting more frantic as time ran out. He hates missing the presentation of the teams and the singing of the anthems.

"By three minutes to the hour, he was excusing us as we brushed past quietly grumbling spectators and took our seats in the West Stand by the halfway line. It was a super match, the crowd cheering to the rafters as Ireland pulled ahead to win. O'Driscoll scored a beauty on the stroke of half-time. He filled in the detail, when my knowledge of the game fell short. I kept asking what must have seemed foolish questions, but he took them in his stride. After the game we headed back to the bar again. He introduced me to his friends, keeping a fair distance between me and the big guy from the North who had been in his company before the match.

"We dined at Roly's Bistro and shared the couple's menu. It may sound naff, but it was lovely."

"On Sunday we strolled through the leafy suburbs of south Dublin." Grainne's voice warmed as she remembered that crisp, dry morning, the leafy suburbs forming a canopy of autumnal russet-toned leaves about them.

"As we were walking he started quoting poetry,

'On Raglan Road on an autumn day, I met
her first and knew
That her dark hair would weave a snare that
I might one day rue;
I saw the danger, yet I walked along the
enchanted way,
And I said, let grief be a fallen leaf at the
dawning of the day.'

"Well, the words of Kavanagh's poem came back to me in a flash. They had never meant much when I was studying them at school, nor had they ever been expressed so poignantly. There was clearly more to this big man from Tullamore than some well-rehearsed Irish blarney. I had really warmed to him even in that short time. I wanted us to be close and intimate, I didn't want him to suffer the poet's fated let down," Grainne smiled, her eyes twinkling playfully.

"In a lowered tone and timbre he closed with that last haunting verse, as we turned onto Elgin Road.

'On a quiet street where old ghosts meet I see
her walking now
Away from me so hurriedly my reason must
allow
That I had wooed not as I should a creature
made of clay.
When the angel woos the clay he'd lose his
wings at the dawn of day.'

"We have been a serious item ever since." A smile lit up her face as Grainne gazed into the fire.

"Is that the sound of wedding bells I hear?" Thornton quipped, flashing her a grin.

Grainne laughed and, turning to look at Mike, she decided to exercise her right to silence.

Chapter 26

The stranger freewheeled into 2 Springtide Gardens. It was just after nine p.m. He guided the scooter into the space in the garage beside the camper van. He took off his helmet and rucksack, tossing them in the back seat of the van.

He tipped a wink to the little girl who was heading for the house next door. Dressed in a wetsuit, she had clearly been swimming as children do from the harbour pier at night when the tide is in. Her long blonde hair was matted and frazzled. She inched past him nervously, her head tilted timidly away. He needed not to ask her name. He knew everything about her.

She was Ailish McParland, just turned seven. She attended My Lady's Primary School in Whiteabbey. She enjoyed Irish dancing every Tuesday night and was top of her class. Mary Savage was her best friend, except for the time they had fallen out over some boy called Niall. Her father, Ciaran, lectured in Sports Science at The Belfast Metropolitan College, while her mother, Mary, taught chemistry at Fortwilliam College. He drove a silver Mondeo, she a white Hyundai I20. They bought the house in Portstewart three years ago. James's father had left quite a tidy sum. Ailish was their only child.

She turned towards him just before she went into the house. The young girl was clearly unnerved but she was blissfully unaware that this brief encounter was a prelude to one much longer, and utterly more unsettling, later on.

The stranger headed for the town centre. He felt a brisk walk as the sun went down would sharpen his appetite.

He took the shortcut to the harbour. The sun was just retreating behind Dominican College that sat watchfully on the promontory overlooking the waterfront. He chose the coastal path that wound beneath the school, along the shoreline. A young couple with a friendly golden retriever sauntered by. The dog snuffled tufts of grass, and marked its presence. It responded reluctantly to the second tug of the lead.

An older couple passed him hand in hand. How many years had they been in love he wondered? Had their union been for fifty years or more? Had children and grandchildren been most of their joy in life? How he had wished that their lot could have been his own in years to come.

The path ran out as it reached Portstewart Strand, a magnificent golden strip. Within its towering dunes, the hallowed links caused havoc, playing with the minds of many dreaming, but newly crushed, golfers. Most were brash heavy guys from USA, with more money than craft and a quaint 'Thatched Cottage and Shawled Women' view of Ireland.

He recalled the summer years ago, when Bob and Sally gave up their beloved Newcastle for a holiday on the north coast. He was fifteen and had entered for the teens' windsurfing championships.

The tide had been full and the wind raced rapidly out to sea on the first day. This caused the waves to rear up and be difficult to ride. He had found this out quickly, but not quite quickly enough, to his cost. A huge one tossed him from his board and he appeared coughing and spluttering to the amusement of onlookers.

He recalled the muffled laughter as he walked up the beach wearing little more than a red face and an air of wounded pride.

"What a wuss," he heard from a voice that sounded more than a little familiar. He turned to see Gemma Davis mimicking his embarrassing fall from the board, as she toppled onto the sand with an exaggerated grimace.

"I suppose that's your competition over now. smarty pants."

"Well, if you must know, it's not," he remembered saying. "It's the best of three attempts and I can't be any worse than that tomorrow."

She liked the modesty in him. She had become used to it over the years in the same class together, his stubborn will to win with a gracious manner in defeat, his genius for maths and science and his conscientious attention to detail. They had been friends and rivals for almost eight years.

"Fancy an ice-cream or are you going to take a second tumble and give us all another laugh?" she said turning with confidence, knowing that he would not be far behind.

"I didn't know you were coming here for summer," he said, drying himself as he walked.

"You never asked," she retorted, a smile playing on her lips. "We have a holiday house along the Strand Road. We come here every summer."

He recalled her bubbly conversation and pretty smile. He agreed immediately to the invitation to tea that night, where he met her parents for the first time. In the morning they met on the beach just after breakfast.

He recalled the race along the strand to the Barmouth, two miles away, where the beach meets the River Bann and Castlerock sits on the other side. Their hearts pumping like pistons as they raced, then fell exhausted onto the sand. There had been almost nothing between them, the winner almost too close to call.

"Looks like I pipped you again," she said with a playful grin, although she knew that was not the case.

He had chosen not to respond.

The windsurfing competition became a sideshow to hanging out with her. His lack of focus led to a couple more ignominious spills and a finish well outside the medals. He would wake early every day and leave Bob and Sally a note, 'Gone to meet Gemma. Back for tea. Have a super day. Love you both'.

They hired bikes and did their own special tour of the north coast, taking in turn the choice of venue. Gemma picked the caves at White Rocks and the Rope Bridge at Carrick-a-Rede, whilst he chose the Giant's Causeway and the walk along Ramore Head. On a quiet path among the sand dunes at Portrush East Strand, he stole his first kiss. She responded with a smile and offered her lips a second time.

All too soon the holiday was over. They shared the last evening looking out to sea as the sun went down behind the Skerry Islands. They had fallen in love.

Chapter 27

The stranger was third in line at Morelli's. The best fish and chips on the north coast, he thought. He asked for extra salt and vinegar and lifted a can of Diet Coke. Best not to go to work on an empty stomach, he supposed.

It was almost eleven p.m. when he ate the last piece of battered fish and downed the Coke.

On the stroke of the hour, he picked up his phone and dialled a number. A familiar voice said, "Hello." The conversation lasted for just a minute or two. The plan for the following days was in place.

He settled into a comfy chair, with a coffee in hand and switched on his iPad. In minutes he was watching 'Cruel Sea', the documentary about the fated Penlee Lifeboat. Tears welled up every time he watched it, although he knew every word of the radio transmissions. The coxswain's final words still rang in his ears, "Falmouth coastguard from Penlee Life. We've got four off at the moment. There's two left on board…" Then the painful silence, the coastguard's vain, timely transmissions, his anxious tone.

It had just past two a.m., when he pulled on his black ski suit and shouldered his rucksack. Then he stole out the back door and passed through the gate and on through the one to the rear of the adjoining house. All was quiet. The kitchen window was not quite locked just as he had left it. The gap was barely perceptible. He prized it open and slipped inside. He waited until his pupils widened and his eyes became accustomed to the dark. There was the familiar fusty smell of damp and nearly dried clothing, rinsed through hastily and hung on the line strung from a hook beside the kitchen door and the one embedded in the pelmet above the kitchen window. He moved with the stealth of a leopard closing in on a grazing gazelle. The hallway was like he supposed many other holiday foyers would be. Dusted with sand and cluttered with bikes, plastic buckets and spades. Coats dangled from hooks fitted to the wall. Ailish's wet suit hung on a clotheshorse by the door.

He paused at the bottom of the stairs. All was quiet. He winced as the third tread creaked. Enough to cause him to stir, but not enough it seemed to waken Ailish's sleeping parents. The curtains were drawn across the window at the head of the landing. They were cheap and unlined allowing for a margin of light. Just enough to pick out the slumbering forms of John and Mary McParland, who had thrown back the duvet because of the heat. He slipped his hand into his rucksack and pulled out a Gerber Air Ranger knife. The blade glinted as the moon appeared fleetingly, through a gap in the bedroom curtains.

He moved to John's side of the bed. The alarm clock on the bedside cabinet was set for seven.

He considered the paradox of this. For that would be the time when they could inform the police about their missing daughter.

He tapped him gently on the shoulder. There was little response at first, just a flailing right arm as if to chase away an annoying fly. His eyes opened at the second touch. He rubbed them hard, bringing the scene slowly into focus.

John must have felt that he was in some sort of wakening nightmare, the type that one seems unable to escape from. For the figure in the dark clothes and ski mask must be a figment, mustn't it? And the knife, just apparent in his hand, had to be part of the same illusion, didn't it? But this was no delusion; this was the start of his own dreadful reality.

"Be absolutely quiet," the stranger whispered. "No heroics please or I will kill her," he said pointing at Mary. "Now slowly and very quietly waken her. She must not scream, John."

John did what he was told, cupping his hand gently over his wife's mouth as she came round. Her uncontrollable urge to scream silenced only by John's forceful right hand.

"I'm going to take Ailish. I don't want to hurt any of you. So do exactly as I say."

He brought the blade close to John's throat.

"Nod once if I have your undivided attention."

The helpless couple did as they were told.

"Don't dare to move. I'll just be a minute."

The parents sat up in terror as the stranger left the room. There was to be no courageous attempt to disarm. No frantic rush to the window or wasted cry for help. They were speechless, unable to take in what was happening. Oh, they had seen the appeal on the news. But it didn't really register. And anyway these things always happened to other families. Didn't they?

He stole into Ailish's room. Neither Paddington nor her threadbare comfort blanket would be much succour to her just now. In seconds she was sedated, the ethelyne having the same instant effect as on Megan Reilly. He wrapped her in the black blanket he had used with Megan and cradled her in his arms. He carried her into her parent's room. Mary sat forward in horror. Then he raised his finger to his lips.

"Not a sound, Mary," he whispered. "I'm going to take her now. Nod once if you want to see her again. I thought you would. Now listen very carefully. We need to trust each other. There will be no tethers or gags or blindfolds, just a simple pledge. Will you agree to this?" he said, placing the blade at Ailish's throat and raising his voice to focus their thoughts.

They nodded.

"You will not alert anyone until seven o'clock. Your alarm clock should keep you right, no police or relatives or well-wishing neighbours. Do I make myself clear?"

Again they nodded.

"If you stick to the rules, you might have her back tomorrow. Disobey me and you will never see her again. Do you understand? The ball is in your court."

He pocketed the girl's iPhone, carried her down the stairs, and left by the back door. The parents considered a hurried 999 call. But what if he was watching. What if police were already on an emergency call? You heard of this more often now, police delays to respond to emergency calls. The risk was too great. The prize for trusting him was all they wanted. They had no alternative. The next five hours would be the worst of their lives.

The helpless girl was carried across one shoulder through the gate at the side of number two and into the garage. He set her on the back seat of the camper and opened the compartment. He placed her gently inside, then inserted a cannula and attached another syringe driver. The dosage was a little more than that he had given Megan, as the girl was bigger and heavier. He wrapped her in the blanket, checked her airway and closed the hatch.

He returned to the kitchen for the last time. He washed out his cafetiere, collected his iPad and Columbian dark roast and left. The engine roared to life with the first turn of the key. He opened the garage door and was careful on exit. The up and over flap creaked as it closed. The scooter sat in the corner. It had done its turn, its purpose had been served.

It was one of those touching moments in life. He had restored the bike from a rusting heap two years ago and gone to England the following year for a 'Mods' convention in Brighton. Scores of smartly dressed young men and women cheered the old footage of beach fights, as Mods and Rockers got it on, down on the sand. It was May 1964 and it looked like fun. He considered how it would give the investigators something else to get busy with. They might even admire the precision of its reconditioning he supposed. He turned out of the driveway and headed for the main road.

Two doors up, Mrs Croft was having another restless night. Things had not been so good since her gall bladder operation. The Doxepin seemed just as ineffective as had the Temazepam or Halcion she had before. The sound of an engine caused her to peer through the curtains. The street lighting was good, the result of another complaint to the council. On a scribble pad beside the telephone, she noted the number of the light blue camper as it turned left at the corner, Y110 HYM. She thought it an unusual combination of letters and numbers, nothing like the regional plate on her Vauxhall Corsa.

The dark haired, bearded driver was not familiar to her. In his forties she thought. But, as the vehicle moved further away, it got more difficult to be certain without her glasses. And anyway, it had become so difficult to estimate people's ages the older she got.

She picked up the phone and dialled 999. Then hesitated and cut off the call before the operator had time to answer. She had been scolded once or twice before, something to do with the inappropriate use of the emergency response system. Dogs barking and Mr Brown coming home drunk and singing of his lost love Machushla, didn't seem to be important to the police anymore. She was not going to invite another telling off, by some young constable, still wet behind the ears. It would do in the morning, around about ten a.m., just after *The Archers*. She popped another couple of pills, swilled them down and headed back to bed. The Doxipan was finally taking charge.

Chapter 28

The stranger took the overland route towards Dervock. The narrow country roads were deserted. Most of the police service, he assumed, was taking what it regarded as a well-earned rest. The parades had passed by peacefully. An uneasy compromise had been reached in north Belfast and now the Orangemen were tucked up for the night.

Many would be for Scarva in the morning to watch the re-enactment of King William's glorious victory at the Battle of the Boyne.

Skeleton crews would be on patrol, scouring the major highways for wilful drunks who had chosen to get behind the wheel. With clear roads and no enforced detours he could have been sitting with his feet up and a well-earned cup of his Columbian by five a.m., bypassing the towns of Stranocum, Kilraughts and Cloughmills. Then crossing the bridge at Broughshane and on through Muckamore, Dundrod and Maze would finally lead to Annahilt. The last few miles would take the van to the little cottage off the Moneyscalp Road, just outside Newcastle. The perfect route, he thought, *if* you happened to be heading that way.

As he crossed the River Bush a mile from Dervock, his thoughts returned to his beloved Gemma.

Chapter 29

The first day back at school after the summer break is always special, pupils dying to offload their stories to those willing to listen. He recalled how holiday tales changed with age.

Stories on return to second and third years were of new friends and the exploits of gangs of mates, of games of football on the beach and fishing trips that made you retch. But talk was never of the opposite sex and membership in the gangs was, for them, distinctly prohibited.

Coming back to fourth year meant tales of advancing social mobility. Mixed cliques became the order of the day. The rules of membership had changed. Boys now enjoyed the company of girls in sleek swimsuits and bikinis, who dressed up to the nines at night and hid their youthfulness with layers of make-up.

Girls liked guys who made them laugh. Not the fools who thought the way into a girl's pants was to act the lad and introduce them to vodka from a quarter bottle in a brown paper bag, the type of youth who did not need the constant sway of a fishing boat to make him retch and follow through. The vodka had this ability, especially when taken neat.

They also liked the guy who was handsome and filling out, showing some definition across the shoulders, inside the rib cage and down below. Indeed the chest area and that below the waist were becoming quite an attraction for boys and girls alike.

At this stage in life, the hard man stepped forward along with the guy whose stories could never be topped. In his year it was Geoff Bogle. A pitiful guy with an uncoordinated gait, a less than handsome form and a glass chin, which exposed itself when first he put his hardness to the test, behind the bicycle sheds, on Friday afternoon at lunchtime. He had picked on the wrong guy, but then almost anyone would have been wrong for the misfortunate Geoff.

By the return to autumn term in fifth form, talk was of summer romances and pining for lost loves. Hearts that were left fractured by brief but memorable encounters. But it was not the same for Gemma and him.

School changed forever after that week in Portstewart. What they had enjoyed was not some updated version of *Grease*. He was not like Danny Zuco, though maybe she could pass for a modern day Sandy. There were no awkward moments between them in the playground. No 'Tell me more. Tell me more. Did she put up a fight?' as the chorus in the musical enquired. And most certainly no inflated tales of intimacy in which Zuco had indulged. What they shared was special and would remain between them.

He recalled the feeling of warmth every time they were in class together, the endless hours spent strolling down long corridors between classes and at break and lunch times, his sense of pride when she took his hand as they walked, marking him and informing other latent lovers that he was off limits.

The secret texts in English class with the phone turned to 'meeting' mode as Mrs Clarke addressed the wipe board.

He recalled the first time he told of his love for her. Well it wasn't quite like that, one of the wonders of technology. He had sneaked a peak at a message from her while teacher was reading a short passage.

'What would you say if I told you that I was somewhat fond of you', it said. He fumbled with the typing with his left hand and at the same time, tried to show some interest in J. Priestley's *An Inspector Calls*. He remembered that Ian McFarland made a ham-fisted attempt at explaining the nature of the relationship between Arthur and Sybil Berling. He had clearly some serious study ahead before the exam.

'I would say I love you', he replied. Then he blushed, not at the nature of his retort, but rather because Mrs Clarke had asked a question and had caught him terribly off guard, something to do with whom he thought most responsible for the death of Eva Smith.

"I'm sorry, Mrs Clarke, I was miles away," he had said, earning himself a stern scowl. "What was the question again?"

Gemma looked briefly at the message and then looked more attentively again, it was just what she wanted him to say. She replied in kind, when Mrs Clarke addressed the board again. She appended a line of 'x's' to her message.

Fifth year went by in a flash. By Christmas, the pressure was building as they prepared over the holidays to face the mock exams in January. They studied together right up to Christmas Eve, taking it in turns to go to at each other's houses. Bob and Sally were hugely fond of Gemma, her perfect manners, the humour and wit. But above all how good she was for their beloved foster son, how truly happy she made him.

They spent Christmas Eve rushing around Belfast in a last minute panic, grabbing toys and clothes and CDs for Gemma's closest cousins. He recalled how sad she looked at times realising that he had no mum or dad or brothers or sisters or aunts or uncles or cousins to buy for, just Bob and Sally and her. But those who mattered had already been taken care of. A framed photograph of both of them for Bob and Sally and for Gemma's parents. They would take pride of place on each mantelpiece.

It was four o'clock when they stopped outside Malcolm's Jewellers. The snow had just started to fall and shoppers took refuge under porches and bus shelters. They looked along the line of wonderful rings, bangles and bracelets – wishful thinking for two so young. He led her to the corner window where Chichester Street turns into Arthur Street and antique jewellery takes pride of place. Fobs, charm bracelets and rose gold watch chains sat centre stage with well-polished second hand rings. He considered the sad tales that many of those bands must keep secret.

In one corner birthstones sat glinting. There were garnets and agates, opals, topaz and amethysts. But one sat imperious, it symbolised the month of March. Gemma's birthday was on the twenty-fourth. An aquamarine shimmered from the delicate clasps of its white gold band. He could tell it had caught her eye.

They went inside to plush surroundings. Escorted to a private room by a kindly lady named Pat, who fetched all shapes and sizes of the gem for their consideration. She laid each one on dark blue baize to amplify their beauty. But none could outdo the one that first had taken her fancy. The one she had seen in the window, the one that fitted so perfectly on her right ring finger. Not her engagement finger, that was for another day.

Chapter 30

By the time Easter came around the pressure was intense. It was late that year, and spring was already in the air. Snowdrops and camellia bloomed along the leafy lane at Shaw's Bridge, spanning the River Lagan. Lilac was still some time away. In a quiet copse in Barnett's park, two jays sat on a sycamore branch. One tenderly preened the other. They nuzzled from time to time, unconcerned by the inquisitive onlookers. He looked into Gemma's eyes.

"Folklore says that jays are life partners, soul mates, if you like. They are always true to each other. When one passes on, the other is quick to follow." His eyes met hers and their lips came together, their long embrace undisturbed by an impatient cyclist ringing his bell and muttering under his breath about the youth of today.

"Happy birthday," she said, drawing a small red box from her pocket and flipping it open. The tiny diamond was set perfectly in white gold.

"An expensive month for a birthday," he had retorted as she slipped the band onto his right ring finger.

"You're my soul mate. I never want us to be apart. We will be just like the jays," she whispered before their lips came together again. A less prudish cyclist raised an ironic cheer.

Chapter 31

The exams were tough that year. Politicians had been concerned that there was too much emphasis on coursework and too many second chances to improve one's marks. Testing had lost its rigour and they had just brought it back.

The stranger recalled the long post-exam weeks made bearable by Gemma's constant company in Newcastle. The cottage had never known such joy and laughter. The Mourne Mountains became their playground. They raced up to Hare's Gap and through the Brandy Pad, or along the Devil's Highway towards Slieve Donard. They had their most cherished moments in a tiny granite shelter beside Lough Shannagh.

She had never before felt the tautness of his almost naked body next to hers or the surge of excitement as they touched each other intimately, kissing and fondling one another.

Bob and Sally could almost hear the wedding bells and kidded them both constantly at dinnertime and when watching the sun go down at the end of another perfect day. It was by the kitchen range one night that Sally winced. Not the grimace of someone with a headache or a touch of indigestion, more like a person who was truly unwell. She tried to pass if off. Bob could not.

The hopeful, and those less so, gathered with eager and fated expectation. The great hall at Sullivan Upper School buzzed with excitement and fear. It was results day, 18 August.

There were beaming smiles and down-turned faces in equal number.

He looked down the list. The string of As and A stars no less than he deserved or than classmates had anticipated. He had taken it in his stride, just smiling modestly with each congratulations. Gemma was more animated but not giddy like some, who became completely scatty. She hugged her friend Chloe and then ran and threw her arms around him. She had come out on top with ten A stars to his eight. But this was not about competition anymore. This was the joy and celebration of each other's huge achievements.

That night they dined at Fontana with Bob and Sally. Prosecco flowed freely and the food was as superb as always.

A mere month later Sally was gone. Bob followed her one Easter morn, the following year. The stranger expected that Bob too knew the legend of the jays.

Chapter 32

It was four thirty a.m. when the CCTV picked up the image of a pale Volkswagen camper as it passed along Main Street in Newcastle. The street was empty, except for a staggering drunk taking a rather lengthy route home. The vehicle swung out of view, turning right, heading for Bryansford. It came to rest just off the Moneyscalp Road in the shadow of Bernagh's craggy mountaintop. The cottage was secluded, well away from prying eyes. It was perfect. The vehicle pulled into the garage. The driver took his precious cargo from the back and went inside. The journey had been just as planned. Now what would the following twenty-four hours hold in store?

Chapter 33

Eamon Lynch had trouble sleeping that night. He had tossed and turned for an hour or two, before heading for the spare room. Amidst thoughts of Megan Reilly, he fell into a fitful slumber. He woke in a sweat when the image of her bloodied corpse entered his subconscious. He hoped the frightful dream would not become reality.

This was no time for sleep he reflected, there was no shutting out the terrible truth of what was happening. It was time to be at his desk again, waiting for something, anything. He dressed, ran an electric razor across reluctant stubble and headed in to work.

By 6.50 a.m., he was at his desk. The night shift sergeant brought him coffee and a piece of toast. He tried to cheer Lynch up with talk of holidays and retirement. But Lynch was bound to his own dark world. He found himself clutching Ramsey's taunting note from seven years ago. The pictures of the shaven head, the party frock, and the lifeless girl now stared at him mockingly.

Thornton joined him. Sleep had clearly been a stranger to him last night as well. He set a hand on his friend's heavy-laden shoulder.

The iPhone twitched in Lynch's pocket. He hesitated and looked at Thornton, reluctant to bring the message to life. He thought implausibly that if he left it where it laid it could not harm him, that the import of its message would be caught, suspended, in time. Deep down he feared the culprit had moved with the times. That technology would tell of Megan Reilly's fate, and there would be one more morbid addition to his metal box of forlorn communications.

He held it at arm's length and pressed the button.

Megan Reilly's listless body appeared before them. Her cropped head, crimson dress and scarlet tethers led them to their worst fears. But the tale they told was incomplete. It was not the finished article they had dreaded it might have been.

The macabre metal chamber, lay open beside the bed. It had been Ramsey's means of dispatching his quarries. This was not yet Megan Reilly's fate. Perhaps there was a glimmer of hope for her.

He scrolled to the chilling message and read it aloud.

"Hope you like the clues I left. Here are a couple of snaps to whet your appetites. I trust you will do better than you did seven years ago. I've given you a chance. There will be one more. Don't squander it or another young girl is going to die."

It was signed 'Scarlet Ribbons'.

The ten-figure grid reference was the last thing he had added.

Lynch was on the phone in seconds.

"Hello, controller," he said impatiently. "Have you got a pen handy? I want to know the precise location of this grid reference 08920 59062. It's Chief Superintendent Lynch here. It's about the missing girl."

The controller got straight to it, knowing precisely the website to go to. Senior officers had a knack of asking for things yesterday. He had always worked on the principle that one solution given makes you handy to know and that two can make you invaluable.

"Hello, sir, it's Gard Owen Henry. The reference is in the North in Binevenagh forest near Castlerock."

Lynch thanked him and set down the phone. Then he turned to Thornton.

"It's yours now, Mike. She's in a forest near Castlerock."

Thornton lifted his own phone and dialled.

"Duty Inspector, please. Detective Chief Superintendent Thornton here. Tell him it's urgent."

Inspector Bob Harris was on the early shift. He picked up the phone.

"Morning, sir. How can I help you?"

"Inspector, we believe we know the location of the little girl who was taken from Donegal last night."

He read the number and the inspector repeated it back to him.

"I'll go there immediately, sir. The GPS will bring me to the exact location. I'll be ten minutes."

Thornton set down the phone and looked at Lynch. "There's something different about this guy. He's taunting us. We need more help with this one."

He was handed a cup of coffee. He had just sat down to gather his thoughts when his phone rang.

"Mike Thornton here."

"Good morning, sir. It's Jean Harrison. We've just had a report of a girl taken from a house in Portstewart last night. She is seven-year-old Ailish McParland. It was menacing this time, almost a carbon copy of Ramsey's abduction of Hannah Graham.

"The parents, Ciaran and Mary, were held at knifepoint. He threatened to kill Ailish if they reported it before seven a.m. The area around the house is being preserved. Detective Inspector Dave Carruthers is at the scene. He has requested forensic technicians, photographers and a full search team. The parents are being taken to Coleraine station. Detective Inspector Carruthers has asked if you wish him to start house to house enquiries immediately."

"Tell him to wait until we have put all that we have together. We don't want to be going back to people again and again.

"Thank you, Jean. It looks as if Megan Reilly is about to be recovered. Our stranger has adopted Ramsey's criminal alias, Scarlet Ribbons. He texted this, along with some photographs and a grid reference, to Eamon Lynch. If the coordinates are accurate, she is somewhere in Binevenagh Forest. Start putting out feelers for the investigation team. See who's not on holiday. We'll be running this one from Maydown. Did you have any joy with Tony Rogers?"

"I did, sir, and he would be delighted to help. He's making his way up here as we speak."

"That is great news. Can you see what DI Tara Ritchie is doing? I'd really like her on board. Tell her she can pick most of her team. We need it put together quickly. I'll be with you at eight thirty a.m.

"Eamon Lynch is clearing it to have a couple of his team work with us. They have the background knowledge of the Donegal abduction and can bring our guys up to speed. Grainne Burrows has agreed to work alongside our press officer. Can you see if Alan Mooney is available please? I want to consider a media release as soon as possible. Everything needs to be ready to go by midday. Oh and see what Dr Eileen Parks is doing. She worked on the Ramsey case. We need a psychological profile of this guy."

Chapter 34

"We've got her, sir. Precisely where he directed. She's alive," said the elated duty inspector. "She's on the way to Coleraine Hospital. The paramedic said that she may have known little about it all, she was quite heavily sedated. A syringe drive was fitted. It's been preserved for examination."

Thornton did not need to repeat the message, the choking sound of uncontrollable emotion told him that Lynch had overheard. The big Donegal man wiped away his tears and gathered himself. For a moment he said nothing, but Thornton knew the sense of great relief he felt. The girl was alive and he would not have to face the cruellest of encounters with her parents, John and Sheila. For a family man like Lynch, such an encounter was especially dreaded.

"We got her, Mike. Thank God we got her," Lynch uttered.

A minute later Kate Lynch picked up the phone. She smiled and sobbed at the same time as her husband relayed the news. The girl was alive. The real Eamon Lynch would be coming home that night. She took a pen from the writing bureau and added Mike and Jayne Thornton's names to the ever-growing retirement party list. Eamon Lynch returned the metal box to the drawer, thankful that its contents had not been added to.

Chapter 35

The guard raised the barrier as Thornton drove through the gates at Maydown. He made his way to the incident room that was enjoying some technical upgrading. Computers, fax machines and phone lines were being tested as the team started to arrive. Video links were being established to combine the ongoing enquiry in Donegal with senior command in both police services.

His office was just off to the right. He settled into his seat when DI Tara Ritchie knocked and walked in.

"Morning, sir, Jean Harrison phoned me. I made it as quickly as I could."

Tara Ritchie was a peeler's pup. Her dad had been one of the last of the old breed. An impressive man of six feet four or five, with the balls to lead from the front and thereafter to face the wrath of the ever increasing politically correct at the higher levels. They winced on occasions when he rose from a swivel chair in the Gold Command Room, pulled on his fire retardant suit and riot helmet and headed for the heat of the fray on Belfast's angry streets at two a.m.

Tara had inherited many of his qualities. She was tenacious almost to a fault, as many a hardened criminal had found to his cost. She wasn't afraid of taking risks but was not reckless.

She had led an investigation into a ruthless paramilitary gang in south Belfast which was into extortion, prostitution and people trafficking. The operation had taken three years of painstaking intelligence gathering, enquiry and witness protection. She never flinched even when her critics questioned her capabilities. She had the last laugh, sending Crazy Billy Christie and his cronies down for sixty years in total.

She did not tolerate shirkers or guys or girls who could not 'hold their water' when the drink was in.

"No gossip outside the team," she would remind a squad. "No pillow talk or acting like the man in the big picture, in front of some snooping hack in the John Hewitt bar, some Friday afternoon. If I hear about it you'll be out and be out for good. No second chances."

They all knew that she was not one for making idle threats and respected her for it. She was willing to work around the clock and right then that was just what Thornton needed.

"Morning, Tara, it's great to see you. How's your dad? Still spending as much time in Tenerife?"

"Not so much now, sir. My sister had a baby boy last year. It's his first grandchild and she called him Chris."

"Now there's a surprise. I don't suppose your dad had any say in it?" Thornton smiled.

"Well, he says most definitely not. But I'm not so sure. He certainly spends enough time with him. He was so put out when Alison announced she was sending Chris to nursery five days a week. Dad managed to negotiate Wednesdays and Fridays for him and mum. You'll find him on mornings walking his grandson through the Commons at Donaghadee, cooing and getting on like a young thing. He has his own table in Bow Bells. He tells me the cherry scones are to die for and the coffee not too bitter and, typical of dad, he always gets a top up on the house."

Thornton thought of the image of this tough retired copper, who could put the fear of God in you, strolling proudly through the park. He was happy for him. Chris Ritchie had truly earned his retirement. He was one of the good guys.

"Sit down please, Tara. This is a difficult one. We are dealing with a very unusual criminal. It has huge similarities to an investigation I was involved in seven years ago, but something is different this time. I'm not sure what yet. We have the same calculated means of taking the first and second children, the same use of map reference to indicate where the first child would be found, but there is no evidence of sexual abuse with Megan Reilly and she was recovered alive. The paramedics think that she may have been completely unconscious throughout the entire ordeal, she was heavily sedated."

"I know something of the Ramsey enquiry from seven years ago. We used it as a case study on my detective inspector's course. You had your critics, sir. Personally I would have done exactly the same as you, if that's any consolation." Ritchie met his eyes.

Thornton cleared his throat, feeling slightly uncomfortable at the thought of classes of students dissecting his past mistakes. "That means a lot to me coming from you, Tara. Perhaps I'll give you my side of the story some time. Now let's get down to business. You will be working with former Detective Sergeant Tony Rogers. He will be your HOLMES (Home Office Large Major Enquiry System) indexer. He's the best there is. Have you got the team you want, Tara? "

"I have, sir. You will know most of the names. Detective Sergeant Brian Black is my number two. He will link in with Tony to ensure that all actions are assigned, completed and logged. Detective Constables Barry Mulligan, Kate Delany, Steve Buckley and Beth Chapman are on general enquiries. Shauna McCree is item reader and Tom Donnelly will do disclosure."

"A great team, Tara. Thank you. Now let's get down to it."

Chapter 36

By nine thirty a.m. the major incident room was abuzz with activity. Tony Rogers was chatting with his old mate Barry Mulligan about his new diet and how he had looked somewhat out of place in his budgie smugglers at his first pilates class. Beth Chapman was dressed to the nines as usual. She was teasing the amorous Steve Buckley about his latest hairstyle and the little bit of skirt she had seen him with sneaking out of Filthy McNastys bar with last Saturday night.

Tom Donnelly was putting things in order. It only worked for Tom, if everything was in its place. He was obsessive, but then the best disclosure officers generally were. However, when Thornton stood up to begin all idle chat was dropped instantly as the room snapped to attention, ready to give their all to recover Ailish McParland alive.

"Good morning, everyone. Thank you for making yourselves available at such short notice. I must thank DI Ritchie for putting together such a super team. Tony, it's also great to have you back in the fold."

Rogers took an ironic bow, which raised a smile from Kate Delaney and a caustic quip from Barry Mulligan.

"To my right is Grainne Burrows, the press officer for An Garda Siochana. She will be working with our own Alan Mooney, who I have spotted in the corner. Good to see you again Alan. On my left is Garda Superintendent Frank Keenan who is heading up the enquiry in Donegal.

"I have had a brief prepared on the abduction of Megan Reilly from Portsalon yesterday morning. Please take time to become familiar with it. I am delighted to tell you that she was recovered alive just over two hours ago. We have a forensic and photography team currently at the scene. A mobile support unit is conducting a search. I am expecting an update from them shortly. Detective Inspector Ritchie has put together a short questionnaire and we have local CID on house to house enquiries in Portstewart.

"Our abductor has clearly upped the ante since his first crime. We need to accept the possibility that this could have more serious consequences for young Ailish McParland.

"A press conference is at one p.m. Alan and Grainne will work on its format together. We will not involve the parents this time."

He turned to Ritchie.

"Tara, I need everything done so far indexed. I want to have the parents interviewed and their statements recorded.

"There is the outstanding action regarding a partial registration number, which needs to be followed up.

"I want enquiries into all CCTV recordings throughout the province from two thirty a.m. until six a.m. this morning. All speed traps are to be checked over the same period of time. We are looking for a light coloured Camper Van partial registration Y110H. Start with Newcastle, County Down. If this guy is following Ramsey's pattern then he may well be heading in that direction.

"I need contact made with all Regional Intelligence Units and analysts. We must find out if there is any information that may point towards other children potentially at risk. We have to assume that he will strike again, if we don't catch him first,

We will meet back here at midday. Our own Crime Operations department and the Garda National Surveillance Unit will brief us then. "

There was a bustle of activity as Thornton and Keenan left the room. DI Ritchie was distributing tasks with purpose and foresight. Every member of the team knew precisely what was required of them. She expected everything done by eleven forty-five a.m. She wanted to make sure all would be ready for the twelve o'clock review.

Chapter 37

Eamon Lynch collected Sarah McGivern just before heading for Portsalon. As family liaison officer, it was important that she was there when he broke the good news to John and Sheila Reilly.

The village was starting to waken as they rounded the corner. Early morning golfers were making their way to the first tee. Setting off in hope rather than expectation. It was a pleasant morning for a few unhurried holes.

Runners scampered along the beach. Women in Lycra fought the good fight against intolerably aging cellulite. Middle-aged men with heart monitors tried to rediscover their youthful tone and vigour. Seagulls squealed as they settled on a shoal of herring, which had entered the bay. Black-backed gulls dominated proceedings like playground bullies at a lunchtime kick about. A brace of northern gannets soared high above, content that they had eaten their fill as the fish rounded Malin Head an hour before.

The inviting smell of frying bacon stirred Lynch's appetite, as he pulled up outside site A42. A portly man sat in the shade of an awning at the set next door, reading *The Independent* and waiting for a bacon butty and a strong cup of tea to properly start the day. He barely acknowledged their arrival but slipped subtly inside. Thirty years of policing had given Lynch a distinctive gait and air.

Sarah McGivern could barely contain herself as the door swung open and John and Sheila stood in nervous expectation.

"We've got her! She's alive!" Lynch roared as he welled up once again, all thoughts of decorum set aside as they hugged and cried together.

"Oh, Sarah and Mr Lynch, how can we ever thank you enough? Where is she? Is she okay? Did he hurt her?"

"When can we see her?" Sheila blubbed. John silently accepted the warm embrace of the big copper and looked forward to feeling Megan's weight on his shoulders once again.

The sixty mile journey to Coleraine hospital was one filled with emotions. John and Sheila stood tearfully as they saw their lovely daughter for the first time again. It was clearly shocking that her golden hair was missing and a drip was fixed to relieve her dehydration.

The peace of the private room was broken as Megan's eyes opened.

"Mummy, Daddy, what happened? What am I doing here?"

"It's okay, don't worry Megan. All in good time, sweetheart," John said as he sat by her side on the bed stroking her forehead where her blonde locks used to tumble down. "We have a lot to tell you."

Chapter 38

The stranger followed what was now becoming a familiar routine. The cottage was just as the brochure had described. The door led straight into the front room with its original stone floor. The two bedrooms were compact but homely. Pocket sprung orthopaedic mattresses had replaced their latex foam predecessors of the 1970s.

He thought that in its day it must have been bleak in winter. The long laneway becoming impassable during the harsh chills of 1947 and 1963, the occupants having to rely on rations and fortitude to see them through. The absence of electricity and running water, which they would have suffered through, was something that would be simply intolerable today.

In the corner of the kitchen, the wood-burning stove was casting unnecessary heat given the delightful morning. The four hours of sleep had left him refreshed and ready for another day. Ailish McParland lay unaware in the bedroom to the rear of the cottage.

He settled for his traditional morning fare. The eggshells still bore the remnants of the hens' uncomfortable lays. The yolks were bright orange and the whites formed narrow circles as they met the searing fat. A welcome sign of freshness, he had been told. They hissed and spat at him, before translucence gave way to pure white.

The bacon was cooked in seconds; flash fried in the hottest of pans. The flaccid rind turned golden brown and crisp as the smoked streaky rashers sang a similar song to the eggs. It was Sprott's finest, sliced from a side kept wrapped in muslin at Orr's butchers in Holywood. The best money can buy in his opinion.

There was little that now attracted him back to the handsome town. One thing was the bacon. More important were the annual tributes paid to Gemma and also to Bob and Sally at their gravesides. It could only ever be a time for reflection and reminiscence. There were never any floral tributes. For vibrant blossoms led to giveaways and curiosities, clues to someone who really cared. Although he cared deeply, he never took the chance of being discovered.

He washed down breakfast with his favoured Columbian dark roast, which he finished in the rear garden overlooking the bay.

He wondered how Lynch and Thornton would have greeted his seven a.m. message. He imagined they must have felt huge relief. But the way that Ailish McParland was taken and the tone of his message should have given them cause for concern.

The enquiry would be moved to Maydown and Thornton would be in charge now. The stranger imagined him assembling his team. He wondered if he would re-employ the delightful Dr Eileen Parks, a forensic psychologist of some distinction. As useful as tits on a boar he had concluded, full of theories and hypotheses and all sorts of good ideas, but they had amounted to nothing more than bullshit seven years ago. They had not managed to save even one little girl's life he thought scornfully.

He imagined the joyful relief of John and Sheila Reilly in Portsalon: the mother's momentary unsteadiness, reaching out to claim her husband's steadying arm, as she came to terms with the joyful news, the father's stoic words of thrill and thank you, the tears of joy and disbelief that their beloved daughter was coming home. He was happy for them. Perhaps they might get the chance to thank him one day. Speak up for him if ever he was put before a court. Say that he had shown them compassion when they had expected none.

Chapter 39

The stranger thought of his return to the home when Bob and Sally died. The last two years had gone in quickly. He and Gemma were on top of their form in lower sixth. This led to talk of Oxford or Cambridge.

He remembered his eighteenth birthday on 12 May. It was his last day at the home. He woke early. He strolled down Cultra Avenue and cut off along the coastal path just before the yacht club. Mrs McNeill was out as usual walking her border terrier, Barney.

He sat on the wall at Seapark and took in the view. He remembered his younger days, with Bob and Sally, racing from the lapping waves to the warmth of an ample towel, his teeth chattering as Sally dried and cuddled him and poured a hot cup of chocolate from a well-used flask.

He reflected on the start in life they had given him, a start without which he may never have survived. Never have come out with a better than even chance of being happy and successful. When he reached The Dirty Duck pub at the end of the esplanade he turned for home. He thought of the joy he would have there, the swill of his first pint as a legitimate patron, listening to Ken Haddock's mellow tones in the background.

Mrs Crombie was waiting for him with a heap of birthday cards and a loving smile.

It was Mrs Crombie who had collected him from the police station eleven years ago. She had supported his fostering and cried with him at both Sally's and Bob's passing. She had watched the boy become a youth and now that youth was a young man.

"Something special about today is there?" she joked.

"You could say that, Mrs Crombie."

"Well, don't be shy. Open them up," she said excitedly.

He recalled sitting in the comfy armchair in the bay window. The one from which he had stared impatiently as Bob and Sally came to take him to their home nine years ago.

"This one's from the lads in school. It's a bit naughty so I'll spare your blushes. This one is from Gemma's parents. It just wishes me a very happy birthday and invites me for tea tonight. The big one is from Gemma. If you don't mind, I'll read this later and spare my blushes this time."

He recalled picking up the last one. He did not need to open it. He spotted the handwriting straight away.

"And this one's from you, Mrs Crombie," his voice wavered as he remembered all the time he spent in the early days sitting crying on her lap, trying to erase the bitter memories of his young life.

He did not employ the same hurried frenzy with which he had opened the first three. For much as the others were special, this one was very special indeed.

On the front of the card was of a boy with a quizzical look and a question mark above his head.

"What lies in store for you?" the caption read.

He peered at her tearful eyes and opened the card.

A smiling young man and woman sat astride the globe.

"A world made just for two," was the retort.

He was speechless. She had captured the moment and his desire precisely.

"There's a gift to go with it Jamie," Mrs Crombie said, pushing the small present into his hand.

He unwrapped the packaging with the same amount of care and tilted back the lid. He picked up the Monte Blanc fountain pen and read the simple message below.

'May you and Gemma write your own enchanted history together!'

The last envelope was formal, marked 'Private and Confidential' and headed Ernest Johnston and Sons, Solicitors.

It read:

'Dear Sir,
I act on behalf of the late Robert and Sally Heron. I should be most grateful if you would call with me at the earliest opportunity. I wish to discuss the arrangements made for you within the deceased parties' wills.
Yours faithfully,
Robert Johnston.'

Chapter 40

He met Gemma shortly after breakfast at the Shell Service Station on the main drag for Bangor. He stuck out his thumb jokingly as she pulled up beside him.

"Going my way?" he jested as he eased himself into the front seat.

"Your R plates are barely dry," he teased. Gemma took no notice. She leaned across with a cheeky smile and gave him a kiss.

"Happy birthday, sweetheart. I couldn't wait to see you."

They were words he never tired of hearing. She always greeted him with the same simple admission.

Gemma signalled and entered the traffic flow on the busy bypass. Her confidence behind the wheel far exceeded her experience. Merely two days before she had driven her instructor to the test centre on Jubilee Road in Newtownards. A serious man with a well-trimmed moustache had questioned her earnestly on the Highway Code before checking her parking ability and then directing her onto the network of roads which she had practised on, almost to distraction, over the past seven weeks. The vehicle had seemed to be on remote control as they proceeded up Bowtown Road. The perfect place for an emergency stop, she thought.

The instructor checked his mirror and braced himself. She was right.

Chapter 41

"Where are we going?" he had asked.

"It's a surprise! Now close your eyes!"

The journey took about fifteen minutes and he recalled having to struggle earnestly to keep his eyes shut tight for the duration. The smell of the sea was in the air. He could faintly hear the rush of the tide.

Gemma rolled to a gentle stop, and turned off the engine. "You can open them now."

Donaghadee lighthouse was first to catch his eye, then the lifeboat that rocked to the rhythm of the incoming tide..

"Out you get," she implored, as she threw open the passenger door and took his hand.

A man with a well-lived-in face, a flat cap and a toothless smile approached.

"Many happy returns, James. I'm Harry Lemon and I'm your boatman for today."

In minutes the *Miss Daisy* passed through the harbour walls and set course for Copeland Island. Nine years had passed since they had been there last. This time they were the only passengers.

"Do you remember going to the island in P6?" Gemma asked.

"How could I forget," he had said. "I seem to remember you jumping from the rocks and panicking as you found yourself out of your depth. A huge grey seal was eyeing you up from a rock. I can still see the look on your face."

"That's an exaggeration and you know it," she had said. "Do you remember we were asked to make something to remind us of the trip? Boys collected shells and flotsam and fused them with glue and sticky tape. Girls created braid from marram grass and plaited each other's hair. The teachers made themselves busy helping the less able or disinclined. But there was little help they could have given you as I recall.

"You made this fisherman's weave," she said, lifting her sleeve and revealing it around her right wrist. "I almost forgot about it, until this morning that is. The thought of us going back to Copeland Island sent me rummaging around until I found it. You exchanged it for some chicken sandwiches and a Diet Coke. I never told you, James, but I fancied you even then."

The stranger looked back with joy on that wonderful birthday trip to the island. This time they had both jumped from the same rock and surfaced, spurting water and gasping together. He had wondered if the seal on the rock had been there nine years ago. They had dried each other off and stood naked in the sunshine.

"I love you, Gemma."

"I love you too, James. I never want to be without you."

They had lain together on towels behind a windbreak. The temptation to make love for the first time was almost unbearable. They resisted. They both felt it was something to be savoured when they were properly hitched. A prying cormorant kept look out, from a rock near the shore to make sure they were undisturbed.

Half an hour later, they hopped across the gap between the pier and the boat and headed for the harbour. In another hour they were sitting on one of the huge harbour bollards, the one beside the decaying crane. They had eaten 'ninety-nines' from the Cabin Ice-cream Parlour. A treat enjoyed by generation after generation. It didn't get any better than that.

Chapter 42

Thornton just had time to freshen up before the midday conference. He drew the blade across his gritty stubble with an uncharacteristic level of inaccuracy. A folded piece of toilet paper staunched the flow of blood from the nick on his chin. He thought he must remember to take it off before the meeting. There could be no signs of nerves or uncertainty to the team.

The mirror was not about to lie, it never had before. He had aged considerably during the last twenty-four hours. He sprayed a generous amount of Hugo Boss in the usual regions and pulled on a new shirt. There was something therapeutic about the experience. The garment was pristine and uncontaminated, unlike most other things in his current world of shit.

He lifted his phone. Rachel answered.

"Hi, Daddy. Mummy's in the kitchen drinking coffee with Barbara's mum. Please tell me you'll be home for my birthday, Daddy."

"All the tea in China couldn't keep me away, princess."

It was a phrase that Rachel had become well used to. The days and nights on which his job had robbed her of his company. But she knew that when her daddy said something, that was precisely what he meant.

"You have a great day with Barbara. Can you put Mummy on now?"

He gathered his thoughts for the couple of seconds before he heard his wife's voice.

"Hi, sweetheart. How's it going? Any word on the little girl Megan?"

"We found her. She's alive and in hospital. It would appear he didn't physically harm her. But he took another girl last night, from Portstewart. We are following a number of enquiries. It's remarkably like Ramsey's work seven years ago. You know I don't like to follow hunches but I think our stranger may be heading for Newcastle. That's where Ramsey struck next. Just off the Bryansford Road as I recall."

"Be careful, Mike. Try not to burn yourself out, pet."

"I won't sweetheart. Now I have to go. There's a conference in fifteen minutes and someone has just arrived at the office. Love you, Jayne. Have a good day and keep an eye on Rachel."

"Bye, darling," she said. "See you soon."

Chapter 43

Dr Eileen Parks knocked again and opened the door at his beckoning.

"Hello, Mike, it's good to see you. Pity about the circumstances."

"Sit down please Eileen. I see you have a copy of the Ramsey file. Let me quickly fill you in on this new boy. There are a lot of similarities, too many. I need a profile on our latest culprit and any comparative analysis with Ramsey would be helpful."

"I'll draw something together for you quickly. Tara has provided me with a comprehensive summary of the incidents since Megan Reilly was targeted and abducted. I'll join you in the briefing room when I'm ready."

Thornton thanked her and closed the door quietly as he left the office.

The incident room was its usual buoyant self, when Thornton took his place beside the lectern. For the last half hour, DI Tara Ritchie had been busy, ensuring that all actions were signed off and the reviews were ready.

"Sir, I've drawn together a sequence. With your permission we will first address outstanding matters from yesterday. We will then move to this morning's work."

Thornton nodded his approval and the DI continued.

"The parents have undergone a preliminary interview. Needless to say we can rule out any involvement in the abduction. They were unable to shed much light on how Ailish was targeted. They bought the house three years ago and rent it out for much of the year but they always spend July there. There is a group of families they meet up with each year. They had little to tell about the occupant in number two. He was not there very often. In fact, they had never met or seen him. The landlord said he paid in cash.

"Ailish had told them of the brief encounter she had with him when she returned from her evening swim at the harbour last night. She had found him 'spooky' and she thought he looked a bit familiar. Like someone she had seen before but could not quite remember from where. She had only left the company of her four friends as she turned into the park.

"They mentioned another incident that happened just as she broke up for school this summer. It was something that she said merely in passing. A man was training a black Labrador to be a guide dog. He had approached Ailish as she was walking home from school. They only lived round the corner. The man had invited her to stroke the dog. They spent some time talking about pets and family and holidays. The dog's name was Sheba. The handler told Ailish that Sheba was taking her final test the following week. He had asked Ailish if Sheba could walk her home. He said it would be good practice for her test next week. Sheba and the handler walked Ailish to the gate and Ailish gave the dog another stroke and wished her good luck for the test the following week. She told her parents that the man in the rental next door looked a bit like the guy with the dog but she could not be certain.

"We were awaiting a call back from DVLO on the partial number plate Y110H. We have now sent them what we believe to be the precise number.

"House to house enquiries revealed that pensioner Lily Croft, who lives two doors up from the MacParlands, couldn't sleep last night and heard the noise of an engine starting. It was after two o'clock. She saw a light blue camper van pull out of the driveway of number two. She watched it turn left at the end of the street. She describes the driver as in his forties with dark hair and a beard. It's a bit ropey as she was not wearing her glasses. But she is pretty sure. She recorded the licence plate number, which she is certain of. It's up there on the screen, sir; Y110 HYM. She says she didn't report it at the time because she had been given a telling off to for reporting matters in the past. She was waiting until ten a.m., after *The Archers*.

"Inspector Paula Harvey is in charge of the search of the scene where Megan Reilly was recovered. I'll ask her to brief us."

Paula pointed at the map on the screen.

"The cottage is just where I am pointing. One hundred metres up a laneway off Bishops Road in Binevenagh Forest. There were two different sets of tyre tracks that we identified. The scientists and photographers believe that the first set you see is a match to those found at Portsalon.

"You can see that the second set has a much narrower gauge. From a small motorcycle, scooter or even a mountain bike. I believe this may have some significance to the search at Springtide Gardens. You will be briefed on this in due course.

"There had been little care taken to wash dishes or clean up generally. Two cups beside the sink have the remnants of coffee in them. He left a dirty plate and a knife and fork on the table. There were also a number of fingerprints recovered. It almost seems too convenient, as if they were left for us to find."

Harvey moved to the next picture. "The metal cylinder in the photograph is made of aluminium. It's light and would be easily transported. You can see how the lid could have been closed over. The scientist said that it would have created an airtight container. He reckons that anyone inside would have air enough for only a couple of hours.

"I am now showing you the tethers used to bind Megan. The scientist said that the knot used is known as an Anchor Hitch. It is quite unique. Ramsey had used the same knot. This image shows locks of hair left behind on the duvet cover. Once again the offender was careless.

"Needless to say, all exhibits have been removed for examination. That's all I have at the moment, sir."

"Thank you, Inspector. What about the search at number two Springtide Gardens, Tara?"

"I was coming to that, sir. Inspector Hinds, can you please take over?"

Inspector Karl Hinds lit up the screen again.

"There was very little care taken to remove any evidence. There was an unfinished plate of fish and chips and an empty can of Diet Coke on the kitchen table. The scientist recovered prints from the Coke can and also from the television screen. The can and the cutlery should also provide us with a DNA profile, though that will not be ready for a number of days.

"You are now looking at a photograph of the garage. In the corner you can see a scooter. It's a 1979 Vespa 75 Primavera and beautifully restored. There was some of what the scientist described as forest debris caught in the tyre tread. The initial opinion is that it was this vehicle that left the tracks at the cottage in Binevenagh Forest, where Megan Reilly was recovered. There was a particular lichen caught in the tread that is distinctive to the forest.

"There was also a set of larger tyre marks. The scientist says they are the same as the ones recovered from Portsalon. Unless he has refitted the tyres onto something else, we can deduce that the vehicle is the same at each of the scenes.

"This next photograph shows the rear window at number four. It would appear that this was the culprit's point of entry. He had used a piece of blue tack to prevent the window lock from closing completely. He must have prised it open later on. We recovered some dusty footprints from the draining board and the kitchen floor. They were fairly well preserved. The scientist said that the pattern suggested some kind of high quality climbing shoe.

"We put a dog through the house. It picked up Ailish's scent straight away from the bedroom and followed it first to the parents' bedroom and then out through the back door. The trail led the dog through the side gate at number two to the garage. That's about it, sir."

"Thank you, Karl," Thornton said, turning towards Tara.

"What about speed cameras and CCTV, Tara?"

"Nothing of significance caught on speed cameras. There was, however, an interesting sighting on the camera in Main Street in Newcastle at four thirty a.m. this morning. A light blue Volkswagen camper van, registration number Y110 HYM, headed up the street and turned onto the Bryansford Road. We lost it there."

"How long would a journey take from Portstewart to Newcastle?" Thornton enquired.

Tony Rogers was ready with the answer, he knew better than anyone how Thornton's mind worked and he had done his homework.

"Going by the main roads, it is ninety-one miles, sir. Route planner suggests a time of two hours and four minutes.

I would suggest that the culprit took a less obvious route, if indeed that was where he was heading. That would certainly add to the time."

"Thank you, Tony, always one step ahead of me. So he would have had to be clear of Portstewart by 2:10 or 2:15 a.m. at the very latest. A '74 Mark Two Volkswagen camper would top out at about sixty or sixty-five miles per hour max. Tara, have someone examine some realistic alternative routes and talk to Mrs Croft and the parents again. If the child was not taken by 2:25 a.m. at the latest, then the vehicle which drove through Newcastle in the early hours is not the one we are looking for. At the moment, though, it is the best we have got."

Thornton took some satisfaction from his instinct to direct the action. He had gone with his hunch. Now they had to find out who owned the vehicle and where it was. That would not be easy. He felt sure it was in the area.

Tara Ritchie directed the actions. She was impressed by his insight under such circumstances.

Thornton was about to address the team when Jean Harrison burst into the room. She excused herself, walked straight up to him and handed over a slip of paper. Thornton read out its contents.

"Vehicle Registration Y110 HYM refers to a Mark Two VW camper van. Date of first registration: June 1974. Re-registered in Northern Ireland three months ago. Current owner, Mr William James McCluskey, 49 Weatherford Heights, Belfast."

Thornton could barely contain himself, his pulse raced and his jaw tightened – a man with a real grudge, one with a liking for young girls. Was this the lead they were waiting for? He pulled up a picture onto the screen.

"Some of you will recall the name," he said, pointing to the picture that flicked up on the screen.

"Jimmy McCluskey was on the Ramsey enquiry seven years ago. I later sent him down for six years. He's currently out on licence. I believe he has the potential to be very dangerous. We need to find him and we need to find him fast!

"Tara, have local CID call with his neighbours. See if any of them know where he was going on holiday and if they had seen the camper van parked at the house at any time."

Two inconspicuous men sat in the corner of the briefing room waiting their turn. They had become well used to blending in with other people over many years on surveillance in dangerous pubs and clubs along each side of the border. Detective Inspector Pat Whelan had worked for the Garda National Surveillance Unit for ten years. John Allen was his counterpart in the North. They knew each other well. Cross-border operations were more regular now. Major manoeuvres by dissident republicans were thwarted regularly. Like the 'Provos' before them, they leaked like a sieve and dropped their guards when the drink was in after Gaelic matches on Sundays or at point-to-point meetings throughout the island. Republicans loved their pints and ponies.

Whelan cleared his throat and addressed his audience.

"We located the suspect, James Elliot, at 3:42 p.m. yesterday afternoon. We had a hit on his phone. We found him bunked up in an isolated cottage off Railway Road just outside Buncrana. The cottage is managed by a local letting company. Elliot had booked it for a week.

"He was not alone. There was already one other man at the house when we set up surveillance. During the course of the next few hours, three vehicles arrived. We photographed four men who entered the cottage. Three of them are known paedophiles in the South. The fourth is not known to us. They all carried overnight bags and a considerable stock of beer and spirits.

"There was no sign of a light coloured camper van at the premises and Elliott's Volkswagen Passat was parked at the front of the cottage.

"The men left the cottage just after eight o'clock. We followed them to the Drift Inn and were able to listen to their conversation in the bar. Perverse as it was there was no mention of Megan Reilly. There were no unique coded conversations.

"Back at the cottage, a team gained entry and put a cadaver dog through the house and outbuildings. If there had been any remains, the dog would have scented them.

"We installed listening devices and a number of cameras that kept us in touch with all that went on during the night. Much of what we picked up was indecent but there was no evidence or indication that these men had anything to do with Megan's disappearance.

"We will continue with surveillance until stood down. The material we have will be of great interest to DI Looby at the National Bureau for Crime Investigation. He will liaise with colleagues in the North."

Detective Inspector John Allen re-entered the room and was next up.

"I have just checked up on William James McCluskey. He told his probation officer that he was going on a touring holiday around Ireland for the first three weeks in July. He explained that the nature of the trip meant he could not give precise locations where he would be at a particular time.

"We were led to understand that he had recently purchased a camper van. This would appear to tie in with the information we received from the vehicle licensing office and the sighting of the VW in Newcastle this morning.

"I have teams ready to go in both Belfast and Portadown."

Then he turned to Thornton. "I'm just awaiting the order, sir. We can flood the area with teams in plain clothes. It may well be our only means of locating him."

Chapter 44

Tommy McConville set down the phone and pondered the conversation for a minute or two. He had come a long way since that day in 1989 when Mike Thornton saved his daughter, Nancy, on Alliance Avenue.

Thornton's efforts had not been wasted. Nancy shone at school and at college. She was now vice-principal at Holy Cross primary school. She married Colum Tracey, a county footballer, on a glorious spring afternoon in 2004. Two years later a set of twins was born. Lucy and Paddy were Tommy's pride and joy. He spoilt them relentlessly as grandparents tend to do.

He had turned well and truly from the Armalite to the ballot box, rising quickly through the ranks of Sinn Fein. He had been party to the discussions, which led to the IRA ceasefire in 1994.

Both Gerry Adams and Martin McGuinness valued his wisdom and past military involvement. It carried great street credibility. He had convinced many hardline republicans to support the peace process and the new police service, the tale of Thornton's heroism never losing its appeal to even the hardest cases.

He was one of the party's delegations to the Good Friday Agreement in 1998. Tommy was to the fore, when the thorny issue of decommissioning of IRA weapons was addressed. On 7 August 2001 an agreement was reached.

He sat on Belfast City Council and the Policing Board. He was influential in his local Community Restorative Justice group. Now he was fancied as a candidate for the Northern Ireland Assembly elections in 2016.

Tommy had much to thank Thornton for. He picked up the phone.

Chapter 45

The gathering turned towards the knock on the door. A petite young lady of twenty-one or so prised it open apologetically.

"Excuse me, Mr Thornton. There's a man on the phone. He wouldn't give me his name. He said that he needs to speak with you immediately."

The briefing room fell silent as Thornton left and went to take the call, caught in time and circumstance until he returned.

Mike Thornton sat at his desk. He contemplated momentarily the forthcoming press conference in an hour's time. He had still not decided how much he was going to expose to the public. The two press officers were to meet him in twenty minutes to decide.

There had been a number of occasions in his career when he had wished that the 'buck stopped' with some other poor bastard. This was one of them.

He picked up the phone. It had better be urgent he thought.

Immediately he recognized the voice. A little more refined than before with the lower tone of an older man, but still unmistakable. Thornton pressed the secure button.

"Hi, Tommy, it has been a long time. How are you?"

"I'm well, Mike. Someone on the Policing Board told me you were thinking of retiring."

"Not just yet, Tommy. I've a daughter to educate. You seem to have forgotten, I started much later than you. I was delighted to hear of Nancy's promotion. You must be so proud of her. Vice principal at the school you attended how many years ago, Tommy?"

"More than I care to remember, Mike."

The tone of the conversation changed.

"Mike, I have some information that may be helpful to you. I take it we are on a secure line?"

"We are, Tommy."

Thornton knew the quality of information that Tommy could provide. He had never asked him to compromise his position in the republican movement. He knew that he would never turn. Nor did he want to think of him in some witness protection programme, alone and cast off from friends and family in a soulless estate on the outskirts of Rotherham or Swansea or Kilmarnock, never knowing what the next knock on the door might bring. Banished from his beloved Ireland forever.

In twenty-five years or so, Tommy had called him only twice.

In the early nineties, an off-duty soldier had stumbled into the Shamrock Club on Ardoyne Avenue. A dangerous enough place for your average non-regular or a renegade from the Newlodge Road, but for a drunken 'squaddy' shouting his mouth off about his glorious Queen and country, the danger could have lethal consequences.

The IRA had sent for a hit team, while some had taken up positions outside to watch from darkened entries and curtained windows for unwelcome police or army patrols. He would most surely have been dead within the hour but for Tommy's timely intervention and the prompt arrival of the Ardoyne

Patrol, a 'hairy-arsed' crew of police officers, with a reputation for straight talk and taking no nonsense.

On this occasion, it was to check the club register, to see that everyone was properly signed in.

Rumours had been rife, so the story went, of guests not being signed in. Checking membership cards and individual names on the register could be time consuming. To most it seemed more than a coincidence that the soldier's drunken rant when asked for his name invited a laying on of hands by a burly sergeant and a hasty frogmarch from the premises into the back of an armoured rover. The spotters returned to their pints. The hit team was stood down. The soldier went via Tennent Street station to Palace Barracks and from there to England the following morning. He spent three weeks in a cooler in Colchester, contemplating the timely intervention.

The second was when an elderly pensioner was attacked and raped in her home. The young man involved had learning difficulties. The IRA were in no mood to show him any compassion.

Tommy had taken a longer view. Personally, he couldn't have given a shit about the young fella. Part of him thought that broken knees and elbow joints might be just what he deserved. But the discussions concerning the Good Friday Agreement were at a critical point. The Unionists were edgy about sharing power. Sinn Fein did not want to explain why the body of a young man, with a mental age of ten, lay with two bullets in its head in some derelict house or back alley.

Nor could he just simply disappear. There could be no more Jean McConvilles or Columba McVeigh's. No more vanishing without a trace in the middle of the night. The spectre of the 'Disappeared' still haunted the republican movement. Beaches and bogs across the border now disclosed the terrible secrets of the past. For it to happen again would most certainly derail their plans for power within a new assembly in the North.

"Mike, yesterday's appeal from Donegal has not gone unnoticed, though needless to say there will be no names or addresses."

"That's understood, Tommy."

"About twenty minutes ago I took a call from a guy in South Armagh. The appeal had asked for information about suspicious activity or something unusual. He said he had done some work on a light blue Volkswagen camper van about three months ago. The vehicle had been recently re-sprayed.

"The man had asked for a compartment to be fitted under the floor at the rear of the vehicle. He wanted it to be finished with lead. He tried to feed some bullshit about a racket he had, smuggling booze and cigarettes from France. The cubicle was large enough to carry a young girl. The lead would help to mask the smell of what lay within.

"He was in his mid-forties, about 5'10", with long, dark hair and a beard. My guy recalled that the vehicle had a personalised number plate. He was sure that it started Y110. And Mike, this conversation never took place. If I get any more I'll let you know."

"Thanks, Tommy. That ties in with what we already know. We believe the registration is Y110 HYM. It was caught on CCTV in Newcastle at four thirty a.m. We think the driver and vehicle are hidden in some holiday let in the area. There was another girl taken last night, Tommy. You will hear about it on the one o'clock news. We know she is in danger and we believe he may be ready to strike again. Would you put out the feelers, Tommy? We need to catch him."

"I will, Mike. Give me an hour or so before you put your own resources to this. I have an old friend living in the shadow of the Mournes. If anyone can find out where this guy is hiding, it's him. We don't want any compromising situations. Your guys will be spotted immediately and then some people won't know why they are there. They might come to the wrong conclusion. There are still a few 'On the Runs' spending the summer months with friends in the area."

"I can give you till two p.m., Tommy. After that, I have to put my teams on it."

Thornton returned to the briefing room

In north Belfast, Tommy McConville scrolled down the list of names and numbers on his mobile. He paused at Francis MacSorley and pressed call.

The MacSorley family had been smuggling and sheep farming in equal measure for as long as friends and folklore could recall. The Kingdom of Mourne was a lean place to make a living. But the MacSorleys were doing well as they always had. The farm was on Tullyrea Road on the slopes of Slieve Commedagh. The farming community was tight knit and suspicious – 'sheep rustlers' had been ruthless over the last few years. That was until they dropped in on the MacSorley farm in the early hours of a crisp April morning.

The 'pikeys' had seemingly failed to do their homework. As the last sheep was being hurried onto the back of the trailer, the single barrel of a Remington shotgun settled between the shoulder blades of Paul Patrick Ward. Few words were exchanged as he was led away to the sound of his brother Kevin's futile plea. The sheep were returned to their fold. Kevin Ward drove off, thankful to be alive, wondering how he would break the news to his mother. Paul Patrick Ward had a remarkable conversion that night and MacSorley's pigs dined handsomely in the morning, finding the unusual piquancy of their breakfast positively delectable.

Little escaped the eye or ear of Francis MacSorley.

A staunch republican, Francis was a one-time member of the Army Council. He never quite saw eye to eye with the hardliners from South Armagh. He found them to be an arrogant and insolent lot, more concerned with their business interests and bank balances than 'the cause'.

Unlike some, he had supported the Good Friday Agreement. He watched the speedy rise of Tommy McConville through the Sinn Fein ranks. It now appeared to him that the North was becoming more Irish than the South, with so much more emphasis on teaching the Irish language. Protestants were now becoming curious for knowledge of the native tongue and Irish Dance classes were springing up on the loyalist Shankill and Newtownards Roads. Unheard of in the past, much of this was down to Tommy.

It never did any harm if you could do a favour for someone so well placed.

"Hi, Tommy, how are you friend? That was a meaty discussion on the Nolan Show last week. I thought the big retired peeler was going to get the better of you. You turned it nicely on him with that inference about police and loyalist paramilitary collusion in the 1980s. It certainly took the wind out of his sails. How did you find out that he had been a member of one of those secret units around that time? I suppose it pays to do your homework. What can I do for you?" Francis chuckled.

The conversation was over in minutes. In another five, MacSorley had contacted a few carefully chosen associates. He used a pay as you go phone. One could never be too careful. He expected to have the information within the hour. Thirty minutes at least before Tommy needed it. A favour not to be forgotten, he considered with a smile.

Chapter 46

Eileen Parks was at the front of the briefing room as Thornton settled into his seat again.

As well as the Ramsey case seven years ago, she had worked on a number of other abduction enquiries. Some of those assembled were sceptical about the worth of forensic psychologists in such cases. But Eileen had a unique knowledge of Ramsey. She had spent many long hours interviewing him after his arrest. Thornton believed her insight would help distinguish between him and the current predator.

"Peter James Ramsey had a dreadful childhood. He was the product of an unloving and unstable relationship. His father was unbalanced, a man with a dysfunctional personality, prone to mood swings and bouts of deep depression. The mother was psychotic. She was much more forceful than the husband. She beat him regularly as he slept and was prone to delusions and other bizarre behaviours. She completely controlled her spouse. She had always wanted a girl and despised her husband's inability to provide her with one. He walked out on her shortly after Peter was born. She took to dressing him in effeminate clothing when he was a toddler. Dolls and dolls houses were his playthings and at home she called him Petra.

"He spent many hours frightened and crying in a small dark cupboard beneath the stairs. She beat him regularly when she caught him playing football with his friends. He was never allowed to do physical education at school. She was always taking photographs of pretty young girls with blonde hair and goaded him with them. She displayed them in his room. On his seventh birthday she put scarlet ribbons in his hair and dressed him in a red party frock. A former teacher of his told me that he was very aggressive to girls in his class, especially those with long blonde hair.

"He told me that on one occasion when he was ten years old, his mother threatened to castrate him, to turn him into the girl she had always wanted.

"He took to self-harming when he was in secondary school, using knives and blades to inflict painful wounds on his arms and legs and around his groin.

"He was taken into care when he was twelve. Three months after he arrived at the home, a cat was found strung on a clothesline with its throat cut. It was believed that he had done it. He never admitted to it.

"When he came out of care, he returned to his mother, who completely dominated him. She assisted him to get young girls. A middle-aged woman is rarely suspected. She would entice them into her car, drug them and bring them to the house.

"At that stage there was no penetration. Just lurid fondling, which she directed. It was as much to satisfy her depravity as his own. When he had his way with them, she would leave them off close to where they had been taken. The children were so disoriented they could give the police very little.

"We think the episode that put him behind bars fifteen years ago was the tip of the iceberg. I believe that his early childhood engrained in him a loathing for young girls. He became a clever, calculating paedophile that would never have stopped.

"The current subject appears to be equally meticulous and highly intelligent, but he's different. Megan Reilly was not sexually abused. In these cases the risk of being caught must be outweighed by the impulse that compelled the kidnap in the first place – most abductions of this nature would result in the child being molested, probably raped and possibly murdered. So why wasn't this the case with Megan Reilly? We should not disregard the possibility that his behaviour will evolve; the next victim may be molested. It is not uncommon for those initially obsessed with child pornography to develop stronger urges that compel them to target, abduct and abuse children.

"We should also consider that this might be some kind of acting-out of childhood trauma. It is likely that he, like Ramsey, had a difficult childhood. He too may have spent some time in care or fostering. There are certain factors that I find grimly significant: the escalating violence towards the parents and the presence of the aluminium tube. I feel sure that he will use it.

"However, his reckless disregard for leaving clues and evidence conflicts with the self-assured planning of everything else. This leads me to conclude that he is not afraid of being caught. This man may have planned something even more horrific, but for now he appears to be goading us."

Detective Inspector Tara Ritchie addressed them.

"I have received the District Intelligence Unit's reports, sir. There is one that is most significant.

"Rachel Smyth is seven years old. She is an only child and lives in Bangor with her parents, Tom and Ingrid. She attends Ballymacormick Primary School. About a year ago a man started appearing at school at break and lunch times. He was in his early forties and had dark hair and a beard. The children were fascinated by the control he had of his wonderful black Labrador dog. It wore a bib saying, 'Guide Dog for the Blind in training'. He said that the interaction with the children was essential to the dog's tuition. It would sit and let the children stroke it. It would lift either paw on command and respond to its master's every command. He always insisted that the boys would befriend it first and then the girls. Children would give the man their name and he would then invite the dog to greet the child, using their name. Rachel Smyth was last to try. She was intrigued as the dog ambled up to her on command and sat at her side. On a second command it walked round her and sat on the other side. She rewarded the dog's obedience with a treat, which the man had given her.

"He appeared to ask more questions of her than any of the other children. About her family and the kind of dogs that lived in her park. Whether she had a dog and where she thought was the best place to walk one when on holiday.

"The headmistress stated that he would turn up at cycling proficiency classes. She never thought of checking any further than the photographic pass he presented. Everything seemed normal. He had asked if he could bring Sheba into the playground when the children were practising. Said that it was vital to her preparation for a final assessment in four weeks' time. He was very plausible and seemed utterly devoted.

"Around the same time, a woman reported a man fitting this description walking what appeared to be a trainee guide dog along Ballyconnell Road on the outskirts of Bangor. He appeared to her to have a particular interest in number twenty-five. This is where Rachel Smyth's family resides. She reported it to the police, who made contact with Guide Dogs for the Blind. They confirmed they were not training a black Labrador called Sheba.

"A couple of weeks later, the parents made an interesting call to the police. They were heading down for a long weekend at their holiday cottage near Newcastle. A green Volkswagen camper van appeared to pick them up a short distance out of Bangor. It followed at a discreet distance until they arrived at their cottage. At the time they thought little of it as Tollymore Caravan and Camping Park is a short distance away. But the vehicle turned up at the end of their driveway the following morning. When Tom Smyth approached the driver made off. He gave a similar description to other witnesses. He reported the incident to the police along with the registration number. There was no record of it. They are currently at their holiday home."

Thornton realised the significance of this. The camper van could have easily been re-sprayed just before its renovation in South Armagh. The description of the driver has been confirmed too often to be coincidental. The sighting of the VW camper van as it passed through Newcastle earlier today created a huge sense of urgency. He shared these concerns with the team.

"Tara could you please get in touch with air support. I want the helicopter here immediately. I'm sending you and Detective Inspector Allen to talk with the family. I want you to discuss with them putting the house under surveillance. In the meantime I will contact the Regional Assistant Chief Constable for the area. He needs to know what's going on.

"Detective Inspector Allen, I want you to keep your party on standby until you have spoken with the family. Make provisional arrangements for surveillance units and armed response back up. I also want a forensic team and a medical officer ready to react.

"We can't take the risk of this lunatic upping the ante again and we don't want a hostage situation developing.

"Inspector Whelan, pass on my sincere thanks to your team on the ground in Buncrana. They may stand down."

Chapter 47

Maydown Station had wonderful facilities for appeals. For the last hour the techies had been setting up video links with international networks and newspapers. The USA was now hugely interested in the investigation. Both CBC and CNN were running the appeal as live feeds to catch the east coast early risers in Boston, New York and Washington.

The last of the media had just taken their seats when Thornton entered with Ciaran and Mary MacParland. The parents were too emotional to make any sort of meaningful plea. Thornton rose.

"Ladies and gentlemen first of all can I thank you for attending at such short notice. Seven-year-old Ailish MacParland was taken from a house in Portstewart last night. We believe that the person who took her is in his late thirties to early forties. He has long dark hair and possibly a beard. We think that he is driving a light blue Volkswagen camper van, registration Y110 HYM."

"We are keen to hear from anyone who may have seen this vehicle at any time, especially within the last forty-eight hours.

"We are currently following a number of lines of enquiry, which I am unable to disclose at this time. However, we cannot rule out the possibility that the perpetrator will strike again. I am therefore asking all parents to be particularly vigilant.

Know precisely where your children are at all times. Ensure that doors and windows are locked at night.

"I am not taking any questions at the moment. What I can tell you is that Megan Reilly, who went missing from Donegal, was recovered alive and well this morning.

"My appeal is now to the person responsible for the abductions. If you are watching this appeal, I want you to consider Ailish's parents, try to place yourself in their position. You are in control. Only you can choose the outcome. You treated Megan Reilly with consideration. You allowed her parents to reclaim their daughter. Please show the same compassion to Ailish MacParland. Let her come home safe to Ciaran and Mary. Thank you."

The relevant quiet of the room erupted into a journalistic frenzy as Thornton and the parents slipped out the back door. Headlines could now include an element of joy tempered with cold reality. Many of the hacks were speculating where the culprit would strike next. Had he headed for the Newcastle area as Ramsey had seven years ago? On this one they needed to be ahead of the game.

For the next hour or two, the telephones were hot and heavily engaged at the Slieve Donard, Burrendale and Enniskeen hotels. The rooms with stunning views were snapped up first. Then every other bedchamber in the vicinity sold out fast. As far away as Newry and Newtownards rooms were going for more than twice the going rate. Business was booming. Feeding on the well-worn adage, 'There is no such a thing as bad news, just a missed opportunity'.

The bar manager at the Slieve Donard braced himself and called in extra staff. Journalists were well known for their alcoholic excesses and jocular late nights, however grim the occasion. At present they were tight lipped and silent as to why the sudden rush on rooms. A couple of large whiskeys would soon change all that.

Chapter 48

The stranger watched the appeal with interest from a corner table in McDaid's pub overlooking the bay. He had been there a number of times. Felix the barman was always available for a timely observation.

He was muttering about the inadequacy of the current legal system. How filthy perverts who abducted children should be strung up, that the public purse should not have to stretch to keeping them in prison in the lap of luxury.

His words had caught the attentions of two middle-aged backpackers who clearly held different views on social justice and prisoner rehabilitation.

The stranger eyed the sizeable slab of beef and Guinness pie on his plate. The pastry was browned and yielding to the fork's gentlest touch. The bowl of champ beside it oozed with butter. In the jug, the onion gravy was a work of art, rich and thick, with a hint of thyme.

"Can I get you anything else, sir?" Felix enquired.

"Could I get just a little mustard and a piece of wholemeal bread to mop up this excellent gravy and would you put up another pint of Guinness? I do believe it's the best pint in the North."

There was an extra inch to his height as Felix pulled the pint. The secrets of a good pour were to offer it not too cold in a dry glass and to clean the pipes regularly. Then it must be left to settle about an inch beneath the rim. Only complete the job when the bubbles disappear from the creamy froth.

Not just the best in the North, Felix mused, but the best fucking pint in the world.

The stranger was interested not so much in what Thornton had said but in what he had not. He had chosen not to mention the sighting earlier of the camper van in Newcastle. He smirked; Thornton had done precisely what he had anticipated. By now he would be pulling in all his resources to locate the vehicle and the cottage where he would hope to recover Ailish MacParland. Everything was going precisely to plan. He washed down the last mouthful of golden crust and left a handsome tip.

"I'll be on my way now, Felix; some things to attend to. A great pie and a wonderful couple of pints. Oh, and by the way, I agree with you, they should hang the pervert." Again the backpackers raised their eyebrows in silent disapproval.

Chapter 49

The stranger fastened his cycle helmet under his chin, undid the lock and straddled the bike. The Battaglin make was not so well known now. Its pale blue tint and aluminium frame replicated the model ridden to victory by Stephen Roche at 'The Giro' and 'The Tour' in 1987. His success at the World Road Racing Championships some months later completed the hat trick, only the second man in history to do so. Not bad for a mechanic from Dublin City.

The Shimano 600 gears kicked into action as he rose from the saddle and peddled hard up the hill. By the top of the incline he was questioning the wisdom of indulging that second pint. The view was spectacular, rugged and unchanged with time. People seemed like ants down on the beach. Some scurried about, busy playing games and plunging into the waves. Others were more sedate as their ages dictated. A boy was struggling with his kite, which appeared to have a mind of its own. The stranger thought of its restrained existence, always at someone else's beck and call. No real freedom to enjoy or the ability to show off its true potential, just another soaring climb and fall or an imperfect pirouette, then a nose dive into the sand, as the pilot ran out of skill, another fractured stay to mend. He pondered briefly how long it would take Megan Reilly's fractured mind to heal, and then returned to the business at hand.

He needed to get back to the cottage to make sure that Ailish was okay. The syringe would need to be replaced. But there was one more call to make before that. This was to be his final challenge, after which he would be as content as he could ever hope to be.

The wind was at his back as he rounded the bend. The road was narrow with passing stage points every two or three hundred metres. A boy racer almost drove him into the hedge as he sped past, gyrating to the rap music blaring from the open car window.

The driveway to the house lay just ahead on the right. He grasped the brake and slowed to a standstill. The tiny puncture made earlier had the desired effect just before he rounded the last bend. By the time he sidled to the gateway, he was running on the rim of his back wheel.

The scent of freshly mowed lawn took his fancy. The house's driveway was lined with flowerbeds ample with Aster, Coreopsis and Dahlia. Hydrangeas and Oleander were in full bloom along the borders. The woman was in her forties. This was not an educated guess, but a fact he had known for some time.

He had never imagined her to be quite so tall and attractive. He had never given her appearance that much thought. Just saw her as a mother spending the final few hours with her only child.

The stylish Armani sunglasses swept back her auburn hair, ready to be replaced when the gardening was done and she returned to the sun lounger on the decking. She was watering rockroses not twenty feet from where he was dismantling the rear wheel.

He could feel her eyes upon him, as he stripped the tyre from the tube, undid the valve and slipped the rubber from the rim. He inspected it thoroughly, exaggerating the difficulty he had finding the hole. He pumped it twice but seemed unable to locate where the air was escaping from.

"Is there anything I can do to help you?" the woman enquired setting down her watering can and walking towards him.

The stranger smiled and nodded.

"That's very kind of you. I can't seem to find the puncture. Perhaps, if I could trouble you for a basin of water and a towel, that would be helpful. I would walk it back to the cottage but it's a couple of miles away and someone is waiting for me. I don't want to be late."

The woman nodded. "Why don't you bring it round to the kitchen door? We should get it off the road, and besides, it's quite a way to be carrying a basin of water."

"Thanks, I really appreciate it," the stranger replied with a hint of warmth.

He lifted the cycle and followed her to the rear of the house. The view from the garden was spectacular. A friendly retriever called Bella bounded over to him and snuffled his crotch. He gently guided the bitch's nose to the side and tickled her ears and under her chin. She pawed his leg when he gave the slightest indication of stopping. He had not counted on this. The dog would merely add to the challenge. It would need to be dealt with later.

"She's a rescue dog. We got her four months ago. Her name is Bella," the woman said as she approached the stranger and set down the basin.

Two young girls were playing Frisbee on the lawn. Quite proficient for seven-year-olds he thought. They must have honed their skills with mums or dads on lengthening spring nights in back gardens. He watched with envy. How he wished he had enjoyed such simple pleasures with his beloved daughter. But the opportunity had been ripped from him so cruelly. He watched as little Rachel's hair floated from her scalp like feathers as the summer breeze picked up and then abated, allowing her silken locks to fall again and settle. Her mother watched with pride, unaware that the girl's golden curls would be leaving her forever that night.

The stranger pumped the tube and lowered it into the basin. The girls came closer, watching intrigued as he fed it through the water and waited for the bubbles to rise. He had almost completed a full circle when a gentle burble accompanied the stream of bubbles that burst the settled surface.

The little girls whooped and the stranger put his thumb over the tiny nick and raised it from the water.

"Would you take the towel please?" he asked Rachel, almost giving away in that instant that he knew her.

He turned to the other girl. "Now could you release the air from the valve? The tube needs to be entirely flat before we can mend it and I can't take my finger away from the puncture or I'll have to start all over again."

The girls were all too willing to help.

"I've never seen a puncture fixed before," said Rachel.

"Everyone should learn to mend a puncture," the stranger remarked, smiling benignly at the little girl.

"Now I want you to dry off the tube. What's your name?"

"It's Rachel."

"Well then, Rachel, you make sure it's completely dry. I'm going to remove my finger just as soon as all the air is expelled. Then I'll mark the hole with this pen. It's water resistant and won't come away when you dry the rubber.

"Now, Rachel, give it a real good wipe down."

The little girl did precisely as he said. "That's as dry as I can get it."

"That's perfect. Now take the puncture kit out of the saddle pocket and remove one of the patches. Not that one Rachel, a smaller one will do."

The little girl peeled away the protective layer and stuck it firmly over the puncture.

"How does that seem?" she enquired.

"We'll soon find out."

The stranger fed the tube on to the wheel rim and replaced the tyre. He took the pump and attached it to the valve. The resistance of the air pressure increased as the tyre expanded to his rhythmic compressions. The stranger pressed down hard. The tyre was ready to go.

He replaced his helmet and mounted the cycle.

"Thank you so much for your help. Perhaps I'll see you again. I'm only down the road."

"Call in anytime, it's nice meeting some of the neighbours. My husband will be home in the morning."

"Perhaps I will."

The stranger rose from the saddle and pedalled along the driveway and onto the open road.

The wind seemed even stronger at his back as he freewheeled along the road. She had not recognised him from their last encounter. But then again his hair was longer and his beard less well trimmed.

The woman did not realise how quickly he would be taking up the invitation. But not at the time of the morning she should have expected and not with the friendly smile she would have anticipated. The dead of night would mark his unexpected call.

He thought of his schooldays and the dark words of poet Edna St Vincent Millay:

> 'Into the darkness they will go, the wise and
> the lovely.'

Young Rachel had each quality in abundance.

"Well, you learn something new every day don't you," Rachel's mother said to her daughter with a smile. "You'll be able to tell Daddy all about it tomorrow."

The woman returned to her watering can, averting its flow just in time, as she spotted an unhurried bee collecting pollen from one of the blooms. The girls returned to tossing the Frisbee.

"Good catch!" Rachel shrieked, acknowledging her little friend's one-handed field. Her return was not quite as impressive as a gust of wind took advantage of its poor trajectory and dispatched it to the highest branches of a cherry blossom tree.

Something for daddy to do first thing in the morning, Rachel thought.

Chapter 50

It was 1.50 p.m. when the stranger dismounted the cycle and steered it into the porch outside the front door.

He loathed the fact that he must leave behind another well-restored artefact for the police and scientists to paw over. Perhaps one day it might take pride of place with the Vespa and the camper van in some morose exhibition at the Police Museum in east Belfast. An interpretation of his crimes displayed beside them, undoubtedly a distortion of the truth, showing no compassion for one whose heartbreak had unavoidably led to the need for vengeance.

Ailish lay sleeping on the bed. He checked and found the syringe driver was half full. Another four hours and then a change he thought. The next one would see her through till the morning.

Part of him wished that he could return her to her parents right now. But that was not part of the plan.

An aluminium tube lay on the floor beside the bed. He tested the hinges and locking mechanism. They were perfect. He fetched the crimson party frock and laid it on the bed beside the girl.

A good fit, he thought.

The smell of percolating Columbian dark roast distracted him. He poured an ample mug full, reclined in a restful chair and thought again of his lovely Gemma.

He thought of his final days at Sullivan Upper. The past seven years had simply flown by. Talk was about the forthcoming exams, of summer holidays and of university.

Both had hoped for Cambridge. Only Gemma was accepted. She had felt his disappointment even though he had tried so hard to hide it. For her it was off to study English at Caius College in October. For him it would be Mathematics at Queens in Belfast. The thought of their impending parting was tempered only by the promises to meet every other weekend. It had seemed as more than he could bear to be apart from her at all.

The annual prom came and went. Guys and girls who had disliked each other intensely in first and second years were now long-term items. He pictured Gemma's evening gown that night, the plunging back and neckline doing justice to her elegant form. A stylish crimson fascinator sat above her 1950's style chignon, matching her red lipstick. Silver high-heeled sandals peeped from beneath the flowing black evening gown, raising her to his height. Her painted toenails were perfectly presented.

"You look stunning, sweetheart," he had said, proud that she would be on his arm that night. Glad that she would be on his arm at every other such occasion. He pinned an orchid to the strap of the dress and escorted her to the waiting stretch limousine.

The night had passed in style. Staff and pupils mingled like friends. The informality of the occasion untethered by school rules and propriety. Even Bryan Freel steered clear of the Jägerbombs just long enough to enjoy the dance floor. He was seen later at a corner of the bar knocking them back with the legend that was Mr Martin. Mr Martin was more than proficient at teaching modern history but positively outstanding at guzzling all things alcoholic. Poor Bryan was on a hiding to nothing. His imbalance and distorted features soon bore witness to that.

The last shot had come back up as sharply as it went down. His cheeks puffed out by an untimely regurgitation, swiftly followed by a swaying, stumbling retreat through the bar to the sanctuary of the toilets. He made it just in time. Prim Ms Coulter stared sourly at Mr Martin. His gluttonous guzzling left her unimpressed. It appeared that he was heading for another wigging in the morning from the senior vice-principal. Best to make the most of it, he thought as he lowered the pint of Guinness and sought out another impressionable youthful contender.

The principal's speech was rich with irony and wit and had raised a cheer. The late night party ended on the beach at Helen's Bay where friends reflected on school days now departed and hugged each other for the last time. The dying embers of the wood fire brought that chapter of their life to a close.

Their results were nothing more or less than had been expected. They celebrated at Fontana, exchanging the Pinot Grigio of the GCSE celebration for a fine bottle of Bollinger. As they sat sipping the last of the champagne she had taken his hand.

"James, I have some news for you," Gemma whispered. "Please don't be cross with me, but I've given up my place at Cambridge. I can't bear the thought of being without you. I've been accepted into Queen's. We can share a flat together."

He was both elated and moved by her decision.

University life had flown in. They took a flat in Fitzroy Avenue and held some of the finest parties of fresher's year.

Study came easily to both of them, so exams were never particularly daunting.

On a bright May morning at the end of first year, a familiar shop assistant greeted them at Malcolm's jewellers. She smiled as Gemma chose a single diamond set among sapphires on a white gold band. This time he slipped it onto her left ring finger on a window seat in the Merchant hotel. A curious few applauded his proposal as he rose from his right knee and kissed his new fiancée.

That summer they backpacked around Europe. Slumming it most of the time in hostels or in tents underneath the stars. But one day would always be special. It was 14 July. The day that he had tumbled from the surfboard on Portstewart strand. For on that day he found his soul mate, his own loving jay.

The trip on the gondola along the Grand Canal was over too soon. The tuneful gondolier serenaded them with Santa Lucia as they stepped onto the red-carpeted jetty and were escorted to the foyer of the Gritti Palace Hotel. The valet, more used to Louis Vuitton or Tumi luggage, set down their Berghaus rucksacks and thanked them for the generous tip.

The room was incredible. The silk damask walls and oriental carpets a rich contrast to the painted woodchip and Tesco rugs in the flat. The view from the balcony of the Basilica Di Santa Maria was simply stunning.

They dressed for dinner and drank cocktails in Bar Longhi. He had a Bellini, she a Strawberry Daiquiri. He had wondered how many Bellinis Hemingway had guzzled down over the long years of crude self-indulgence at the bar.

The maître d' escorted them to a table beside the canal. He held Gemma's chair until she was ready, easing it comfortably behind her as she sat. He placed freshly pressed cotton across her lap. They dined like celebrities and talked the night away. It was just after one a.m. when they fell asleep in each other's arms. In the morning after breakfast, they caught a taxi to Marco Polo Airport. Five hours later they were on the Dublin Airport shuttle bus, heading up the motorway to Belfast, and back to reality.

Chapter 51

Tommy McConville sat impatiently awaiting the call. Thornton had given him until two p.m. and time was fast running out. He was not let down.

"Hello, Francis. What have you got?"

"Well, Tommy, needless to say the lads have been very busy."

Truth be told Francis had been sitting on the information for the past half hour. It did no harm to emphasise the full extent of your efforts.

"There were plenty of houses we were able to eliminate immediately. About an hour ago my son, Tiernan, was on the Moneyscalp Road. He had a clatter of leaflets with him promoting the farmers' market in Dundrum this Sunday.

"Number forty-one is just beside Malachy McShane's farm. It would appear that the boyo we have been looking for has been almost a next-door neighbour of mine for the last few days. Within a stone's throw, you might say.

"The bold Malachy was in a talkative mood. He told Tiernan that a light blue camper van had turned into the driveway next door at about twenty to five this morning. He had been up foaling a mare, which was having an awkward labour, when the van arrived.

"Tiernan called at forty-one. The house belongs to the Sweeney's. I know the family well. I called with Liam Sweeney. He told me a man called McCluskey from Belfast had taken it for a week, ending on Saturday. He gave me a key to the back door. He's not the type to ask any awkward questions. He's one of the old brigade. I will have someone drop it down to Newcastle station. I am sure the enquiry team will be encouraged not to ask too many questions?

"Tiernan knocked a few times and was just about to head off when a man in his forties opened the door. He had long brown hair and an untidy beard. Tiernan told him about the Sunday market in Dundrum. The guy said he would be gone by then. That he was only there until Saturday. He appeared to my son to be a bit on edge.

"He asked Tiernan if there was a shop within walking distance. Tiernan told him about the wee store in Bryansford about three quarters of an hour's walk away.

"The man had a black Lab that seemed very friendly. Is that any good to you, Tommy?" Francis enquired knowing that what he had given him was like gold dust.

"Great work, Francis. I'll not forget this. It might be a good time to put in a bid for the land you were looking at. You may find that it will be needed by Roads Services sooner than expected. There should be a handsome profit in it for somebody in four or five years.

"There's likely to be a bit of action in that area for a while now, Francis. The 'sneaky beakies' will be all over the place. Tell your lads to stay well clear. We don't want any embarrassing compromises. No nosy fucker sticking his neb in where it is not wanted."

"You have my word on that, Tommy."

"I trust I'll see you at the Ard Fheis next March, if not before, Francis. Rath Dé ort, God bless you, Francis."

"Slán agus beannacht leat, Tommy," Francis replied, saying goodbye to his friend.

Francis fumbled in his pocket for his other phone and dialled the number.

"What have you got?" a voice replied.

Francis went into great detail about the morning's events. It paid to keep your MI5 handler sweet as well.

Chapter 52

The second hand of the clock in Thornton's office had almost completed its last rotation of the hour when the phone rang. The voice on the other end was unmistakable.

"Well, Tommy, how did your friend get on?"

They talked for a couple of minutes. Once again Tommy had not let him down.

"That's great stuff, Tommy. Thank you. I hope it's not as long until we are in touch again. Good luck with the assembly elections next year. If all goes well we can have lunch in that wonderful members' dining room. I was there once before. A DUP assembly member on the justice committee invited me. He thought I might know a well-placed 'Shinner' who could ease the way for some sensitive police reform. But that's a story for another time. Please pass on my best wishes to Nancy and tell her I will be watching her flourishing career with interest. Bye, Tommy."

"Goodbye, Mike. Let's hope you recover the kid alive and catch him before he strikes again."

Thornton informed his boss of the situation and then phoned DI Tara Ritchie.

"Hi, Tara, have you had an opportunity to talk with Rachel Smyth's parents about our proposal?"

"Not yet, sir, we are five minutes away. The Duty Inspector is at the house at the moment. I'll get back to you with their decision."

"Put your phone on speaker mode. I need John to hear this as well."

There was a short pause until the hands free kicked in.

"We have identified the house. It's forty-one Moneyscalp Road. It's about three quarters of a mile from the Smyth's holiday home. The owner of the property has confirmed that a Mr McCluskey rented the cottage for a week, ending this Saturday.

"He was seen driving into the laneway in the camper van at about 4.40 a.m. this morning.

"John, I have spoken with your boss. We agreed to have the command centre in Belfast, with a forward location at Newcastle station. The local superintendent has agreed that the regular beat and vehicle patrols will operate out of Downpatrick station. Your teams will have complete control at Newcastle. Your boss has already sent teams to meet us there.

"The helicopter has just arrived back at Maydown. I'm making my way down. I'll see you shortly. Good luck with the parents."

Chapter 53

The two young girls were playing in the garden as the unmarked police car drew up outside the door. Rachel Smyth was easily recognised. Her long blonde hair was tied up in bunches to make it more comfortable through the heat of the afternoon.

Ingrid Smyth struggled to come to terms with what the police were telling her. The thought of someone stalking her daughter over a period of time made her feel ill. How she wished her husband was there. She had never needed him more. She would have to phone him.

"Mrs Smyth, I understand that what we are telling you must be hard to take in," John Allen stated from a seat beside the pensive mother.

"I have plenty of experience of this type of situation. You will all be perfectly safe. My team will have the house and gardens surrounded. We would prefer if Rachel stayed at the house under our care. Things must look as natural as possible. If the suspect sees anything out of the ordinary, he may just move on. We cannot rule out the possibility of an accomplice who may be watching the house.

"The officers who will be here with you are highly skilled and will look after all of you. Is the other little girl staying tonight?"

"She is. She arrived this morning. Her parents flew from Dublin an hour ago. They are heading for Florida. I can't even get in touch with them. I have to phone my husband, Brian."

Ingrid Smyth picked up her cell phone and dialled the number. She fought hard to hold back tears as she explained the situation.

"Oh Brian, of all the nights you have to be away. Is there any way you can get home tonight?"

"There isn't, sweetheart. There are only two flights a day; the last was ten minutes ago. I am sorry, love. Can you put the police officer on, Ingrid?"

The conversation lasted a couple of minutes. Reassuring words and phrases interspersed with probing questions.

John Allen handed the iPhone back to the concerned mother.

"Well, Brian, what do you think?"

There was a timely pause as she listened and responded with an occasional nod.

Then it was her turn. "I will be careful. No, I won't let her out of my sight. I love you, sweetheart. See you tomorrow."

She set down the telephone, gathered herself and sat down.

"He's agreed to your proposal. What do we do next?" Ingrid Smyth asked.

Chapter 54

It was just after three thirty p.m. when Mike Thornton rolled into Newcastle station.

"Great work, Tara and John. I take it you already have the Smyth's cottage under surveillance?"

"I have sir. We have officers in cover to the front and rear of the home. A quick reaction team is supporting them."

There was a buzz of expectation in the briefing room when a major operation was going down, John Allen thought to himself. These officers had the most caustic wit, which balanced on the edge of political correctness, toppling over on more occasions than he would have preferred.

"Guys, can I have your attention please?"

The room fell silent as John Allen spoke.

"The code name is operation Binion. Communications will be on secure net 1. Gold Command is operating from our Belfast office; ACC Barnett is Gold Commander. We are video linked to them and with the investigation team at Maydown.

"DCS Thornton is Silver Commander. His call sign is Binion Control. There are two main sites significant to this task. Detective Sergeant Niall O'Connor is Bronze Leader at the first site. He and his team have been given their call signs. Niall is Binion Alpha 1.

"Detective Sergeant Hazell Kennedy is lead at the second. Her call sign is Binion Bravo 1. Ian Rea is in charge of our quick reaction teams, call sign Binion Charlie 1.

"The first site is forty-one Moneyscalp Road. We have reliable information that suspect James McCluskey is staying here. His captive, Ailish MacParland, may be there. Both the front and rear entrances are already under surveillance.

It would appear there might be a window of opportunity for us, when he walks his dog to the shop in Bryansford sometime later. We need to be ready to go at a moment's notice. When we do react, we will have about an hour and twenty minutes. Niall, your team will need to be at the top of its game."

The young detective nodded in the direction of his boss. He knew precisely what he meant.

"There should be a light blue Volkswagen camper van, registration Y110 HYM, in the garage, which you can see on the aerial photograph. I want this photographed and examined. I want photographs of the front and rear tyres. A cadaver dog will examine the vehicle. You are also looking for some kind of void to the rear of the chassis.

"I want a tracking device fitted to monitor its movements without compromising ourselves. Flight control at RAF Aldergrove has Scout One on standby.

"We have managed to get a key to the back door. The survey map on the wall shows all the areas of dead ground surrounding the building. You should have plenty of cover to get a team close without being seen.

"Inside the house, I want evidential cameras and listening devices at every appropriate location. There should be a blue racing bike in the front porch. I want it photographed and a tracking device attached.

"If you find Ailish MacParland, you must call for medical backup immediately. We are less than ten minutes away. Under no circumstances will you try to dismantle any devices. At this point one of our Quick Reaction Teams will move immediately to arrest the suspect."

Mike Thornton interrupted John Allen with something less than his usual good manners.

"Ladies and gentlemen, be under no illusion as to the responsibility placed upon us. The eyes of the world are watching. Our primary objective is the welfare and protection of everyone party to this operation. Ailish MacParland may already be struggling for life. You will take no risks whatsoever with the lives of either her or Rachel Smyth. The culprit used a knife during the last kidnapping. He has ramped up the violence. We cannot rule out that he is prepared to use it. This leaves a couple of possibilities, including the development of a hostage situation or the presence of extreme danger to the girl or a member of the team. If you find him in a position either to wound or inject her, he must be stopped at all costs. Check your rules for firearm engagement."

The room fell momentarily silent, broken only by a familiar sound.

"Binion Control from Binion Alpha 2. The target has come out of the front door and is on the move. The dog is beside him on a lead. He is heading for the road. Now turning right onto Moneyscalp Road. Bravo Alpha 3 standby, he is heading in your direction."

There was a pause before the receiver sprang to life again.

"Binion Control from Binion Alpha 3, target is now in sight. Bravo Alpha 4 stand by. Suspect is just passing the junction at Planting Road. He should be with you in ten minutes."

"Binion Alpha 3 from 4, roger on that."

Chapter 55

A scurry of activity followed the radio message at the target's rental. Detective Sergeant Niall O'Connor left in a hurry to take up his position with his team.

They moved in under the cover of a delivery van. The driver reversed up the driveway and came to a stop at the rear beside the shed, out of sight of prying eyes. The handler brought the dog down the ramp. A team was already through the back door and making its way through the house. The kitchen was mostly neat and tidy. A cafetiere had been rinsed out in the sink. The remnants of ground coffee blocked the plughole. Niall O'Connor made his way quietly though the kitchen door and into the hall. He could not rule out the presence of an accomplice.

The team to the rear of the house opened the shed.

"Binion Control from Binion Alpha 5. Vehicle as described is in the shed. Registration is confirmed as Y110 HYM."

"Binion Alpha 5 from Bravo Control, roger."

"Binion Control from Binion Alpha 4, suspect now at the junction with Bryansford Road."

"Roger, Binion Alpha 4."

Thornton turned to John Allen.

"He's making better time than we had anticipated. At this rate he'll be back within the hour."

John Allen took the radio mike.

"Binion Control to all call signs, wait out. Suspect making good time. Re-calculation of time frame now reduced to fifty minutes. Please confirm by response."

Each of the call signs replied in order.

The key almost fitted the lock. The officer extracted it and filed down one of the jagged peaks. The second attempt was even closer. Again the rasp scraped delicately at the metal. On the third occasion it entered unobstructed and the lock turned. Twix the Springer Spaniel was on an extended lead moving inside the vehicle. There was an occasional show of interest, but not the sort that caused her tail to thrash like a wiper blade. An officer was at the rear of the vehicle, using the same key as had opened the driver's door. The perfect fit caused the lock to spring. He stood looking at a sizeable void sealed with lead. The dog moved to the rear of the van. The void was about three feet square and a foot deep. The smell of Jeyes fluid leapt from the empty space, masking any other scents that may have once been there. The dog recoiled immediately. As the handler was closing the compartment, the hint of a crimson tether caught his eye. It was barely visible beneath an oily rag in the corner. He photographed it, then removed it carefully and placed it in an evidence bag, logging its discovery. He reached into his packet for the roll of ribbon he had been given at the briefing, identical to that which had bound Megan Reilly. He cut it to the same length as the piece that he had recovered and placed it exactly as the other had been.

"Binion Control from Binion Alpha 6. Target in shop."

There was now a sense of urgency at the house. Inside the team moved from room to room. Techies were mounting concealed cameras and listening devices. They never stopped marvelling at the advances in modern technology. The photographer took snaps from every conceivable angle. If a forced entry was required, the team would know every inch of the dwelling. The first bedroom door lay open. The team searched it quickly, checking the wardrobe and chest of drawers. They were empty. The search of the second room produced the same result. There was evidence that the bedclothes had been disturbed. A crumpled sleeping bag lay on the floor.

The door to bedroom number three was closed. Niall O'Connor drew his Smyth and Wesson pistol, alerted his colleague to do the same and pushed it open cannily.

"Binion Control from Binion Alpha 6. Target now leaving the shop."

John Allen raised the mike.

"Control to all call signs. You must be clear in twenty-five minutes. Binion Alpha 1, any sign of the girl?" For a few seconds there was silence.

"Binion Control, there's no sign of her, sir. There is also no sign of a metal cylinder or sedating equipment. We will not have time to search the loft or for voids beneath the wooden floors."

Thornton felt his heart sink as he looked at John Allen and Tara Ritchie. He had been so sure that she was there. But if she wasn't there, where was she. Did McCluskey have another place? Was she in a derelict building or hidden underground nearby?

"Binion Control from Alpha 4, target turning onto Moneyscalp Road. He's fifteen minutes away."

The search dog was enjoying a little treat, wagging its tail and being congratulated by its handler. Then it was back in its cage. The handler sprayed a masking agent over the area where the dog had searched.

In another ten minutes the team would be done. An officer took a small tracker from his pocket. He reached in under the rear onside wheel arch. He paused. It was too obvious.

He lowered himself onto his back on the ground. He placed the device behind the first exhaust pipe clamp but removed it almost immediately. He shuffled back a little further. The second clamp had the same subtle features as had the first. The tracker fitted easily alongside the exhaust pipe housing.

"Find that, you bastard!" he mused, as he crawled from beneath the camper.

A pinhead camera and listening device lay in wait near the locking device of the rear door. They did not need a front view. The mirror and the sun visors were too obvious. He was bound to check them. In the house the last of the devices was being tested. All were in perfect working order before the team climbed into the van. Sergeant O'Connor was last to leave. He locked the back door, slipped the key into his pocket and took his place in the passenger's seat. They had done their best in the time available.

At the end of the driveway they turned left and rounded the bend four hundred yards up the road, as McCluskey came into sight of the cottage half a mile away in the opposite direction.

The debriefing room had a sombre air at four p.m. that afternoon. The teams had worked hard. There was a protective ring around each of the houses. At the Smyth's cottage everything was carrying on as normal. Now they would wait until McCluskey made his next move.

Chapter 56

"How do you take your coffee, Tara?"

"Just the same as Eileen will do nicely, thanks, sir."

Thornton topped up the cup with a little cold water and sat down between his two colleagues.

"That was a real blow," he exclaimed.

"Mike, are you sure we are looking in the right direction?" Eileen Parks enquired. "What about the parents of the children who were taken seven years ago. They would have known enough about the case to be potential suspects."

"I am quite confident we can rule them out. The Baillies go to Donegal every year on the anniversary of Emma's abduction. They cast a wreath into the tide at Downing's beach. Eamon Lynch and I attended the first commemoration. This has nothing to do with them. The Grahams sought a new life in Canada a year after Hannah was killed. The Orans are both dead. The mother committed suicide three years after Holly was killed. The father supposedly drowned during a violent storm off Rathlin Island two years ago."

Thornton continued, "The body was never recovered, but when they found the wreck, his life jacket was tangled in the lifeline, and a chunk of his scalp embedded in one of the cleats. It was concluded that he had struck his head as he tumbled from the boat. The dinghy was still in the galley. Days later what were believed to be his clothes and boots washed up near the island's harbour. His former in-laws confirmed they were his. The coroner was satisfied that he had drowned and returned a verdict of accidental death."

"Okay, so we can reasonably exclude the parents from the original Ramsey case as suspects?" Eileen asked.

Thornton paused and stood in silence for a moment, thinking; he figured it was best to leave no stone unturned.

"Tara, have someone call with James Oran's former in-laws. Get a financial profile as well, double check there are no discrepancies, no large withdrawals from his account around the time of his death."

"Yes, sir."

"Other than Elliot and McCluskey, is there anyone else with an axe to grind?" Eileen continued.

"Not to my knowledge. You will both recall that the investigation was reviewed independently; it was done by the book."

Tara Ritchie interjected, "Not everyone saw it that way, sir. McCluskey certainly didn't."

Lynch raised an inquisitive eyebrow at Thornton.

Thornton sighed. "There was an issue concerning a source during the investigation. Some months before the kidnappings began, local detectives were running a source in Newcastle. At the start, he appeared to be well placed and reliable. His information led to us locating a major cannabis factory near Ballykinler. Drug Squad mounted an operation and made five arrests. Subsequent searches of their properties and of social networks helped to dismantle a major crime syndicate.

"In time his information became less consistent. We believed local criminals were feeding him inaccurate information. We even considered that the cannabis find had been set up as well. Another syndicate moved in fast on the heels of the arrested to feed the swelling market. They brought Ketamine and Crystal Meth to a customer base already hooked on skunk. It created an epidemic of addicted teenagers. Violent crime has gone through the roof.

"Six months ago, he told his handler about a consignment of drugs coming in to Kilkeel harbour on a yacht, the *Emily Rose*. Well, everything was in place. The boat was under surveillance from when it left Portpatrick harbour. We detained it as it berthed. Apart from a few iffy magazines, the craft was clean. Not so much as a half smoked spliff. We later discovered that the consignment went to Warrenpoint harbour on a freighter from Amsterdam two hours before drug squad officers boarded the *Emily Rose*. Twenty kilograms of uncut cocaine with a street value of five million pounds made its way across the Narrow Water and into the Republic.

"The source was assessed at headquarters and subsequently removed from the register.

"On the day before Holly Oran was taken, he called the enquiry team at five thirty p.m. A detailed description and a photo fit of Ramsey had been broadcast on the one o'clock news that day. He reported that he had seen a person fitting Ramsey's description in Donard Park at about four thirty p.m. McCluskey brought it to my attention, but the source's handlers said he had been anxious for some time to get back on the register. The extra cash fed his growing desire for crack cocaine. By that stage we had received over sixty calls from all over the province and beyond. As far as I was concerned, this was just another one that we simply couldn't investigate. We had no idea where Ramsey had headed after Castlerock. We could as easily have sent officers to pick up on sightings in Broughshane or Belcoo. In the South, there were spottings as far west as Achill Island and as far south as Skibbereen.

"As it turned out, he may well have been right, but how was anyone to know? The findings of the review were not disclosed to either the public or to the parents of the children."

"Are you sure that this never leaked?"

"I cannot be certain. McCluskey knew of it obviously, but how would sharing the information serve his purpose?"

Chapter 57

The stranger reclined in an easy chair beside the hearth. Everything was going according to plan. He switched on his iPad and opened his music app. He scrolled down his classical list. For a while he was indecisive as he hovered over the two pieces. Decisions, decisions, he thought. Was the wonder of one of Bach's Brandenburg Concertos or the haunting melody of Bruch's First Violin Concerto what he needed at that moment?

He contemplated and then guided the arrow between the two composers. There was only one piece suited to the occasion. It had to be Beethoven's fourth. He fitted his headphones and sank even deeper into the chair.

The thrill of Murray Perahia's interpretation took him back to his student days. It was his final year and the wide world of work beckoned. A position at Methodist College was practically assured. Gemma was heading back to Sullivan to teach English. There had, however, been a little matter to attend to first.

Spring had come early that year. The mild, wet winter had seen to that. Oilseed rape and barley were in profusion in the fields surrounding Cultra Manor. The swifts returned on 4 May, the day before the wedding.

He recalled his anxious wait in the small parish church at the picture perfect folk museum.

It was five past two when the horse drawn carriage turned left onto Meeting Street. The rhythmic clip clop ceased as the coach drew up on the Diamond just outside the church. He recalled Kenny Hayes checking his pockets for the last time. Appearing to be having a moment of panic before smiling towards him and producing the white golden band.

"Just kidding, James," he had said with a wink.

The gathering rose and turned to greet Gemma's radiant entrance and procession. Her father strutted like a peacock. Both of them seemingly uplifted by every beaming smile and best wish, savouring every moment. He recalled the temptation to turn and steal a fleeting glimpse of her. But he settled his gaze on the altar and the empty wooden cross between the stain-glassed windows.

Like a whisper she arrived beside him as the strains of 'Gabriel's Oboe' lingered and faded away, replaced by a fleeting yet serene silence. She was just as lovely as when he had first set eyes on her.

Another song started up. He recalled his days with Bob and Sally in Holywood. How they loved the haunting tone of the mandolin as Finbar Furey's leathery voice recounted the lyrics of the lovely song. The chorus, familiar to most, finally revealing the title of the song in its last line:

> 'I love you as I never loved before.
> Since first I saw you on the village green.
> Come to me 'ere my dream of love is o're.
> I love you as I loved you.
> When you were sweet, when you were sweet sixteen.'

It had been Bob and Sally's favourite love song. How he wished they could have been there to see them. Suddenly he felt their presence, as if they stood beside him.

Her demure smile met his beaming grin. He had always worn his heart on his sleeve. He eased back the veil and their eyes met. A tear of joy crept down the side of his cheek. She smiled.

"You look beautiful, my darling," he had whispered.

Their eyes never parted as they made their vows. The white gold bands rested easily on each wedding finger.

The signing of the register was complete. Family and friends rose as they walked together down the aisle, able to acknowledge the good wishes with a sideways glance or a simple nod. They strode down the aisle as one to Mendelssohn's Wedding March, taking a few strides to synchronise their steps to the rhythm.

At Cultra Manor, the Kennedy room was resplendent, decked in soft cream and beige and scented with camomile. Each table bore an individual floral centrepiece.

Family and friends became reacquainted, trotting out familiar platitudes and pledging to get together more often. They passed the time sipping sparkling wine and scoffing canapés as the camera's lens focused and snapped time and again in Wild Flower meadow. Buttercups were as profuse as the surrounding acres of oilseed rape flowers and barley. In Ballydugan's Weaver's House they posed beside antique spinning mills and looms that once belonged to men creating plain and satin weave or twill. The old and the new captured perfectly together. Then it was the Manor's turn to provide the backdrop.

He had taken in the view across the lough as the camera clicked – just as good as the one from his bedroom window six years ago.

Chapter 58

The day raced in like the tide. Before they knew it, they were alone in the Castleward suite at The Old Inn in Crawfordsburn, The turf fire smouldered in the hearth, the champagne was perfectly chilled, the rose petals on the eiderdown appeared to have been caringly arranged, placed precisely by someone well used to bridal room preparation.

They shared strawberries together on a grand settee overlooking the garden, delicately removing the stalks and feeding each other. The dry champagne enhanced the flavour and made them tipsy.

"One left," Gemma whispered, taking the narrow end into her mouth and drawing him closer. Their lips came together and never parted until the remnants of the last berry were gone.

"I love you more than ever, James," she said as they stood together. She stepped from her sandals, surrendering her elevation. Her wedding dress slipped elegantly to the floor. She undid his shirt and eased it past his shoulders. It fell just as easily.

"Something old," she whispered, unfastening the rose gold necklace and placing it on the bedside cabinet. The catch of his morning suit trousers came away with little effort. They crept down his legs. The absence of shoes and socks allowed him to retain his poise as he kicked them gently to the side of the bed.

Their lips came apart.

"Something new," she sighed, guiding his hands to the bra fastener and assisting its release.

She drew him closer.

Her hands undid her mother's hair clip and her golden locks tumbled down her back.

"Something borrowed," she muttered, releasing him from his Calvin Klein's and ushering him to the side of the bed.

She led his hands along her velvet body and placed his fingers inside her silk waistband. Her hands slid behind his neck. She lowered herself gently onto the bed. He was such an adept counterbalance. Her sapphire-coloured underwear came away in time to her passionate recline.

"Something blue, my darling."

As her back arched up from the cotton cover, she looked at him longingly and smiled, certain that five years of the most intimate foreplay would soon be fittingly celebrated.

Chapter 59

Assistant Chief Constable Barnett picked up the phone.

"That's disappointing news Mike," he said after being briefed. "Do you not think it's time to arrest McCluskey? The media is all over this one. The press office is inundated with calls from around the world. We can't take the risk of another girl going missing Mike."

"You mean I can't take the risk, sir." Thornton replied somewhat brusquely. "It is not the media who are running this enquiry. It is my team who will be putting the case together, sir. We just don't have enough to go on at the moment. The circumstances point strongly towards McCluskey but we just can't be certain. It will be me in the witness box with a high court judge peering over his bifocals if things go tits up.

"There is no sign of Ailish McParland having been in the back of the van or in the cottage. If we move too quickly, it may endanger her. Remember how he reacted the last time I arrested him. He was cute and calculating. He admitted to nothing in spite of the weight of evidence we had. No, sir, we need something more compelling. Otherwise he'll stick two fingers up to all of us this time and walk out the door."

"I hope you're right, Mike. I really hope you are right."

The call ended abruptly.

Barnett picked up the receiver of his secure line.

"Chief Constable, I was just about to call you." For a couple of minutes he listened.

"Yes, I hear what you are saying, sir, but my judgement is to leave him in charge for the moment. If another child goes missing or Ailish MacParland ends up dead that will be a different situation entirely, I will step in. Thanks for the call, sir. I'll keep you informed."

Chapter 60

Eileen Parks placed a hand on Thornton's shoulder, "Mike, is there anything I can do for you?"

"Thanks, Eileen. I would like you to go over everything we have again. Look at the patterns of the culprit's behaviours and the clues he has left. I feel like there is something we are still missing."

"I'll do my best, Mike."

In his office Thornton sat alone with his thoughts. He knew only too well the message that Barnett was sending. He was sure that he would have dated and timed the call. It was time to cover one's back and ACC Barnett had not risen to his exalted rank without that particular ability. He wouldn't be storming in to take over until the case was wrapped up tight as a drum, or something went gravely wrong.

Thornton felt the need to get out of the station for a while, to get his head showered, to sweep away the clouds of doubt that were gathering on the horizon of his mind.

He drove the few miles to Tollymore Forest Park, one of his favourite sanctuaries. He made his way through the barbican gate with its gothic arches, down the driveway to the car park lined with cedar. He parked beside a family enjoying an early evening picnic and headed down the pathway to the Arboretum.

The giant Redwoods and Monterey pines towered above everything else. As a boy he had never appreciated the heritage of the Monkey Puzzle and Eucalyptus trees among which he was now strolling. As far as he was concerned at that age, they were for climbing up and swinging from. The fear of the occasional fall from grace the only impediment to the faint hearted. For him the thrill of the climb always outweighed the danger. Life was about taking calculated risks; he had learnt that from an early age.

He wondered now at the proud oak trees that had furnished the fated Titanic over a century ago. The highly polished stairway leading to the principle dining room must have been something to behold. The ornately carved spindles and bannisters must have helped the Guggenheims, the Astors and other wealthy passengers keep their balance as the vessel tilted gently to and fro.

The Shimna river's tranquil babble seemed willing to bear the burden of his restless soul. He handed it over for a while. Just then he needed that release. The sights and smells of nature helped to free his beleaguered mind and uplift his spirit. He had discovered the therapy of birdsong some time ago. He listened to a chirpy warbler in a nearby copse, asserting its courtship rights.

Overhead a raptor soared high, the bird catching the last of the evening sun and perhaps a welcome supper for its fledglings. He had always struggled to tell a buzzard from a hen harrier. But he was sure it was one or other.

He chose the route across the stepping-stones, along the north bank. He kept a watchful eye out for elusive red squirrels and pine martens. They stayed in hiding.

Was it the soaring bird of prey that kept them in cover, or his presence alone that caused them to be shy? The forest was rich with pine and spruce. Vibrant displays of red campion and ox-eye daisy filled the spaces between the clumps of trees, providing a habitat for insects and small mammals. Foxgloves were profuse along the firebreaks.

A water vole surfaced and disappeared over the riverbank. His mind was clear now. In the stream, a twig was caught in the swirl of an eddy. How lucky it was not to need oxygen, he thought as it was drawn again and again beneath the surface. He looked away to protect himself from the uneasy connection to it; he knew the investigation was in need of some oxygen. Just enough to reignite the fading embers of the enquiry. His mind started to let in the darker side of the past few days again. He struggled to blank it out.

He stayed a while at the hermitage, enjoying the skilful work of master tradesmen of three centuries ago. As he idled passed the waterfall he caught a fleeting glimpse of a Kingfisher. It was gone in seconds, something to tell Jayne and Rachel about tomorrow when he was home. At the Footstick Bridge he sat down. The sun was caught behind a canopy of trees but there was still enough light and heat in the day. He slipped off his shoes and socks and dangled his feet in the water.

In twenty minutes he was back in the car heading for the office. He passed the shop at Bryansford where McCluskey had been a little more than an hour ago. Further along the road lay the driveway to the Smyth's cottage. He had a sudden urge to see how things were inside. Then he changed his mind and left their protection to Hazell Kennedy and her team. The change of scenery had done him good. As the barrier to the station rose, he felt refreshed again.

Chapter 61

John Allen was concentrating on one of the monitors as Thornton entered the control room. He focused on the screen.

He hadn't seen Jimmy in over six years. Time and prison had clearly taken their toll. The once immaculate slicked back hair was now long and uncombed. The beard he thought to be unbecoming. The pinstripe suit replaced by shabby jeans and a creased denim shirt.

The suspect shifted the coffee table to the side and threw back the deeply patterned rug. He drew a screwdriver from his right hip pocket. For the next two minutes he was busy releasing a floorboard.

He placed the tool in the narrow gap between the planks and prised open the one he had freed. He reached inside and pulled out a small black rucksack. He undid the tassel and checked the contents without removing them. Then he tightened up the braid again and placed the bag on the floor beside the television.

It was never ideal to speculate on what was inside, but it was always prudent to be prepared for something unforeseen. The details of his actions were noted and timed.

"Anything else to report, John?"

"Apart from what we have just been watching, nothing much, sir. He had dinner half an hour ago. He finished with a cup of coffee and listened to his iPod for a while.

"He took a phone call at 16.43 p.m. It lasted for two minutes, forty-six seconds. We were unable to put a trace on it. McCluskey must be using a pay as you go. His regular phone is switched off.

"The Smyth's have just finished their dinner. The girls are in the garden again playing with a Frisbee. Hazell Kennedy is doing a fantastic job keeping everything quiet and low key. Don't worry, sir, if anyone comes visiting that house tonight they will get more than they bargained for."

Chapter 62

It was just after seven thirty p.m. when Tara Ritchie and Eileen Parks joined Thornton in his office.

"Well, Tara, how did you get on with our unrecovered body? What had the former in-laws to say about his disappearance?"

"I called with them personally, sir, it was only three quarters of an hour up the road. I have to say they were quite surprised to see me, but willing to help.

"They said that Oran was devastated by the loss of his wife. He was admitted to Downshire, nursing home, following a bout of severe depression. After his release they saw less and less of him. Shortly afterwards he received some news that really set him back, though the in-laws said he never discussed it with them. He retreated further into isolation and took to gambling and went on regular excursions to casinos in Dublin and the Isle of Man, which I'll come back to later. He never returned to work. He took a medical retirement and became a bit of a loner. He rediscovered his love of painting. He had been very good at school. Land and seascapes were his topics of choice. A picture of Slieve Donard hung above the fireplace in their sitting room. It was an impressive piece but dark, grim even. I'd say it was either copied from a photograph or painted from a position just below the mountain.

"He also started going on challenging survival weekends and renewed his passion for sailing. He bought a new Flying

15. He didn't really do regattas. Being a crewmember or joining in the celebrations had lost its appeal, but he was a member of the Royal Ulster Yacht Club. He could be found there regularly at lunch times. He sat at the same table, a window seat which looked away from Ballylumford Power Station across the bay. A blot on the landscape, he had called it. He preferred the view to Black Head and of the Aran Islands on a clear day.

"The following year, he planned a solo voyage around Ireland. He set off from Bangor marina on the day he drowned. They recalled the coastguard had posted warnings of a severe storm building in the North Atlantic and heading for Scotland and the north coast of Ireland. He paid it little attention. They were of course devastated when he went missing, presumed dead.

"They told me Bob and Sally Heron had left him a small fortune in their wills. It amounted to over two million pounds. This allowed Gemma and him to marry in their last year at university, just before graduation. His will left substantial sums, one million in total, to the Samaritans, Cruise Bereavement Care and Marie Curie. The rest went to his in-laws. That was all they were able to tell me."

"What about the financial checks, Tara?"

"Yes, sir, I was just coming to those. Bob and Sally had invested very prudently in blue chip bonds and shares and in Krugerrands. They had a handsome portfolio.

There is nothing remarkable about his financial activities, charity donations, payments for holidays and sailing club fees, household bills, the usual sorts of standing orders and direct debits. The only oddity is that about three years ago he started to make large cash withdrawals. It was always fifteen thousand pounds. Always made at the end of the month. There was no further activity on any of his accounts or credit cards after he was presumed dead.

"I made some enquiries about his gambling. He favoured the Palace Hotel and Casino in Douglas on the Isle of Man and The Mayfair in Dublin. We were able to link credit card transactions to each of them. The dates of his visits coincided with the large withdrawals of cash.

Both casino managers told me that he was a regular customer. He appeared to be quite a heavy gambler. Always arrived with a sizeable wad of notes and seemed to leave with little at the end of the night. I believe we have taken this as far as we can, sir."

"Thank you Tara. Oran is probably insignificant to the investigation, I just wanted to chase up every loose thread."

"I understand, sir."

"Anything on the fingerprints and DNA yet?"

"We won't have the DNA results for a couple of days, but I'm expecting the fingerprint results in a couple of hours."

"Okay. Eileen, how are you getting on with the review?"

"Well, Mike, there are some details that don't work for me. If McCluskey is our man then he has been very careless indeed. Leaving fingerprints and DNA match opportunities should not be his style, based on the thoroughness of the rest of his planning and his history as a police officer. To be caught once by a road camera is careless. To be caught twice is more than just coincidence. There was no need for either. These were done on purpose, Mike. We have to consider that he may not be our man."

Regrettably she was telling him nothing that he did not know already, but he thanked her for her work.

Chapter 63

Dinner that night was a variety of pizzas, fries and garlic bread from Mario's. The hubbub in the kitchen was a welcome distraction from the grinding hours of waiting. John Allen preferred pepperoni to salami. Irene Parks ordered a Hawaiian but got a meat feast. Tara went for a Margarita with extra jalapenos. Thornton wolfed down a Diavola, the heat distracting him momentarily from the case.

They all needed a short break to tackle the fatigue that was setting in. Conversation moved quickly to holidays and city breaks. Tara was planning a trip to Bilbao and San Sebastian in a fortnight. Thornton was able to fill her in on places to eat and beaches to visit. He held most of the detail back of his last time there with Jayne. Perhaps it was time for their return. Next time Rachel could come with them.

John Allen had just become engaged and was heading to Sorrento in September. There was to be no slumming it either, the Excelsior Vitoria Hotel no less.

Irene Parks was heading back to Boston and New England with her latest partner. She loved the Irish influence in the city and early morning breakfasts along the Charles River.

"What about you, sir?" Tara enquired.

"Oh, nothing special this year, Tara. I guess I'm a bit of a home bird at heart. We've a cottage outside Glenarm. Jayne's there at the moment. It's my daughter's birthday on the fifteenth I made her a promise that I would cut the cake after she blew out the candles. I intend to keep it."

Tara considered her boss, thinking that in many ways he was like her own dad had been at that age. He was decent, courteous and hugely courageous. His rescue thirty years ago of the young girl in Ardoyne was the stuff of legends, the sort of tale that needed no gilding. She didn't imagine it had ever appeared on any promotion application or staff appraisal over the years. Thornton was far too unassuming for that and anyway his huge successes as an investigator bore testament enough to his outrageous talent.

She saw weariness in him now, like a boxer who had taken one punch too many, still on his feet, but losing heart for the fight. Being the boss carried huge responsibilities. She wondered how she would cope in his position. But this was a burden he would not pass down.

Chapter 64

The clock ticked slowly on the wall. It was almost midnight when McCluskey rose from his chair. He picked up the rucksack and headed for the bedroom. He set the sack on the bed and took out a black long sleeved garment. He took off his denim shirt and replaced it with the black polo. He slipped out of his jeans and stepped into a pair of black Lycra trousers and a pair of dark pumps. He took a ski mask from the bag and put it on like a skullcap.

John Allen lifted the microphone. "Binion Control to Scout 1. There is some activity at the target location. Make your way down."

"Roger, Binion Control, taking off in two minutes."

The pilot fired up the engines, received clearance and took off. By road the journey would take forty minutes. He would be there in ten at most. He would hang off some miles away. His presence over Hilltown might spook the odd republican or two with something to hide, supping Guinness in Minni Doyle's. Then they would remember; if you can hear the engine's whine, the spooks are looking at someone else.

They focused on the monitor in the control room. McCluskey placed his iPad in the rucksack and hoisted it onto his shoulders. He left the dishes in the sink, headed through the hallway and checked the front door. It was locked. He returned to the kitchen and undid the latch. It was 11.58 p.m. when the monitors lost him momentarily. The silence in the room was deafening, then suddenly: "Binion Control from Binion Alpha 2. Suspect in garage. He is moving around the area checking for anything out of place. He is inspecting the wheel arches."

There was another pause.

"Now he is under the vehicle."

Niall O'Connor turned to one of his team, glad they had changed the device's original location. Was it back far enough not to be found? Would its position at the second exhaust housing be sufficient? They would know soon enough.

"He's on his feet again. He's checking the void. He's lifted out an oily rag from the corner. He's checking the ribbon. He's replacing them both. He's dusting the door handle for prints. Nothing found. The door is open. He's inside."

In the control room they were now picking up his every movement. They watched as he inspected the rear view mirror and then the sun visors. He was content.

McCluskey reversed the vehicle from the shed. A three-point turn placed him in the right direction. He headed down the driveway towards the road. The tracking device sprang to life.

"Binion Control from Scout 1, target in sight turning right onto Moneyscalp Road. GPS is functioning well."

Chapter 65

Ingrid Smyth was in her daughter's bedroom, sorting out clothes for the morning. She needed every ounce of inner strength to hold back her emotions.

"What time will Daddy be back tomorrow, Mummy?" Rachel quizzed, rubbing her eyes and yawning wide.

"He'll be here just after midday, pet. We are for the three-ringed circus tomorrow night. Daddy booked the best seats in the house, as a special treat."

"Oh, Mummy, I can hardly wait. Will Hazell be here in the morning? I really like her. Can she come with us, please?"

"Perhaps you could ask her in the morning, but she might be busy. Now, young lady, you need all the sleep you can get. Look at Julie, out for the count already."

She kissed her mother on the cheek. In minutes, she was deep in slumber.

Less than ten yards from her bedroom window, a policeman sat in cover. Like an obedient hound, the submachine gun rested easily on his lap.

Detective Sergeant Hazell Kennedy threw a reassuring arm around Ingrid and went to make a cup of tea. Her earpiece came to life suddenly.

"Binion Control from Scout 1, suspect approaching junction with Planting Road in five, four, three, two, one. Suspect turning right. I say again, turning right. Suspect now on Planting Road, GPS active."

Thornton looked at Tara Ritchie and John Allen. This was not what they had anticipated.

"What is he up to?"

"Probably just a decoy, sir. He will be surveillance aware. We have every angle covered." John replied.

"Binion Control from Scout 1, suspect vehicle now four hundred metres from junction with Tullyrea Road. Vehicle slowing to a stop."

The communications room was glued to the monitor. McCluskey fiddled with his right trouser pocket. He raised himself from the seat and pulled out his phone, answering an incoming call.

"Binion Control to all call signs. We have eyes on the suspect. He has pulled to the side of the road. He appears to be taking a phone call. Scout 1, what is his GPS position?"

The co-pilot checked the reference.

"Binion Control from Scout 1. It is 31697 33202."

"Roger, Scout 1."

There was another silence.

"Binion Control to all call signs. We cannot make out what the caller is saying. Call signs wait out."

The teams at all locations held their breath.

"Binion Control to all call signs, telephone conversation has finished. He is removing something from the phone. It must be the SIM Card. Now he is rolling down the window. He seems to have tossed it from the vehicle."

"Binion Charlie 1, I want a team directed to that grid reference and hold the scene until the morning."

"Roger, Binion Control. There in five after the target moves on."

"Binion Control from Scout 1. Suspect on the move again. Now passing Tory Bush Cottages and turning left onto Tullyrea road."

"Back on course again, sir," John Allen noted with a sense of relief.

All was quiet at the Smyth house on Bryansford Road. The girls were asleep and Detective Sergeant Hazell Kennedy was swapping stories with Ingrid Smyth, ever conscious that the vehicle was heading in their direction.

In the next few minutes she may have to react. Go into overdrive. Reveal her ruthless efficiency. Shoot to kill if necessary. Best to remain calm for now.

Chapter 66

Their cottage overlooking Glenarm seemed a long way off. Thornton thought of his wife preparing for another party without him. She would still be up, icing buns and topping up a lemon drizzle cake. She knew exactly what he liked. By now, Rachel and Barbara should be fast asleep. Exhausted by the day's activities. He hoped that the extended spell of good weather was not affecting Rachel's asthma. The higher than normal pollen count had been causing her to wheeze lately. On occasions it was like a high-pitched whistle. Once she had struggled for breath, she had become agitated. The tightness in her chest had caused panic. Her heart rate and respiration climbed unnaturally, terrifyingly. They had feared she might suffocate. The fluticasone for a while seemed ineffective. He thought she might lose her struggle until the rhythm of her breathing slowed, the heartbeats became countable again and the panic paled. It was three years now since that terrible episode.

When all was ready Jayne would curl up with a half-cup of coffee in her Marks and Spencer pyjamas and listen to some music. Ed Sheeran was her current favourite.

He thought about tomorrow. He would be there for the party, even if it were for just an hour or two. Right now he sensed a long night ahead, another sleepless night. He felt dryness behind his eyes. The type caused by dehydration. He raised a water bottle to his lips and lowered it again when it was empty. The effect was immediate. The grittiness was gone. He felt refreshed and up to the task again.

Tara Ritchie forced a brew into his big right mitt and offered him a biscuit.

"Caffeine will be the death of me," he said. "Ah, McVitie's chocolate digestives," he uttered. "The only sort for nights like these." He dunked it for a second or two then pulled it out just before it reached saturation point and fell into the beaker. The crunch was failing fast as he popped it in his mouth.

"Any chance of another please, Tara?"

She offered up the last in the pack.

"Only if you have had one," he insisted pushing the packet towards her.

"Watching my figure, sir. I have to be in shape for those beach bars in San Sebastian. I want to be able to enjoy all those tapas bars and regional wines you made sound so inviting."

In truth she would have enjoyed a first, but just then she felt his need the greater.

"Binion Control from Scout 1. Suspect vehicle turning left onto Bryansford Road. He is passing the Outdoor Pursuit Centre."

There was a pause.

"Now approaching the town."

Inside the vehicle McCluskey lit a cigarette and shifted from radio mode to disc. The strains of Tony Bennett were unmistakable. McCluskey allowed the artist the first three lines before joining in, "I'm going home to my city by the bay. I left my heart in San Francisco. High on a hill it calls to me."

"Binion Control from Scout 1. Vehicle now approaching target location."

The moon hid under a blanket of cloud as the van pulled past the driveway and then reversed until it was hidden from the open road.

"Binion Control from Scout 1. We no longer have eyes on."

Constable Stephen Grey peered through his night goggles from a thick rhododendron bush just yards from the vehicle. A throat mike picked up his every intonation.

"Binion Control from Binion Bravo 2. Now have eyes on the suspect vehicle. It is parked about ten metres off the road, out of sight of the house."

Around the cottage and within, highly trained officers made ready.

Hazell Kennedy turned to Ingrid Smyth.

"This may be it, Ingrid. Everything is under control. Go to the bedroom and pretend to be asleep. I have three officers covering each side of the house."

Ingrid passed a darkened team member in the hallway and entered the bedroom. However much Hazell Kennedy had tried to reassure her, this was now for real and she was scared.

"Binion Control from Bravo 2, suspect still inside the vehicle. No movement as yet."

Ten minutes passed and McCluskey had not appeared. It seemed like an hour as tension mounted.

"Binion Control from Bravo 2, suspect is opening the van door. He's finally out of the vehicle! The rucksack is on his back. Now he is taking cover!"

The mike went silent. Fifteen seconds became thirty. Then a minute passed.

"Binion Control to Bravo 2. Situation report."

There was no answer.

"Binion Control to Bravo 2 sit. rep." Again there was no reply. John Allen turned towards Thornton.

"What the fuck do we do now?" Allen asked.

Thornton thought hard and quickly. At the house uneasy officers almost broke their cover, fearful for their colleague. Wondering if the suspect's knife had been put to use.

"Give it a minute, John. Perhaps he is standing right on top of him."

The silence seemed to last forever. Then suddenly, "Binion Control from Bravo 2. Suspect now using natural cover and approaching the house. Now at the crown of the bend. I have lost him."

"Binion Control from Bravo 3. I have the suspect in view. He's heading for the left side of the house. The moonlight is on the other side."

"Shall we take him now, sir?" Allen enquired.

"Not yet, John, let him get into the house. Then we've got him."

"Binion Control from Bravo 3. Suspect has checked the side windows and is moving towards the front door."

Trigger fingers started twitching all around the cottage. Hazell Kennedy unsheathed her Taser and moved closer to the door. He would feel its paralysing impact the second he stepped inside.

"Binion Control from Bravo 3. He is testing the door handle. He is reaching into his rucksack. He has something in his hand. I cannot make it out."

Thornton thought of the duplicate key used to such good effect in Portsalon. He was tempted to give the order to move. He held back.

"Binion Control from Bravo 3. The suspect has shouldered the rucksack again and is turning away. He is heading down the driveway under cover."

"What is this guy at, sir?" Tara Ritchie enquired.

"I don't know, Tara. Perhaps he was spooked. Maybe he knows we are on to him."

The phone rang. It was ACC Barnett.

"You should have taken him then, Mike. The Chief is here at Gold Command with me. What the fuck are you playing at?"

"Sir, with respect to you and the Chief, what have we got? A parcel packed with circumstantial evidence, but nothing concrete. A guy being nothing more than a little creepy at the house. We would be lucky to sustain a charge of civil trespass. A good lawyer would drill straight through it. And what about Ailish MacParland or have both of you forgotten she is still missing. How does the Chief suggest we get her back if McCluskey clams up?

"Ask the Chief if he will go and explain to the parents why their child is dead. I suggest you give me some space or come down and take over."

He slammed the phone down, with unusual force.

"Sorry, everyone, I would have preferred you had not heard that conversation. I doubt I will be top of the list for the next position at the top table," he said with more than a touch of weariness and frustration.

"Binion Control from Bravo 2, suspect has returned to the vehicle. He is on the move again. Heading down the driveway in darkness. Now turning right."

"Binion Control from Scout 1, suspect vehicle on Bryansford Road again. Turning right towards Newcastle. Now turning right onto Tullybrannigan Road."

The operations room was stumped. Vehicle now reversing into driveway at grid reference 44868 86663. Have lost sight of target."

The control room fell quiet again.

Chapter 67

The stranger switched off the engine. He checked his watch. Ten more minutes would be sufficient. He felt elated at the precision of his plan. Perfect in every detail and always one step ahead of his pursuers.

He contemplated the next few hours. Then he thought again of Gemma. But that was nothing strange. For every waking hour he thought of her.

Their first year at work had been an exciting one for both of them. At night they helped each other with lesson plans. Taking A Level classes was challenging. Saturdays were devoted to sport. Then there were the distractions caused by family planning. This did not come so easily as everything else in life appeared to, months ran quickly into double figures and worries about fertility were only barely eased by the doctor's timely reassurances.

It was 2 September and another new school year beckoned. He recalled the sheer delight tinged with disbelief that accompanied the five simple words.

"I think I am pregnant."

He thought about the state it had put him into, jumping for joy and struggling to get the next sentence out with any sense of composure.

"How do you know? I mean, how you can tell? Are you all right? I think I need a seat."

The months had flown in. It was the morning of 14 July when Gemma shook her husband awake and declared with equal panic and joy, "James, I think it is time. My waters have broken."

The journey to hospital was quick but restrained. Her labour was long. He had thought of the irony of her putting up with all the pain and him finding it more difficult to bear.

It was 1:35 a.m. the following morning when he held her for the first time. Holly Gemma Oran had arrived into the world.

At 7lbs 10oz, she was their pride and joy. The next seven years flew in so quickly. At eleven months and three days she took her first unstable steps, it was on a Sunday in May, five faltering strides before she stumbled and fell into her adoring mother's arms.

They listened to the babble that only she could understand. Three months later she called him Dada. At three, they took her to the zoo and the botanic gardens where she questioned them beyond their wisdom. They taught her 'please' and 'thank you' and discouraged the frequent use of 'no' when things did not go as she would have liked.

She was reading and counting well before her first day at Holywood Primary. She showed her mother's gift for English and his own for Maths and Science. She shared them eagerly with those less able.

The annual nativity play was a highlight. In P1 she had been Casper, the wise man who travelled from India with his gift of gold. The next Christmas she was Balthazar who brought frankincense. She never got the chance to play Melchior, or perhaps even Mary, a role that always fell to a P3 girl.

He recalled the times playing rounders on the beach, the shouts of "Faster, Daddy!" as they ran together along the sand. He shared his extra speed with her. Clasping her hand tightly, allowing her to take exaggerated strides, until the pace went beyond her. Then he would sweep her into his arms and they would laugh together.

The days at the swimming pool too, how she had shrieked when the ridiculous Mr High-Knees appeared, kneecaps breaking the surface as he strode towards her; his own invention of a perfectly harmless villain.

Holly had loved the weekends. Especially those after the hour changed in spring. Daddy and Mummy packing cases in the boot, the journey down the road just before rush hour, the feeling of exhilaration as the car pulled off the Bryansford Road onto Tullybrannigan Road.

He recalled the cruel night she was taken in July. The day had started so well. The sun was high as they left the cottage. The walk through Donard Park had been more exhilarating for her than was usual, for they were heading for Slieve Donard and its matchless summit.

There was a scurry of activity in the car park. Men and women fastened gaiters and extended titanium poles, old hands and novices setting off together.

They took the route through the forest of Scots pine and oak. The track was uneven and tricky before they reached the Ice House. The Glen river serenaded them until they arrived at fifteen hundred feet. How raucous this song became was dependent on the rainfall, which was timid on the day of the climb.

He recalled the moment as they crossed the stream for the last time before the assault on the summit. Holly was filling a water bottle when the man approached. An innocent encounter he had thought. The man stopped and cupped his hands to take a drink. The water had dripped from his bearded chin. The chat moved quickly to the ascent that lay ahead, the rugged elevated slalom to the saddle and the wall, the rest before the final ascent and five hundred feet or so of unrelenting incline. Then would come the thrill of the summit and the view.

On a clear day four countries were visible from the peak. Five if you counted the Isle of Man. On the stillest days the wind was always wild and whistling. The man had asked Holly if she felt tired.

"I'm okay, thank you, Mister. I think my daddy may be struggling a little more than I am," Holly had quipped, giggling. The man had walked with them to the saddle between the two peaks, exchanging conversation, then swung right up Commedagh.

As he sat in the van, hot tears streaking his face, the stranger was furious that he had not sensed the danger. If he had just seen the one o'clock news that day his whole life could have been different. If they had left the house just two hours later, he could have protected them. They would still be here. He wouldn't be alone. The uncanny photo fit and description would have been enough to postpone their ascent to the summit until another day, to call the police and have the man accosted at Hare's gap on the other side of the mountain. But he hadn't seen the news, the photo. He didn't know he was laughing with a monster beside the river, shaking hands with a man that would take everything from him.

He recalled how tired they had been as they returned to the cottage shortly after five p.m. Just a quick shower and shave before a trip to Nardini's and the circus in the park. As a child it had been his delight to go with Bob and Sally. Now it was his Holly's turn to gawp with wonder. The entertainment did not disappoint. At 11.50 p.m., he had tucked her into bed. He remembered his joy as he hugged and kissed his tired daughter and told her of the treats in store for tomorrow.

It was one thirty a.m. when he felt cold steel at his throat. The darkened figure wore no mask. His words still haunted him.

"I hope you enjoyed the walk to the summit, James. Holly was doing ever so well when we met by the stream." Ramsey had laughed at James's recognition and confusion.

"Let me run you through the formalities, Mr Oran. I will be taking Holly. Waken your wife and tell her not to bleat or I will slit her throat."

He obeyed.

"Good, James, now take these ribbons and tie her feet and hands."

He recalled the feeling of sheer helplessness and guilt, his beloved Gemma's fear, the look that searched for some response from him. When would he react and rescue her? Disarm or overpower the intruder? But he could not. It was just too dangerous, with the blade at his throat he would be dead instantly. Instead James did precisely what he was told. The intruder then tied him tightly to the bedstead.

For a moment he left the room. He still had flashbacks of Holly in Ramsey's arms. The taunting leer as Ramsey met his eye, a second before he stole their daughter.

Then there was the waiting, the terrible waiting, the unbearable anguish. All night he had fought with the tethers, chaffing his wrists until they bled. Finally he managed to prise his wrists from the crimson shackles. Then came the desperate call to the police.

Constable Jayne Winter was their family liaison officer. He recalled her arrival. She kept them informed as the search for Holly progressed, told them the news when she had been found alive. Jayne had shared their elation. She drove them to the hospital and walked with them to Holly's bed.

Their relief was short-lived. Holly lay barely alive in A & E, the tiny gown unable to mask her injuries; her bruised and battered body, the streams of blood already congealed down her legs, her shallow, stilted breathing and Gemma's frantic pleading with the doctors as they struggled to save Holly's life.

He remembered the moment when they had stopped, his horror as the doctors solemnly took a step back, the silence, and the dawning realization of what this meant. He rushed to her side. Taking her in his arms, he begged her to stay. Beside him, clasping her daughter's hand, Gemma made a desperate plea, begging the doctors, begging him, begging anyone to do something. Jayne Winters had hugged her, cradling her from behind, as though trying to hold her together. But her world, her life, had been torn apart. Her daughter's life was ebbing away and there was nothing she could do.

It was too soon for them to be apart forever.

He would never forget the moment that he held her last, as all life left his daughter's broken body.

Then she was gone.

Chapter 68

Tara Ritchie ran into the room.

"Sir, the fingerprint results are back. We don't have a..."

Ritchie stopped short as she caught sight of Thornton's face.

Thornton knew already what she was going to tell him. They did not belong to McCluskey. They were not on record, though they would have been seven years ago, he thought, taken from a parent as part of the enquiry. Destroyed later, when James Oran had been eliminated from the investigation.

The registration on the wall now glared mockingly at him. Y110 HYM. A personalised plate, some had said. Irene Parks came through the door.

"Mike, I have the connection with the number plate."

He had already made it, as the significance of McCluskey's location had dawned on him, as he realised it was Oran. The reason for McCluskey's arrival at Tullybrannigan road was clear. It was the place from which Holly Oran was taken seven years ago, the last of Ramsey's victims to die. Tomorrow was the anniversary of her passing. McCluskey was only a partial player in the scheme, the one to lead them on a wild goose chase, the one seeking long-awaited revenge.

How could he have missed the clues? The partial plate caught on a speed camera on the Foyle Bridge should have registered, Y011H. The completed mark captured on CCTV in

Newcastle the following morning, now slapping him in the face. Read in reverse, as it would be in a rear-view mirror, it was so obvious: MYHOllY.

"I see it, Irene. How the fuck did we miss that?" He shouted, pounding his fist into the desk in front of him. The uncharacteristic show of anger silenced the room.

His phone twitched in his pocket. It was Tommy McConville.

"Mike, I have some news for you about the camper van."

Again Thornton knew what was coming. There would be two. One for Oran and a ringer vehicle for McCluskey. A second one had been similarly converted. Tommy confirmed his suspicions. Somewhere in Tyrone or Fermanagh he would hazard a guess; though the precise location would remain a secret.

Rachel Smyth was just a decoy too, a taunting diversion. It wasn't the Smyth girl that was in danger. His own daughter was the real target.

Thornton snapped into action.

"Tara! Call Ballycastle police! Send a car immediately to twenty-three Tully Road. He will be going for my daughter!" Tara looked horror-stricken as she grabbed her phone, not waiting to ask who 'he' was.

"John, send a team to Tullybrannigan Road immediately! Arrest McCluskey. Seize the vehicle. Have the house sealed until the morning. Use a local Mobile Support Unit if you have to. Ailish MacParland isn't there. McCluskey never had either of the girls. He is an accomplice. James Oran has Ailish. He's not dead. It's all about my failure to save Holly Oran!"

Thornton snatched up his mobile and dialled Jayne's number, his heart skipping a beat when she picked up. He wasn't too late!

Except the voice was not that of his beloved wife.

"Hi, Mike, it has been a long time. Remember me? I have just had a most interesting half hour with Jayne. I must say I did most of the talking; the Zolpadine left her a little woozy after all. As she knew it would, quite the policeman's wife. She needed some extra encouragement to take it.

"That was quite naughty of you not to tell her about the case review those years ago, and not to have told me at the time. Now, who do you imagine let me in on that piece of information? Think hard, Mike!" The voice spat out his name, full of vitriol and hatred, thinly veiled.

"You know what I'm talking about? The sighting of the man fitting Ramsey's description in Donard Park, a short distance from our holiday home. Not just a report from some well-intentioned member of the public, but from a registered informant!

"And you failed to investigate! Your sloppiness, your total fucking ineptitude, cost my daughter her life and destroyed my wife too! You cost me everything, you fucking bastard! Have you any idea what it is like to lose the dearest things to you, Mike?" Oran's voice had become hysterical, he was screaming. He stopped momentarily and just as Thornton drew breath, Oran began again with a calmness that was even more chilling than the outburst.

"Are you aware, Mike, as I was cradling my dying daughter, you were in the labour ward awaiting Rachel's birth? Well, of course you are. It made the headlines of one of those tacky Sunday papers.

"You listening joyfully as your daughter took her first breaths, me distraught beyond belief, as my Holly took her last. She died in my arms. The symmetry is striking, don't you think? Very fucking ironic. But by tomorrow morning, we will have even more in common, Mike. Then we will see how well you cope.

"Jayne told me about Rachel's asthma. That must have been hard to watch at times, to watch your daughter struggle for breath. I had to tell Jayne that in the morning, asthma would be the least of her daughter's worries. That particular thought did not rest easily with her. I'll give her credit, she struggled, she tried to fight. Just as well the sedation finally took more of an effect. I wouldn't have wanted to kill her. Not when your punishment is just beginning.

"Don't worry about little Barbara. She's fast asleep. Bella, your lovely retriever has been equally fortunate. Curled up in a ball by the hearth, all too happy to gulp down a sedated piece of meat.

"I really must go now. If you're half the detective you're supposed to be, a patrol car will be on its way to your cottage already, I imagine. I should advise them to hurry. I'm long gone but young Ailish MacParland might be struggling to catch her breath by now.

"Let us see how good a detective you are when it's your daughter's life at stake. How many leads you will discount now it means so much more to you? It's only fair Mike. You know what they say, an eye for eye.

"No more stunts or stooges, Mr Thornton. I have what I want."

As the dial tone sounded, Thornton was speechless, reeling in shock. The cold-hearted message had left him numb. His phone trembled again. His eyes settled on the incoming message. It was sent from Ailish MacParland's iPhone. He opened the chilling pictures. The little girl's blonde hair lay like sheaves of corn beside her. The crimson party dress was just visible inside the metal cylinder. A video recording replaced the photographs, the time stamp visible in the corner. Ailish was not moving as Oran removed the syringe and fastened the lid. The shots turned to a ten-figure grid reference. Thornton shouted it out and then repeated it, 48207 91296. The GPS found the location in seconds, though the familiarity of the setting had already hit Thornton. It was her room.

"It's the Tully Road outside Glenarm, sir."

"The bastard has left her in Rachel's bedroom! She's been in there for almost an hour already! She may already be coming round from the sedative; either way, she's running out of air, we need to get her out! Tara, arrange an ambulance immediately and phone Mr Barnett. I need to be with Jayne."

Chapter 69

At Tully Road, Glenarm, a Mobile Support Unit burst through the front door of number twenty-three. Sergeant Ian Walker ran to the back bedroom. The metal cylinder lay fastened beside the bed. On the bed beside him lay the discarded syringe drive. He called out to the young girl, but there was no reaction. He feared the worst. "In here!"

He fumbled with the stiff catches, sweaty palms hindering his efforts to release her. As assistance arrived, having cleared the rest of the house, he forced open the canister. Inside Ailish MacParland was unconscious, He wanted to ease her out of the grim container but there was no time for delicacy, he dragged her out. He checked her airway; she was breathing, just. Relieved, he fell back allowing the ambulance crew to take care of her.

In the main bedroom Jayne Thornton lay bound by the same type of tethers. She was recovering quickly from her sedation and coming to.

He lifted his mike. "Control from Oscar Lima 15. Contact the investigation team – both the girl and Mrs Thornton are safe. The ambulance has taken over and will be taking them both to Belfast City Hospital. Tell the SIO we got here just in time; this guy was cutting it fine. One of my call signs has just discovered a light blue Volkswagen camper van at the back of the cottage. We are retaining the scene until morning. A search team has been arranged to start at first light."

Chapter 70

Thornton's mind was a clamour of emotion as he swerved into the car park at the hospital an hour later. A police car pulled up beside him. Ciaran and Mary MacParland were two steps behind as he rushed through the door into A & E.

Jayne sat devastated on a bed. The short release from reality that the sedation had afforded was gone. He took her trembling form into his arms.

"Mike, what have I done? What have I done? He was here yesterday, he had a puncture, he was talking to her, to Rachel. He came back later, I let him in, I didn't know, how could I know? Mike, he was on me before I could do anything. He had a knife, he said if I dared to move he would kill both girls. He tied me up Mike. I told him about us, about her asthma, even my miscarriages, the stillbirth. I thought he would show some compassion. He didn't, he was so angry.

He blames you for his daughter's murder and wife's suicide. I thought he was going to kill me Mike. He drugged me. Just before I passed out he carried Rachel into the bedroom. She wasn't moving. For all I know she could have been dead. He told me to say goodbye to her."

Thornton tried to comfort his inconsolable wife as she choked out her story.

"Mike, I'm so scared."

"I know, I know, sweetheart." Thornton looked into her eyes. "Look at me, Jayne! I am going to get back to you. I have to go, but trust me, she's coming home."

Chapter 71

Yellow Water Picnic Park straddles the Kilbroney River just out of Rostrevor beside the Newtown Road. It is a popular area for campers and hillwalkers who avoid the more familiar routes into the mountains. It is also less fashionable with police patrols.

It was 3:20 a.m. when the black Range Rover turned off the Newtown Road. The journey from Glenarm had passed uneventfully. Oran imagined the flurry of activity at Tully Road, police patrol cars frantically setting up checkpoints within a thirty-mile radius of Glenarm. Pointless ventures, as he was already well out of range.

Jayne Thornton and Ailish MacParland would be in an A & E department, one of the Belfast hospitals he imagined. Each would be recovering from their ordeal. Ailish would need a little more time. A drip would relieve her dehydration. But she would be safe again in her parents' arms, another thankful family counting their blessings. His precise timing of the last message to Thornton would have ensured her safe recovery, just about.

Mike Thornton would be racing back down the road to Newcastle. Beating himself up no doubt for his failure to spot the clues. He would be removed from the investigation; it would be too much of a conflict of interest. However, he would not be far from it, he would be focused and should not be underestimated. This time *his* daughter's life was at stake.

James McCluskey would be heading for Antrim Custody Suite, trussed up like a turkey about to be plucked. He would be interviewed immediately upon arrival. A superintendent would authorise the interrogation without the presence of a solicitor. The circumstances allowed for that. But McCluskey would say nothing. Not just because it was his inclination. He knew nothing save what he had been told. Jimmy knew the score. It was not for him to prove his innocence.

The neatly thatched roof was the first thing to catch the stranger's eye, the freshly coated walls, the next. The house wore a mask of decency, hiding the truth of its dreadful past, like a jumped-up Ulster politician with a skeleton in the cupboard, putting on the daily facade.

The lodge had been transformed by new owners. Confident they could turn a pound or two and have a little nest egg for retirement. It appeared to be renting well. Obviously by holidaymakers unaware of its brutal past and the back bedroom's dreadful secret. His beloved daughter had clung to life there, her tiny body beaten and abused, waiting for the rescue that had arrived just out of time.

He had booked this week many months ago. Quaint country cottages were a real hit with foreign tourists.

He carried Rachel Thornton through the door and along the stone hallway into the same back bedroom, where his own dear daughter had lain. He set her gently on the bed and checked the syringe drive, still enough for at least twelve hours, he noted.

Her gentle rhythmic wheeze disturbed the silence.

He needed sleep. The day ahead would be long and traumatic. He lay on top of the bed and thought of Gemma. Holly's loss had been devastating and her strength withered with every day that passed. Then there was the prying press, impervious to any human inclination for respect or remorse. Poking their noses into private matters. Only concerned about getting the best story. Setting the context with a stolen snap as they entered court for Ramsey's first hearing. Attaching it to a catchy headline.

As the "Not Guilty" plea rang in his ears, he had tried to get Gemma to the car quickly, but the swarm surrounded them, lenses clicking, lights flashing, questions hurled, no consideration for either of them.

Then there was the endless wait for the trial. The terrible thought of reliving her ordeal for the entire world to witness had plagued Gemma. Eighteen months of hell had passed. She needed closure. She dressed in black for the trial that she had imagined would finally bring it.

But she got none. Ramsey saw to that.

The Dacron fishing line hidden in the waistband of his underwear provided the perfect ligature. The Anchor Hitch made the perfect knot. There had been no suicide watch. Once again Ramsey's cunning duplicity had worked to his advantage. The warders found him on the morning of his trial, partially suspended from the bedstead. His eyes bulged and saliva caked his chin. The Orans' only possible consolation, that it must have been a slow and painful end.

Gemma never recovered. The bouts of depression grew more unremitting. The tearful nights broke his heart. Then there was the day he found her, exactly two years after Holly's death. He had nipped out to the shop as she had asked. Her request for wine with dinner, a hopeful sign he had thought, a flicker of light in a very dark place.

But why had she said goodbye and told him she would always love him? Why hadn't he noticed how strange that was as he closed the front door behind him?

The silence was palpable when he returned. The living room was empty, as was the kitchen and every other downstairs chamber. As he turned to go upstairs the empty frame upon the mantelpiece caught his eye, and he felt a sense of dread. He mounted the stairs, each step harder than the last, the strains of 'Gabriel's Oboe' became louder. He no longer felt the joy it had given them on their wedding day. He crossed the landing to meet the music. Hesitantly, as the music soared to its haunting crescendo, he pushed open the bathroom door.

He had found her bleeding in the bath. The deep gashes to each wrist had already done their work. Beneath her lifeless stare, Holly and Gemma smiled up at him, their photograph floating in the water.

Chapter 72

The sun was rising as Thornton swung into Newcastle station again. He rested his head against the steering wheel momentarily. He needed to stay calm and collect his thoughts, to out-think Oran before it was too late. He knew that he could no longer head up the case. Too much of a conflict of interest, Mr Barnett would now be in charge. He knew everything would now be done by the book. He also knew that this approach might not be enough.

He reckoned they had less than a day to find her. It was now 6:20 a.m., Holly Oran had died at 4:20 a.m. on the fifteenth.

The team were exhausted, John Allen and Tara Ritchie were just coming around as he entered the station, others still lay sleeping, wherever they had found to put down their heads.

Detective Sergeant Hazell Kennedy appeared at the door. The sight of Thornton made her stop in her tracks. She could not imagine how he must be feeling. She wanted to turn away.

"That was great work today, Hazell," Thornton said gripping her shoulder, partly in recognition but mainly to break the ice. "Come and sit over here and give me an update. Try not to feel awkward, please. This is not easy for any of us."

The Smyths were safe. An officer would remain with them until Ingrid's husband returned. Now she and her crew were on standby. Her team was taking a well-earned rest.

Then she updated him on McCluskey.

"The team moved in shortly after you directed, sir. He did not resist. It almost seemed as if he had been expecting us. He said nothing after caution, just smiled and refused to account for his presence at the place of his arrest. No explanation for the dark clothing and ski mask. He was placed in an evidential body suit and brought to Antrim Serious Crime Suite for interview later today.

The house was unoccupied. There was no trace of use. The camper van is under cover. A number of forensic teams have been arranged for tomorrow. The guys are preserving the site where we believe McCluskey discarded the SIM. Mobile Support Units will relieve our team at seven a.m. and start the search immediately."

Chapter 73

Thornton stretched and rubbed his eyes. He must have fallen asleep. The crick in his neck spoke of broken slumber on a rickety chair, beside the draughty window. In seconds he was alert again. The smell of coffee enticed him to the kitchen. The tense murmuring of the team quelled as he entered. Tara Ritchie and John Allen were pouring a second cup. Eileen Parks was half-heartedly chewing a bacon sandwich. Hazell Kennedy was sat with the other members of her team.

What was anyone meant to say? What could they say?

Thornton took the lead.

"Guys, I know you all feel uncomfortable, but that is not what I need from you right now. We will find my daughter. We will find her and we will put this bastard away. But we can't do that if you are tiptoeing around me. Say what you have to. Mr Barnett is taking over. He is making his way down. There will be a briefing at eight thirty a.m. and a press conference at ten a.m." He sat down with a sigh, running a hand through his rumpled hair, and gratefully accepted the cup of coffee and sandwich pushed in front of him by Tara.

Chapter 74

ACC Barnett arrived at 8.10 a.m. A few more technicians, his own media consultants and two senior detectives accompanied him. It appeared that Grainne Burrows and Alan Mooney were to be sidelined for the forthcoming press conference. Tara Ritchie might find herself in the same situation. Nonetheless they would be invaluable for advising on Barnett's appeal and to act as sounding boards.

Thornton stood up as his boss entered the office.

"You must be distraught Mike. I am so sorry. How's Jayne?"

"She's recovering, thank you. She is staying with her sister until I get back with Rachel."

"Do you not think it would be better if…?" Barnett trailed off, silenced by the look on Thornton's face.

"Do you mean if I was not here, sir? If I was at home with a distraught wife instead, waiting for news? I appreciate your concern. But I am staying. I won't interfere. But I want to make my own appeal at the press conference."

"I'm really not sure about that, Mike."

"Can you please tell me what the difference is? As far as anyone is concerned I am now a parent just like the Reillys and the MacParlands. I want to keep the conference within the confines of this enquiry, but I am perfectly willing to organise my own release."

Barnett realised the importance of showing a united front and uneasily met Thornton's eyes. He nodded.

"Okay, Mike, I agree. I will work with my own advisors on the bulk of the release. By the way I brought the main enquiry to Belfast. It will bring everything more neatly together."

Thornton nodded in agreement. He was just about to leave the room when he turned to Barnett.

"One more request, sir. I'd like Detective Inspector Ritchie with me after the briefing. It appears you have brought your own team."

"That sounds like a good idea, Mike, as long as Tara is happy to do so."

"Of course, sir," Tara quickly accepted the offer.

Chapter 75

Barnett stood nervously at the lectern. In truth he had never headed up an enquiry such as this one; never had so much been at stake. He took a sip of water, surveyed the seated audience of colleagues, aware also of those viewing on video link in other locations. The Chief would be looking on with interest.

"Ladies and gentlemen, let us not waste time. Our intention is to recover Rachel Thornton alive and arrest James Oran. I will now ask Detective Inspector Tara Ritchie to brief us."

"Thank you, sir. Ailish MacParland and Jayne Thornton are recovering in hospital. Both are unavailable for interview at this stage.

"William James McCluskey was arrested at 1:53 a.m. this morning. He was interviewed shortly after his arrival at Antrim Serious Crime Custody Suite.

"He has refused to disclose anything about his relationship with Oran or the whereabouts of his accomplice. He denies any knowledge of a plan to kidnap any of the young girls. That was as far as the interviewers were permitted to go without the presence of a solicitor. He is due for a second interview at nine thirty a.m.

"The search is ongoing at his home. A laptop and computer have been seized.

"After McCluskey's arrest, an O2 SIM card was recovered at the place where we saw him throw an item from the camper. Our technical team are currently working on the SIM card. At present we cannot connect it to a phone used by McCluskey. We did not find one in his possession. The vehicle is still to be thoroughly searched.

"A search advisor is planning a sweep of the area along the route that McCluskey took. This will take some time sir. They know to get in touch whenever they find something."

"I am afraid that is all we have for the moment."

"Thank you, Tara. Well, ladies and gentlemen, by DCS Thornton's estimation we have a narrow window in which to recover Rachel. It is fair to say that we have little to go on at the moment. No make or model of vehicle and no direction of travel. Special Branch colleagues are pulling in favours the length and breadth of the province. We have armed response units on stand-by in Belfast and Portadown. A helicopter and Scout 1 are at our disposal.

"Until we come up with something, we need to ensure the other elements of the investigation are tied off, all witness statements taken and logged, the exhibits transferred to Belfast and listed before going to the lab. Ensure the search logs have been properly signed off and exhibited. We don't want any embarrassing encounters with the chief prosecutor. Thank you everyone. You all have your individual assignments. That is all for now."

The group rose as ACC Barnett left the room with his henchmen.

Chapter 76

James Oran sat comfortably in front of the television. He savoured his favourite Columbian dark roast.

The first ten minutes of the release were taken up by ACC Barnett. Quite bland, and with very little to say, Oran thought. He had clearly been on all the media courses. He tiptoed through the minefield of questions from international television and newspaper reporters.

When he finished, a plainspoken reporter from Fermanagh summed up daringly; "ACC Barnett, would it be fair to say you cannot take credit for very much? The kidnapper gave up the two girls who were recovered and you have not the first clue where he or Rachel Thornton are. Is it fair to say you are no further on than when he took the first little girl?"

Barnett's brightening cheeks provided all the answer the audience needed.

Oran watched with keener interest as Thornton made his way to the lectern. He had expected him to be a little more stooped. The weight of emotion must be enormous. A photograph of Rachel Thornton appeared on the screen. Thornton was about to bare his soul. Oran had waited a long time for this moment.

Thornton pointed to the screen beside him. "This is my daughter, Rachel. She should have been preparing to celebrate her seventh birthday with friends and family. Instead, last night Rachel was taken from our home. Her mother was threatened and is in hospital.

"Rachel is our only child. James Oran took her. He told me it was retaliation for my failure to save his daughter, who was a victim of Peter James Ramsey seven years ago. If you are watching, James, I did the best I could. Not a day goes by when I do not think of your daughter and the others we were unable to save.

"You are in complete control now. I want you to consider the grief you have suffered. Is that really what you want for me, for anyone else? I want you to consider my little girl. Do you want her to die, scared out of her wits and alone? Would you wish that upon any child? I wish you had not been denied the joy Megan Reilly's and Ailish MacParland's parents feel right now. Please give Rachel back to us, James."

Thornton sat down in front of an audience silenced by his candour.

Oran, however, remained unmoved. The depth of his grief and the need for revenge had long overshadowed all other emotion; they were all that was left of him.

Chapter 77

It was eleven thirty a.m. when Eileen Parks joined Thornton, the two press officers and DI Ritchie in a conference room at the Enniskeen hotel. Thornton had set up a Skype connection with Tony Rogers, his cherished HOLMES receiver in Belfast. He had a mind for the fine details of both enquiries.

The view of the mountains served as an easy distraction to those with less to contemplate, but this was a time to be busy, a time to push their collective grey matter to the limit.

"Glad you could join us, Tony. I hope you can hear me?"

"Well and truly, Mr Thornton."

"I want to draw together the strands of this case. Sitting around waiting for a lead is not going to get my daughter back. I want to go back to Mr Barnett with a credible plan.

"We need to review what has happened, the similarities between the two men's crimes, and those actions individual to Oran. So bear with me for a moment.

"Let us first assume that Oran has replicated much of Ramsey's plan, albeit he never intended to kill or abuse the first two girls.

"Let us look first at the features over which Oran had more control. With the targeting of the girls, he clearly used a similar method to Ramsey, with the exception that Oran had already identified my daughter as his final victim.

"The means of the abduction: Oran followed Ramsey's lead, raising the level of violence on each occasion. The mode of transport was the same except for Oran's inclusion of a hidden compartment.

"Let us look now at the things over which he had less control. He could not rely on finding a suitable girl who would spend the holidays in precisely the same locations as Ramsey's victims. This had to be more random. Hence Megan Reilly was taken from Portsalon, fifteen miles or so from where Ramsey took Emma Baillie. Ailish MacParland was abducted less than a quarter of a mile from where Hannah Graham was taken. However, to my mind this is coincidental.

"Now let us consider where the children were found. Megan Reilly was found only half a mile from where Emma Baillie's body was recovered. The cottage in which Emma was left is now derelict, making it unfit for Oran's purpose. Has he chosen the nearest available cottage?" Thornton paused, pointing at his audience.

"It was never Oran's intention to leave Ailish near Planting Road where Hannah Graham was found. He chose to leave her at my holiday home, a place personal to me.

"But it may be significant that he used a let on Moneyscalp Road to house McCluskey. After all, the two roads are practically beside each other. This is another significant location for Oran, it was close and it provided a necessary decoy.

"Finally, there are the 'stunts and stooges' as Oran described them to me: the faking of his death, so well planned and executed, and the siphoning of money from his account. The gambling was the perfect scam. Rachel Smyth, again was the ideal foil, the right age and look and holiday destination. The systematic sightings of a man outside her school and house were clearly designed to direct our attention towards her.

"This leaves the children taken: Holly Oran, seven years ago, and my daughter, this morning. Get me the location, Tony, where Holly was left."

"I know it was somewhere near Rostrevor."

Everything clicked into place for Thornton. How fitting would that be to complete his revenge? Help arriving just out of time to save his little girl – the same cottage, the same bedroom, the same fate as Holly.

He turned to Dr Parks. "I share your earlier instinct, Eileen; revenge is more important than escape. He will choose the final location for its symbolism, its symmetry. He is not concerned about being caught; it may even be his intention. He clearly wants to take my daughter's life. What better place than where his daughter lost her own?"

Silence was accompanied by nodding heads. They agreed.

"Tony, do you have it? Where Holly Oran was discovered?"

"I have it 18 Newtown Road. Just beside the Kilbroney River. I pass it frequently heading up the Mournes. Yellow Water Picnic Park is close by. There should be good access through Rostrevor Forest Park along the network of tracks to the rear of the house. A couple of hikers would not seem out of place heading for Eagle Mountain from the picnic park. It's a common route this time of the year.

Thunder's Hill and Lackan More are peaks on the other side of the cottage. I have walked them on a number of occasions. There should be a clear view of the front of the property from either slope, but you would need good lenses. Getting any closer during daylight would be tricky.

"We took a lot of photographs of the house after Holly Oran was found. I'll email them to you. They'll be with you in thirty minutes. They should prove helpful to John Allen and his guys, if you decide to send in a recovery team."

Chapter 78

Thornton lifted his phone and dialled.

"Hi, sweetheart, how are you feeling?"

"Just waiting for my sister to take me back to her house. I had a chat with the MacParlands. Ailish is going home tomorrow. They were devastated to hear it is our Rachel that's missing. Any news yet, Mike? I am almost at my wit's end." Her voice broke as she struggled to maintain composure.

From the other end of the phone Thornton could tell his wife was on the brink of a breakdown. Even her choice of words tried to distance her from the reality. It played better in her mind to think Rachel had gone missing. He didn't want to disturb this illusion; it might have been the only thing holding her together.

"We are following a very strong line of enquiry. I believe we are close to finding her."

"Oh, Mike, please tell me I will see her again," she sobbed.

Then her tone became more frantic.

"Mike, I've just remembered. Just before I passed out I saw him lift her inhaler but not the medication. What if she has a seizure Mike? You remember the last one. We thought she was gone. Mike, this is terrible."

Thornton did his best to console and reassure her, but felt uneasy as he realised that the threat to Rachel increased with every passing hour. They might not have as many hours as he had anticipated. He could only hope Rachel was still sedated.

Though, Ramsey had not afforded Holly the same kindness seven years ago. From the minute of her abduction, she had been terrified, right up until her final breath. He tried not to think about his precious daughter suffering the same fate. As he hung up the last he heard was Jayne's sobbing as her sister took the phone. He would do all he could not to let her down.

Chapter 79

It was twelve thirty p.m. when Thornton walked into Barnett's office. A familiar figure was there to greet him. Eamon Lynch gave a warm embrace that said more than any words could.

"Just here to see what I can do to help, Mike. ACC Barnett got in touch."

Thornton was almost overwhelmed. He looked at the big Donegal man. The tearful eyes told him that he was sharing some of his pain.

"It is good to see you, Eamon."

The three of them sat down.

"Any word from Special Branch yet, sir?"

"Not as yet, Mike. They are still working on it," Barnett replied.

"What about McCluskey? How are the interviews going?"

"Just as you predicted I'm afraid. He is telling them very little. He says they have nothing more than a series of coincidences. There were no fingerprints on the SIM card. It has been examined. Two calls were received in the space of fourteen hours, one just before Ailish MacParland was taken, the second just before he visited the Smyth's house. They were each from the same pay-as-you-go number. We are unable to trace it.

He is denying any knowledge of James Oran, save what he recalls from the original investigation. At the moment we are at a dead end, Mike."

Tara, Irene and John Allen were invited to join them.

This was the perfect platform for Thornton to make his proposal. He led Barnett through the course of his theory. His reasoning was compelling. He knew that his boss was looking for an angle, an opportunity to shine; to show the Chief that he was not just a smart guy with a first in law.

Barnett listened with interest, then asked for some opinions.

"What do you think, Ritchie?"

"I am with Mr Thornton on this one, sir. We have little else to go on and it makes sense."

"Thank you, Tara. How about you, Dr Parks?"

"I have to agree with Mike and Tara. Oran has been meticulous in his planning. He has been taunting us all the way, leaving unnecessary clues. Almost defying us to outwit him. If he doesn't give us a chance, if he goes somewhere completely unrelated to the old case, his game doesn't work."

Barnett mulled over what he had heard. The room was silent for a moment.

"We will go with it, Mike. I'll phone the Chief and tell him our decision. Tara, you are back at the helm. My men will shadow you. Tell them I said it is not a question of rank but experience. We will brief at two thirty p.m. Please have everyone present. Place our armed response teams on full alert. I want to review all risk assessments with DCS Thornton before the briefing."

He turned to John Allen.

"It looks like your teams may be in use sooner than you thought, John. Get in touch with reconnaissance at Aldergrove. We need a map of the area urgently."

"Will do, sir."

"Tara, have someone call with the landlords, Terry and Laura Fearon. We need to know as much as possible about the cottage's security. We also need to know if they use Facebook or other social media, which Oran may have access to.

"I will contact the regional Assistant Chief Constable and Superintendent Brennan in Newry. I want the area placed out of bounds until the operation is over. No emergency calls to be attended without my permission.

Oh, and Tara, telephone headquarters. I want DCI Jenny Mullan as our negotiator. She is the best I know."

Thornton was seeing a different side to his boss. He had no need to include him in the enquiry. More than this he was doing all the right things and his team was responding. He saw a man who may not choose to go out on a limb but would take calculated risks. He liked that.

Chapter 80

James Oran checked on Rachel Thornton. Her wheeze was a little more pronounced now, but she was still peaceful.

He recalled the moment when Holly died in his arms. Twenty-two minutes past four in the morning of 15 July. By his reckoning his revenge would be complete in just over fourteen hours. He inspected the syringe drive. The little girl would be coming round at midnight. He wanted her to experience the same fear that Holly had. It was only fair, he had been powerless to comfort his daughter, and now Thornton would be denied that same opportunity.

Underneath the loathing and the grief, Oran wondered why he felt no stirring of pity for the child; it wasn't her fault after all, but he had spared the little girl's terror for most of the ordeal, unlike Ramsey, he would gain no pleasure from her pain.

He examined the second aluminium cylinder. The locking devices needed a little oil, on this one; the hint of a squeak irritated him. A drop or two of WD40 did the trick. He unpacked the party dress and laid it beside her. A pair of red satin shoes and a matching hair band would complete the ensemble. More than the other girls had worn, but fitting for the occasion he thought.

He toyed with the idea of shaving her head. But that was for later. She would be dressed for dinner and photographed in all her glory, hair perfectly groomed, her unconscious body propped up by secreted cushions; everything almost appeared normal, except for her closed eyes and the absence of her winning smile.

Chapter 81

Barnett and Thornton debriefed the individual officers on their risk assessments. It was John Allen and Hazell Kennedy who were given the most searching scrutiny. Each risk carefully considered, every action and reaction, forensically examined. They came through with distinction.

At two thirty p.m. on the dot, Barnett stood to address the team.

"Ladies and gentlemen, thank you for being so prompt. I am going to invite each of the officers in charge to provide their part of the briefing. The code name is Operation Eagle."

John Allen was first.

"Thank you, sir. The map you are looking at shows the area surrounding eighteen Newtown Road. You can see the forest line runs along the boundary to the rear of the property. It will provide excellent cover to insert a team. I have one on stand-by just waiting for the order, sir. There are a number of bushes running along either side of the driveway. They will give a degree of shelter if we decide to put a team in after dark.

"The turn in the approach to the cottage would conceal any advance towards the front door. The rear garden is grassed. This would allow for a stealthy approach to the back and into natural cover below the window line of the cottage. You can just about make out the panel fence around the periphery, about a metre high.

"I am now pointing at the detached garage to the right of the cottage. It has room for two vehicles. It would provide good cover for a team. We intend to insert one after dark. It is my intention to use a number of listening devices and insert a mini camera through the front letterbox to give a view of the hallway."

John Allen revealed the latest technology. Experienced officers marvelled at the tiny lens, marginally bigger than a match head.

"I spoke with the landlord and his wife. The house has just had new doors and locks fitted. It was burgled three months ago. The front and rear doors are mahogany. Each is fitted with a five-lever mortice lock and a latch. Neither of them will be easy to breach. All the windows have Yale locks. It is a bit of a fortress, sir.

"The couple checked their social networks. There are no photographs of them. The web site is clear of them as well."

"Tell me, John, did Oran collect the key from their home address or at the cottage?"

"At the cottage, sir. It is kept in a key-guard on the wall beside the front door. The passcode is changed after each stay.

"They have a telephone number for him; it's 07985 669748.

"The photographs of the interior taken during the last investigation are most helpful. They were shown to the landlord. He assures me there have been no internal modifications. My recovery teams are getting familiar with them in case we need them to go in. My sergeants are working on their plans as I speak. They will brief us shortly, sir.

"There would not appear to be any suitable locations to deploy marksmen. Any high ground with a good line of sight is too far away, but I want to put a team with a scope on Lackan

More. They should be able to monitor the front and both sides of the house. I can have them in position in forty-five minutes sir. I intend placing a second team to the rear. Both are awaiting your order.

"Unless there are any questions, that is me, sir."

"Thank you John. I see no point in wasting time. Please deploy your recce teams as suggested. Mr Thornton and I will want to review the recovery plans with you before those teams are deployed."

The remainder of the briefing was taken up with plans for medical aid and arrest. The Crime Scene Investigators and forensic scientists agreed what constituted each other's responsibilities.

The Mobile Support Inspector outlined his plan for cordons, search and as an escort in the event of an arrest.

The exhibits' officer reminded the party how things should be properly bagged and labelled. Tara Ritchie insisted that notebooks were written up immediately after the operation and incident logs were signed off.

To many it was old hat, but Barnett was leaving nothing to chance.

Chapter 82

The two police officers were like any other enthusiastic hikers. There were a number of other cars in the park just off the Kilbroney Road. They made good time crossing fields and dry marshland. The ascent to the summit of Lackan More was moderately steep. It took thirty-five minutes. Finding the best location provided a stiffer challenge.

A craggy granite outcrop provided good cover to the rear and sides. It was enhanced by a bird watcher's canopy, a common sight at this time of the year; twitchers seeking out ring ouzel, meadow pipits and red grouse fledglings, to post on Twitter and Facebook. In seconds they would be viewed around the world. The team settled in, in anticipation of a long night.

"Eagle Control from Eagle Alpha 1, in position. Making the connection now."

"Roger, Eagle Alpha 1."

The powerful Kowa Highlander Prominar binoculars rested on the tripod. The addition of 50x eyepieces gave an impressive range. Detective Constable Jim Baillie attached them to the iPad and made the connection. For the next six hours the infrared connection would be redundant.

He scanned the landscape, taking time to get used to the sensitivity of the powerful field glasses. He caught a glimpse of a seagull in flight. The view changed quickly from sky, to forest, to farmland. He scanned locations to either side of the cottage. At the farm next door, a woman stepped from a BMW X5 and collected some groceries from the back seat. The carrier bag bore the TESCO branding. He was impressed by the scope and clarity. Then he settled on the target.

A curious audience gathered around the screen in the control room. The garden was different to how Thornton remembered it. The foliage added to its charm. The cottage had been freshened up, the white walls newly painted, the thatched roof replaced. The wood panelled fence around the border was an added feature. The curtains were drawn and there was no sign of activity.

The binoculars fixed on a black Range Rover parked to the right of the cottage beside the garage. The magnification brought the registration plate into view. Blurred at first and then it sharpened 157LH2007.

Eamon Lynch could not contain himself.

"It is a county Louth vehicle. It may well be a personalised plate. I'll have it checked."

He left the room for a couple of minutes. On his return he bore a contented smile.

"The vehicle is registered to Sean Major, 21 Mariners View, Blackrock. It is on the coast about six miles from Dundalk. I have heard of him. He is an up-and-coming Irish artist. Came onto the scene two or three years ago. He paints land and seascapes, around Carlingford Lough and the Cooley Mountains. They are not my taste. A bit too dark and brooding for my liking, but I'll check to see if he has exhibited recently, they may have a photograph of the artist."

His words made an image come flooding back to Tara Ritchie – the painting of Slieve Donard on a cloudy day above the mantelpiece in Oran's in-laws' house. Dark and brooding was a good description.

She scribbled the name on the wipe board and played about with the letters for a minute, recognising another potential anagram. Sean Major the artist was James Oran the abductor.

She shrieked with excitement, signalling the two names, "We have him, sir."

Thornton fought with his emotions. There was a moment of elation in the briefing room before the reality of the situation settled in again. Oran was still in control. The danger to his daughter's life was still the same. Oran, whether unmasked or not, was still intent on killing her.

Eamon Lynch was busy on his phone, alerting Superintendent O'Hagan in Dundalk. A Garda team would call at Major's house and with his neighbours. They needed to be sure they were dealing with the right person and car. They could not take the risk of it being another ringer vehicle.

The registration mark stared at them like a child with a burning secret to share. 15 7 2007, the date on which Holly Oran died.

Chapter 83

The second team parked at Yellow Water Picnic Site. To an innocent onlooker, they were like any other happy couple as they crossed the stile and strode amidst a patch of bell heather to the pathway. The GPS was tucked neatly inside the young man's rucksack. The binoculars swung innocently from a lanyard around Constable Jill Adam's neck.

The couple turned right along the route to Eagle Mountain. The lane ran out as they headed off the path into tightly packed rows of Sitka spruce and Douglas fir. The GPS guided them to the precise location. They stole stealthily to the edge of the forest cover, within touching distance of the wooden fence.

"Eagle Control from Alpha 2. In position, with eyes on. The curtains are closed. There is reasonable cover to the southern boundary of the property. The garage is about five metres from the fence and is at an oblique angle to the house. Will report any activity."

"Roger, Alpha 2."

Chapter 84

Barnett addressed the gathering.

"Everything is in place, but we haven't got the first clue if anyone is inside. It could be another lure. We need to find out if Oran is there."

He turned to John Allen.

"We need to know what is going on in there. John, what can you do for us?"

"Sir, at the moment, there is little we can do technically. We need the cover of darkness. We know he has not met either landlord. Terry Fearon is on business in Glasgow. That leaves Laura."

Barnett interrupted. "I have been thinking; she could make a call. Tell him she needs to leave something, extra towels or bed linen, for example."

Barnett looked to Thornton.

"What do you think, Mike?"

"That might work, sir. They have the phone number. He can be contacted, told that she is coming down. She could say she is heading off overnight. The fresh towels and bed linen sound plausible. At least we may find out if he is there. But that is no guarantee that Rachel is with him."

"Thanks, Mike. I take it we have someone with the landlords?"

"We have, sir; DC Colly Sloan," Tara cut in.

"Tara, I take it you have never dealt with Oran? You were not part of any of the appeals. You haven't had your face in the press at any time and no television appearances?"

"No, sir."

"I want you to go to the landlord's house. You make the call. Ask if it is convenient to visit. Do not push too hard. Use the Fearons' car. We have no idea if he has been to their house or not. He has covered most other bases."

"I can tell him that we don't like to arrive unannounced when people are staying. That it is a matter of privacy. I will ask his permission in the event that he may have gone out. If Rachel is there he will want to be present. To pick them up at the door."

Barnett turned to Thornton.

"What do you think, Mike?"

"It sounds good to me, sir."

Barnett turned to John Allen. "Put all your teams on alert. Tara, I suspect you know what is coming next?"

"I do, sir. I am up for it."

Chapter 85

"Hello, Mrs Fearon, I'm DI Tara Ritchie. You are aware of an incident at your rental? I'm afraid I'm not in a position to tell you anything more about the operation, however there are things I need to verify with you. Have you ever spoken to Mr Major?"

"No, my husband manages all the bookings. I look after the cleaning and the garden. I am sure it was an online enquiry followed by a telephone call to arrange for key collection. The key is left in the secure lock beside the door.

"We rarely have any dealings with the tenants, Miss Ritchie, unless it is a longer term let and Mr Major only booked for a week starting yesterday. I believe his message stated that he was coming to the region to do some painting."

"Can you be certain that Mr Major has never seen you before? No photographs, no Facebook? This is essential Mrs Fearon."

"I really don't think so. Both Terry and I tend to shun any publicity. There are no photographs on our web page, none even on mantelpieces or tables which are visible from outside."

Tara Ritchie contacted the control room.

"ACC Barnett, I can confirm that Oran has never had any encounter with Mrs Fearon. I am happy to give it a go, sir."

Barnett turned to Thornton.

"It's your call, Mike."

Thornton considered the options. There was no guarantee that either Oran or Rachel were there. They needed to know. If they were not at the house the team would need to think again. But frankly he was out of ideas.

"Let's do it, sir."

"Tara, make the call," Barnett instructed.

Chapter 86

Oran had not been expecting to hear his ringtone but the number was familiar – the Fearons' home telephone number. He let it ring out.

"No reply, sir," Tara muttered, her heart starting to sink.

"Try it again, Tara," Barnett insisted.

Again Oran let it ring. He toyed with the idea of letting it go to message mode, but he could not take the risk of someone arriving unannounced.

"Hello, Sean Major speaking."

The reply almost stuck in Tara Ritchie's craw.

"Hello, Mr Major, I hope I am not disturbing you. It's Laura Fearon."

"Hi there, Mrs Fearon, I was just enjoying a cup of coffee. I didn't hear your first call over the kettle boiling. What can I do for you?"

"Mr Major, I am sorry to disturb you, but if it is convenient just now I would like to bring you some more towels? I don't think I will have left enough. Normally I refresh them tomorrow morning for tenants, but I am going away to my sister's house this evening and staying overnight, and Terry is away in Glasgow for a few days. I am sorry about that. I never like to call without arranging with the tenant first. I can be down in five minutes if that is all right?"

"Call when it suits you, Mrs Fearon. Would you mind leaving them at the front door? I had intended to have a lie down. I have a bit of a headache."

Ritchie had to think on her feet.

"If you don't mind, Mr Major, I would prefer to hand them over. We have problems with petty theft in the area, especially at this time of year. Young hikers come unprepared and take what they can get their hands on. We have been caught out in the past."

"Well, we don't want to encourage any petty pilfering. I will see you in five minutes."

The phone went silent and Tara Ritchie took a deep breath.

She radioed her boss.

"Sir, he's gone for it."

"Excellent work, Tara. Now here are the ground rules. I do not want any heroics. We cannot take the risk of you becoming a hostage. We simply need to find out he is there. We will deal with other matters later. Is that clear, Tara?"

"As crystal, sir."

Tara turned towards Laura Fearon.

"Just one more thing, Laura, may I borrow your wedding rings, please?"

Chapter 87

The route from Cherryhill in Rostrevor took Tara Ritchie past the Church of Ireland on the Kilbroney Road. Her heart was racing as she turned onto Newtown Road. Her mind was awash with 'what ifs' as she pulled into the driveway. The silver Ford Focus came to a standstill yards from the front door. Tara stepped out of the vehicle, collected the towels from the boot and made her way to the porch.

The monitor in the control room followed her every move. Thornton was relieved she was dressed appropriately for the hot afternoon in July.

As she reached the door it opened. The tiny microphone concealed under her pale blue cardigan sprung to life.

"Good afternoon, Mrs Fearon. Thank you so much for bringing the towels." Oran remarked taking the fluffy pile from Ritchie.

"That is a gorgeous sapphire ring, Mrs Fearon."

"Why thank you, Mr Major, it's my favourite gem."

Major smiled and replied, "And your birthstone perhaps?"

The remark left Tara doing her best to hide her discomfort. "Correct, Mr Major, a September birthday."

"I must say you look younger than I had anticipated."

"That is kind of you to say so, Mr Major. Looks can however be deceiving. I put it down to the fresh Kingdom of

Mourne air." Tara tried for a modest smile, unsure if Oran had made her. His eyes gave away nothing.

"Indeed they can be, Mrs Fearon," he said after a moment's pause.

"Now if you'll excuse me, I want to take a doze. I intend to head out later and grab an hour or two of painting before the sun goes down. I rarely use the beauty of the sunshine's glow. The clouds are due to sweep in within the hour. There is nothing quite like the spectacle of mountains in a heavily veiled sunset.

"Goodbye, Mrs Fearon, I hope to see you again."

From the slope on Lachan More, Constable Jim Burns had retracted the distance and sharpened the image.

Thornton gazed at the monitor as if he was watching a sequence from the past: the posture unmistakable, the shoulders broad and impressive, the hair a little longer with a fleck or two of grey. The face haggard from years of grief.

The last encounter had been a solemn one, just after Ramsey had committed suicide in prison.

"It's him, sir," Thornton gasped. "That is James Oran."

Chapter 88

Dusk was falling as the police officers gathered in the ops room. The streetlights flickered outside the station. In an hour it would be dark. The clouds had settled as Oran had predicted, but he never left the cottage; there would be no joyless landscape recreated in oils that night.

On Lachan More the infrared lenses had just been fitted. They scanned the front of the house. All was still. In the cover of the trees to the rear, the observers now numbered four. Two would scale the fence and move to the cover of the garage when the order came. The listening devices lay restlessly in their pockets. The drawn curtains would hide them from the inquisitive inhabitant.

Two hundred yards along Newtown Road a rapid response crew waited in cover in flame retardant suits. The method of entry had been thoroughly discussed. Mechanical access would be too slow; an explosive breach, too dangerous. Ballistic entry was best. A specially converted shotgun, with a 'stand-off' breacher attached, rested readily on an officer's knee. It would take out the door hinges in seconds, the Tesar frangible rounds disintegrating on impact. The door would be hurried along the hallway by a metal 'enforcer'. The noise, it was hoped, would provide a sufficient distraction to get to Oran and overpower him.

In the bedroom to the right of the hall the syringe drive pump hushed. Oran withdrew the needle from the little girl's right arm.

The crimson party frock slipped over Rachel's shoulders as he sat her up. He combed her corn gold hair and laid it back with the red satin band. He slipped on the delicate matching shoes and fastened the silver buckles. He placed Rachel in the armchair and sat down beside her. He replaced the needle and switched on the pump. He turned her head towards the camera and placed his arm around her shoulder. The sedation system was barely visible.

The communication came from the call sign in the trees.

"Eagle Control from Eagle Bravo 2. The curtains in the bedroom to the right at the back have just lit up twice, as if someone has taken photographs."

"Eagle Control to all call signs, hold your positions."

Thornton felt edgy as his iPhone trembled in his pocket. The screen told of an incoming message with an attachment. He knew the number but struggled to open it.

"What does it say, Mike? You have to open it," Barnett whispered placing a hand on his shoulder.

The message was short but savage.

"Here's one for the album, Mike. Enjoy."

The phone fell from Thornton's hands as he viewed the screen, his darling daughter sat unconscious, wrapped in the arms of a fiend.

His inclination was to bolt for the door, to make his way to the house and strangle the life out of the bastard. But that was sure to fail, and then he would never see her alive again.

Chapter 89

It took some minutes for the team to recover its composure.

"Well, at least we know she is in the cottage and still alive," Thornton said, trying to put the team at whatever relative ease could be mustered. He didn't want them to start shutting him out, to treat him as the irrational, emotional parent. He had to remain professional if he was to have any say in his daughter's fate.

"You're right Mike. Now let's get your daughter back and home to her mother." Barnett was on top of his game again.

"Mike, why are you sure we have a few more hours?"

"One can never be certain, sir. But Oran seems to be following a timetable linked to his daughter's death – the same house on the same day by the same means. We must assume that he will want to use the same time of death, twenty-two minutes past four, tomorrow morning. The anaesthetist said it would take her ten to twenty minutes to come round once the sedative is withdrawn. This is only relevant if he wakens her before placing her in the cylinder. We must presume that he will use it.

"I do believe he will waken her. Let her experience the horror which his own daughter was subjected to. Let our inability to rescue her play on our minds for the rest of our lives and place a barrier between Jayne and myself.

"The lab techs have calculated that a child could last no more than two hours inside the cylinder.

"This gives us a window of something similar in time. Say, from two a.m. tomorrow morning.

"He may choose to leave her alone to suffocate. That is what Ramsey did. In this case, it would be the best scenario. We could let him leave the house and arrest him when he is at a safe distance from Rachel. We cannot take the risk of entry before he has disconnected the sedation or he could overdose her. And, let us not forget he has a knife, so she will be safer within the canister, if he chooses not to leave. If he is still inside at two forty-five a.m., we go in."

The team marvelled at his clarity of thought at such a time. He left the room and telephoned Jayne.

Her voice seemed so fragile.

"Please tell me you have found her, Mike. Please tell me she is still alive."

"We know where she is. We are going to get her back alive. We have a good plan but it will take a little more time. The next time I call, she will be safe and in my arms."

Chapter 90

The briefing room was quiet. The atmosphere was tense. Barnett approached the lectern. It was one a.m.

The plan was based on Thornton's assertions. Every detail was picked over. Every officer tested on their function. Paramedics were on standby. John Allen would lead the recovery team. The Chief looked on from headquarters. He lifted the phone and wished Barnett good luck.

At Newtown Road, darkened figures moved into position. Two officers slipped from the cover of the forest to the shelter of the garage. Along the driveway the leafy foliage played host to four other constables. On Lachan More Jim Burns took charge of the binoculars again and scanned the cottage. There was no sign of life as time moved on.

A listening device was settled on the window of the bedroom where the curtains had lit up some time before. At first there was little activity, the room was in darkness. The sombre strains of an oboe mingled with a dull buzzing sound.

"'Gabriel's Oboe'," Thornton whispered. He tried to shut out both the music and the low monotonous hum. Instead he searched for whimpers or cries. There were none. She was either dead or still asleep. But he believed it was the latter. The time to waken her had not yet arrived.

"Eagle Control from Bravo 2. Two more flashes from inside the bedroom."

The last two photographs, Thornton thought. He could barely contain himself. Oran would be attaching them to a message and adding the grid reference. He believed he would be planning to send them just as Rachel's time was running out. At 4:10 a.m., he guessed. But all this was hypothetical. By then the house would have been stormed and his daughter rescued. That was the plan. They would stick to it.

Chapter 91

In the bedroom Oran sat in darkness. Rachel's golden locks had come away with ease. Practice makes perfect, he thought. He switched off the pump and extracted the cannula. He tethered the little girl's hands and feet, the scarlet ribbons tied loosely so they wouldn't hurt her. He placed her gently inside the cylinder. Her wheeze was more pronounced, high-pitched and whistling. He struggled with his conscience momentarily, resorting to thoughts of his darling Holly's fate to secure his resolve as he fastened the lid. It was 2:10 a.m. The knife sat glinting on the bed. He would send the text in a couple of hours. The grid reference would have Thornton scrambling crews and paramedics to the cottage. They would be too late.

Chapter 92

"Would you like a cup of coffee, sir?"

Thornton shook his head.

It was 2:25 a.m.

To the front of the house a large bush rustled as the officer stole from cover.

"Eagle Control from Bravo 3. I am in position at the front door."

The throat mike caught every word. The tiny camera fell soundlessly as it passed through the letterbox. The hall was almost pitch black, the lens sharpened.

In the control room they heard the sound of footsteps from the bedroom. Then a darkened figure appeared on a screen. The knife's keen blade caught whatever light there was. Oran disappeared into the kitchen.

Was this the opportunity they had waited for?

"What do you think, Mike? Shall we take him now?"

"No, sir, we must stick to the plan. He could cut her throat before the final hinge gets taken out."

The figure came out of the kitchen and returned to the bedroom. For a few minutes sight and sound were absent.

Oran sat by the bed. He heard a stirring in the cylinder. First a gentle nudge to one side and then to the other. Then a noise like a head being bumped.

Rachel had awakened.

Her eyes must have taken time to focus. Her senses a little more, until she realised she was bound and entombed. The darkness and claustrophobia caused her to panic.

In the operations room they heard her whimper. The rhythm of her breathing had changed and she was crying uncontrollably. The high-pitched whistle was replaced by a frantic gasping noise, as she struggled for breath. Her airway was closing.

Oran thought of her mother's account of the asthma attacks. He began to look frantically for the inhaler.

Inside the cylinder Rachel Thornton began to seize. Oran froze in alarm as the cylinder started to shake. What was happening? As he rushed to her side, the cylinder fell silent.

Had she arrested? Was she dead?

Hurrying, he released the locks and pulled her out. Her lips were starting to turn blue, her pallor ashen.

This wasn't the plan.

Time and again he had gone over it in the night with his darling Gemma. In his mind, she had been complicit. For although she was gone, her spirit was ever present. She was his conscience. But the atmosphere had changed. Rachel Thornton would not die like Holly had. Natural causes would take her. Gemma would not go along with that, for she had been kind and loving, and this wasn't fair, this wasn't equal.

He checked her airway and started the compressions. The girl was limp and lifeless.

It was not meant to end this way.

The heel of his hand pushed deeper and deeper, ribs almost cracking under the downward force. There was no response.

The sound of his exertions sent the ops room into action.

"She has gone into arrest! Send in Allen now! I am going down there," Thornton shouted as he sped through to door to his car.

In no time at all the crew was at the front door. The hinges disintegrated and the enforcer did the rest. The team followed the remnants of the sturdy door up the hallway, shouting as they went. Creating an unsettling disturbance. Moving with precision into every room. John Allen was headed for the back bedroom.

Chapter 93

Thornton's heart was pounding as he started his engine and veered out of the car park and onto the road. The drive would take fifteen minutes he calculated. In his hurry he had left behind his radio and iPhone. He silently cursed himself, what was happening? Was she alive? Was she safe? He dared not think of what he might find. The mountains were cloaked in cloud. He wondered if his life from this moment would be similarly shrouded. The moon wore a haggard look. He thought of Jayne tossing and turning, her waking with a start and fearing the worst. He turned left onto Sandbank Road. He sped past Yellow Water Picnic area. It was empty.

In front of him the torchlight circled. The officer was in the middle of the road. One laid in cover on a bank some metres away. He slowed and stopped. The sergeant recognised him immediately.

"Any word yet?"

"They have arrested Oran, sir. I am afraid there is no word on your daughter."

Thornton reached the cordon at the driveway. He passed between the rhododendrons and stopped beside the ambulance. Two paramedics were wheeling a stretcher from the house. The light was poor. He could just about pick out the blanket covering the feet, then the legs, then the torso. In that instant, which seemed to last forever, he feared the worst.

At last her tiny shaven head came into view. She wore an oxygen mask. The medic walked beside her. Thornton fell to his knees and thanked God, an entity rarely in his thoughts.

As the stretcher drew up beside him he rose, then stroked her brow and clutched her hand. Her eyelids flickered. The mask grew hazy as she whispered, "Daddy." Then her eyes closed with sheer exhaustion.

Tara Ritchie stood beside him.

"You forgot this, sir," she said, passing him his phone.

Thornton threw his arms around her. "Thank you, Tara, for all you have done today."

The phone was snatched up on the other end almost as quickly as he had dialled the number.

"We have her, Jayne! She's safe now. We are heading for the Ulster Hospital. I am sending a car for you."

The conversation ran to a couple of minutes, him fighting back tears, her not even trying to. Sister Patsy was weeping on Jayne's shoulder. Her mother and father sat speechless at the kitchen table. To bury their only grandchild would surely have finished them.

John Allen approached as Thornton hung up the phone.

"He was still doing compressions when we arrived, sir. The paramedic said his actions saved her life."

Chapter 94

Eamon Lynch appeared bearing a look of sheer relief.

"Oh, Mike, I can't tell you how happy I am. You did it. You got her back."

"No, Eamon, we all did it."

Once again the two aging coppers found themselves in each other's arms. A lot of water had passed under the bridge since their first embrace on a rugby pitch in 1993. In many ways they had passed through the gateway to middle age together. Now the big Donegal man would happily retire.

Barnett remained in the ops room, sensitive enough to realise that this was Mike Thornton's moment. Though admittedly he was delighted with the result and how he had met the challenge personally. He answered the phone.

"Great job," the Chief acknowledged. "I do not have to tell you how much was riding on this one."

Barnett knew precisely what this meant. The pending post of deputy appeared a little closer.

"Thank you, sir. It was a wonderful team effort. But it is a long uneven road to trial. Still much to do, sir."

"Then I will leave you to get on with it. Perhaps a few hours' sleep are in order? I am heading for the Ulster hospital. I have a word or two to say to Thornton."

Chapter 95

Oran stood handcuffed in an evidential suit and gloves in the hallway. Their eyes met for the first time in almost seven years.

Oran broke the silence.

"Detective Thornton, well, this is a surprise. You thought this one out for yourself for once? Pity you didn't manage it seven years ago when it was someone else's daughter's life on the line. All of this could have been avoided."

Thornton looked into the eyes of a deluded and broken man. He saw the weariness, the loneliness, the misery etched into Oran's weathered face. It was no wonder he was mad really; wrapped up in the painful memories of the past, Oran cared not what the future held. There was no escape planned, nothing planned beyond the death of Rachel it would seem. Except, perhaps, his own demise?

The anger that had gripped Thornton in the preceding hours had dissipated upon coming face to face with this man. He was a pitiful creature. And in the end he had saved Rachel. His daughter owed her life to her abductor. Thornton regretted what had happened to James Oran.

"Thank you for saving my daughter, James. I am so sorry I could not save yours."

A beefy constable led Oran to a waiting car.

Chapter 96

The Accident and Emergency Unit was busy as ever. A plain-clothed officer was reading the Daily Mail and trying to be discreet.

"You must be Mr Thornton?" a junior doctor enquired. "Your wife and daughter are in this room. She is coming round nicely."

Thornton eased open the door. The oxygen mask was absent. Rachel was peaceful. Jayne sat stroking her daughter's hand. There was no great scene of raw emotion. Not even a word was exchanged. Two pairs of tearful eyes said it all. He drew up a chair and placed an arm around her shoulders. He placed his left hand over his wife's. A drip fed the cannula in her right arm, the fluid topping up levels of water and electrolytes.

With his entry she stirred. She blinked. Her head turned towards them.

"Mummy? Where am I?"

Jayne could not control her quivering lip or the urge to hug and kiss the daughter that she had almost lost.

"Look at the time, Mike. Eighteen minutes past four. Three minutes after she was born."

And four minutes before Holly Oran had died, Thornton thought. The quirk of fate was not lost on him. He thought of Oran seven years ago. Struggling to keep his loving daughter alive. The symmetry was striking, the irony bittersweet.

Chapter 97

"Chief Constable, good to see you. Thank you for coming."

"It's the least I can do, Mike. How is Rachel?"

"She is recovering well, thank you, sir. They are moving her to a recovery room shortly. I can't tell you how relieved…"

The words stuck. His head lowered as he turned away, unwilling to show his emotions.

In a second, the chief was at his side, a welcome hand of reassurance upon his shoulder.

"Mike, I am pleased for you and Jayne. What a relief. You must be exhausted right now, but I want you to know that you did a fantastic job today, Mike."

Chief Constable Gary Webb was normally a man of few words. Coming from him, this meant a lot.

"If you don't mind I will head on now. The media are all over it. The press office needs a release as soon as possible. I have told them I would talk to you first. Is ten o'clock agreeable?"

"Thank you, sir. Ten o'clock would be great. I take it to be at headquarters?"

"Yes, Mike. I will tell ACC Barnett."

"He was fantastic to work with, sir. He never flinched."

"Nor did you, Mike, nor did you."

He was alone again. Words sprang to mind from his days of study.

'Victory has a hundred fathers, defeat is an orphan.' John Fitzgerald Kennedy, after the Cuban crisis of 1962. A proverb borrowed from Mussolini's son-in-law he believed. Another irony he thought.

Chapter 98

By ten a.m., the police headquarters were buzzing. Worldwide networks had picked up the story. Media and press crews from more than twenty countries were packed tightly into the briefing room.

Chief Constable Gary Webb was flanked by the Garda Commissioner, the opportunity to recognise the success of cross-border operations too good to miss. Mike Thornton was to the chief's right. Barnett to the commissioner's left.

Webb rose to address the audience.

"Ladies and gentlemen, thank you all for coming. This is a day to celebrate. The chief suspect is behind bars and three loving daughters are back in their parents' arms. I want to thank the commissioner for her constant support during the last few days. It was invaluable.

"I cannot begin to tell you how proud I am of the enquiry teams on both sides of the border. They never lost their focus or resolve. From the bottom of my heart I thank them all.

"My best wishes go to Garda Chief Superintendent Eamon Lynch who retires in just over a week."

He turned to face him.

"Eamon, I trust you and Kate will enjoy many more happy years together."

Bashfully, the big Gard acknowledged the Chief's kind recognition.

"This investigation took on a different light when one of our own found his daughter had been taken. ACC Barnett took charge of a most difficult and personal enquiry. He responded to the challenge magnificently. Thank you, Charles, for your diligent, hard work.

"To recover any child is a great feeling. When she is one of a valued colleague it is special. All too often the term is used inappropriately, but Mike Thornton is one of the old school. Long may we benefit from his canny and perceptive investigations."

He turned to Thornton.

"Mike, we have a surprise for you."

The techie made the connection and the screen came to life.

Rachel Thornton was sitting up in bed, the shaven head diminished by her beaming smile. Jayne was beside her. He could hardly believe how quickly she had recovered.

"Hi, Daddy. The doctor says if I am very good I can have a party in my room this afternoon. Mummy made a drizzle cake especially for you. She says that the people who helped get me back can come and have a piece of birthday cake. Will you be here, Daddy?"

"Nothing could keep me away, sweetheart. You better start practising your blow for all those candles. You have seven to put out this time. See you soon."

Seasoned hacks welled up with the rest.

Thornton stood.

"Chief Constable, Commissioner, ladies and gentlemen. This has been the most challenging time of my career. I cannot thank you enough for all your support.

"I have a few words for the media firstly. When Megan Reilly and Ailish MacParland were taken, you were asked not to speculate, make wild assertions or interfere with the families. That is what you did. It made our job more manageable. Thank you for that.

"When Rachel was taken, I had no right to have anything to do with the enquiry, but ACC Barnett saw it differently. Mr Barnett was superb, as were all the members of the team. Thank you, sir.

"Now you must excuse me, I have a pressing engagement that I simply cannot miss. I have a present to buy and a shower and shave that are long overdue. Thank you again."

The pressroom cleared quickly as Thornton left the room. Newsmen and women hurried off to work on catchy front-page headlines.

Thornton shook Charles Barnett's hand. It was not alone a gesture of gratitude, but also one of respect for a man who had not deserved to be underrated.

"Thank you, sir. From the bottom of my heart, thank you. I am sorry if I ever underestimated you."

Barnett smiled, convinced that he had gained a friend that day.

"Call me Charles, please, Mike."

"It will be my pleasure when off-duty and out for a well-earned pint. But at work, you will be sir or Mr Barnett. You heard what the Chief said. I am old school and anyway, more importantly, you have truly earned the right. Please join us at the party."

"That will be my pleasure."

Chapter 99

From headquarters to the Ulster Hospital would take ten minutes at most. As he passed Tullycarnet primary school his phone rang.

"Hi, Mike, can you speak? It's Tommy McConville here."

"Work away, Tommy, I am on hands free."

"I cannot tell you how happy I am for you. I can only imagine your relief."

"You above most would know that feeling Tommy. Rachel is recovering well. She is having a party in the ward in twenty minutes."

"That is great news. I have a little snippet for you, from my source in the office of the First and Deputy First Minister's. You can expect an invitation in the post. So can the Reilly's and MacParland's. Robinson and McGuinness are together on something for a change. I understand that my invite is also in the post. McGuinness wanted a likeminded republican at his side, someone who knows you well enough to keep the conversation going I imagine. He loves the story of your rescuing Nancy. She'll be there as well."

"It will be great to see you and Nancy again, Tommy. Catch up on old times. Will your own contribution to the investigation be off limits, Tommy?"

"Not for public consumption, Mike. But McGuinness has a long reach. He may know already. News travels to the ears of the well placed very quickly. There are also some good arse lickers who will not miss the opportunity to brown nose McGuinness and Adams. I must dash now; I have two grandchildren to pick up from school. They are only there because of you. See you at the 'House on the Hill'. Enjoy the party."

Thornton reversed into a space in the car park just as the conversation ended. He had just beaten the visiting-hour-jam.

He passed through the door. The volunteer receptionist greeted him at the desk and gave directions.

The room was off to the left in the children's ward. Rachel reached out to meet her father's embrace. He wished to give her the biggest squeeze ever but contained himself. Jayne threw her arms around his neck and kissed his cheek. He turned to meet her lips and let his linger there a while.

"Naughty, Daddy," teased the little girl, giggling.

By two thirty p.m., the walls were decked with party balloons and streamers. A colourful poster identified the room; 'Happy 7th Birthday Rachel'. The little girl had added her favourite characters, out of shape but instantly recognisable: Rapunzel, Olivia the pig, Atomic Betty and several Mr Men.

The cake appeared with seven burning candles. The welcome guests counted to three and Rachel Thornton blew like never before. One by one they went out, the last resisting almost until the end of her puff. Daddy added a timely waft and the room rang with applause. They toasted her with Shloer from plastic cups. Eileen Parks wiped a tear away. Tony Rogers did the same. Eamon Lynch took a 'selfie' with the birthday girl. Tara Ritchie squeezed in just in time. John Allen and Hazell Kennedy talked of holidays and well earned rests. Charles Barnett bathed in the happiness in which he had played a major part. He smiled then excused himself. Grainne

Burrows stayed away. This was not the time or place for echoes of intimate encounters from the past. She had made her excuses.

Mike and Jayne hugged their daughter, San Sebastian now firmly on their minds. Inter-connecting rooms at the Maria Cristina hotel, overlooking the Urumea River and Zurriola beach.

Chapter 100

For Tara Ritchie there was little rest. The following day came in quickly. The team sat patiently in a quiet briefing room at Antrim station.

She turned to DC Beth Chapman.

"How are you getting on with McCluskey?" she enquired.

"Not so well, ma'am. Mostly no comment answers and exaggerated yawns. He insists that he has been set up. He registered the vehicle some months ago. He is refusing to acknowledge the purpose of the void or tell us where it was added.

His neighbours saw it regularly in the driveway. We cannot connect him to the SIM card, and the telephone has not yet been recovered. Even if it is, we cannot prove he used it."

"What about the guide dog at the school and near Rachel Smyth's house?" Tara enquired.

"Nothing to do with him he insists, although his dog is called Sheba. We have spoken with the PPS. On the basis of what we have, it is unlikely they will let us charge him. At present, we have little else to put to him. His solicitor is getting restless, wondering when he will be released. I doubt we will be given an extension. We need something more compelling."

Ritchie spoke, "We need to know what Oran says. McCluskey can cool his heels for another few hours. I will speak to the solicitor and the custody sergeant. Have Oran brought to an interview room and contact Thornton. He will want to be involved."

Chapter 101

Tara Ritchie met Thornton in the custody suite.

"Good afternoon, sir. I trust Rachel and Jayne are well?"

"Both doing great, thank you, Tara. They are staying with Jayne's sister."

"Sir, we are holding McCluskey for another twelve hours. The PPS are not comfortable with us charging him. Nothing conclusive at the minute. Oran is in an interview room. He has refused the offer of a solicitor. The doctor said he is fit for interview. He insists that you are present."

The two officers entered the room and sat at the other side of the table and turned on the recorder. Oran was given his rights and cautioned. There was a second or two of silence.

Oran was first to speak. He looked to Thornton.

"Well, detective. I am sure you are feeling very pleased with yourself. I imagine quite a different feeling to that of seven years ago when you interviewed Ramsey. I do not intend to put the children and their parents through the stress of a prolonged trial. I will admit to my part in things here and now. But please do not press me about where the vehicle was worked on or any connections to anyone else who has been arrested. 'No comment' interviews must be so tedious. I do not wish to indulge in one. I will tell you everything I can now. Please permit me to finish without interruption."

Thornton nodded his assent.

"Some months after Gemma took her life, I was approached by a person who told me of a missed opportunity to arrest Ramsey and rescue my daughter. He said that you, detective Thornton, had discounted information revealed by a reliable source. You undoubtedly recall the sighting in Newcastle of a man fitting Ramsey's description just before Holly was taken. How could such a mistake fail to haunt any father?

"He said that the lead had been pointed out to you in the strongest terms and that you still ignored it. He said that if it were not for your dismissal of that sighting, Holly could have been saved. It was your sloppiness that cost my daughter her life. He told me how this had been buried; how you were still 'Mike Thornton', the legend that rescued the McConville girl from that car bomb, celebrated for saving her, and all the time this secret that you were to blame for Holly's death. You were respected; you had a career, a family. Imagine how I felt discovering that as my daughter lay dying, yours was born, a final, terrible irony.

"It was then that I planned to take Rachel. I decided to follow in Ramsey's footsteps. I didn't want to let you or anyone else forget my daughter's case. I despise that man but I knew imitating his crimes would create a couple of suspects at least. Undoubtedly I would have been among them, who after all lost more than I did?" Oran's eyes flashed momentarily in anger before he regained his composure and continued.

"So, I had to disappear. I'm sure you can appreciate, in this day and age, that took time and considerable planning.

"First off, I needed money to keep me going. The gambling sprees were merely a ruse. Croupiers rarely recall correctly how much anyone is spending at the tables; flashing a lot of cash and then making a fuss about using my credit card gave the impression I wanted. Over a long period I put away enough money to keep me going after I disappeared.

"Then I had to establish a new identity in the South. It really was quite straightforward. Six months before my disappearance I applied. All I needed was a copy of my birth certificate, my passport and a witness. The birth certificate took a while to perfect, but for an artist it's not such a difficult document to forge. I had befriended an elderly gentleman in Blackrock, where I rented a house. He acted as my witness before the Commissioner of Oaths, swore to my new identity, my new name, the only one he had ever known me by. The following week, I applied for an Irish passport under my new name, Sean Major. A bank account was opened once my passport arrived. I presented it to the RSA, along with two utility bills. My driving licence was last to arrive, and with its arrival, James Oran was ready to disappear forever.

"My departure was relatively straightforward. I had always been a competent sailor. I became very good indeed, what else did I have to occupy my time anymore? In the months before, I made sure I was noticed engaging in high adrenaline activities and going out to sea in treacherous conditions often against advice. People started to remark how detached I had become.

"I learnt about the currents and dangerous waters around Rathlin Island, how more than thirty percent of bodies were never recovered. On the day, the forecast was accurate. I loaded the boat with an additional dinghy. It was jet black and impossible to see in the dark. A wet suit and an oxygen tank completed the extra cargo.

"The wind was at force six and rising when I left Bangor Harbour. It was three p.m. The sail along the Antrim coast grew more perilous by the hour. It was one thirty a.m. when I rounded Fair Head. Air pressure was falling. The wind had increased to force ten. Gusts reached ninety miles an hour. I never faced a more angry sea, waves coming from different directions, rising steeply and crashing onto the deck. I could barely keep the boat's head into the wind. It took another two hours to reach the cover of Rathlin Island, just out far enough not to be spotted.

"I waited until the storm was at its height. I lodged a piece of my scalp in one of the cleats. A paring chisel had removed it under local anaesthetic some months before. I kept it frozen until it was needed. Next I ripped the life jacket to shreds and tangled it along with my sailing clothes in the rigging.

"At four a.m, the tide turned. I capsized the boat and jumped into the black dinghy. The other one was neatly stashed in the galley.

"There is a strong current that travels west of Ballycastle. It runs out near Corrymeela. I had tested it several times before my disappearance. It spat me out a short distance from the shore.

"I reached the beach about twenty to six in the morning. There was no one about. Fishing boats had taken shelter from the storm. Anglers chose a good morning to lie-in. My car was parked a short distance away with a change of clothes. I left it there the previous night. My Vespa scooter took me home.

"In time, I was able to make a healthy income selling paintings. But I was careful, starting at flea markets and car boot sales in West Cork and Connemara. I only came north to target the children and visit my family's graves. I never even left flowers or wreaths for fear of being discovered.

"I needed stooges to send the investigation in other directions. Elliot was my first choice. You remember he shared a cell with Ramsey whilst on remand. He had an axe to grind too with you, Mr Thornton, and a dark secret from the past. I knew you would latch onto him.

"He was easy to locate. On the day of his release I followed him home. For months, I plotted his movements. His associates are a dubious bunch indeed. Their photographs are at my home in Blackrock. They may form the basis of another enquiry.

"His holiday in Buncrana in July was a stroke of luck. Close enough to arouse suspicion when Megan Reilly was taken. Someone kept an eye on the cottage for me. Private detectives are two a penny these days. As the Garda Siochona's National Surveillance Unit watched the house, my snoop looked on. Something you might share with them some time.

"McCluskey was an even more obvious choice. He hates you with an unrelenting passion, blames you entirely for his demise. Some things we share in common, McCluskey and I. Abandoned by our mothers, years spent in children's homes, wives and children lost forever, albeit in entirely different circumstances. He was my perfect double.

"The children were easy, just a systematic elimination, time consuming, but not difficult. The guide dog was an inspired idea though. Who would ever suspect such a ploy? Teachers and children flocked to meet my lovely Sheba, named after McCluskey's Lab, inviting her into the playground. She is in a boarding kennel on the hills overlooking Blackrock Bay. Please find her a good home, detective, I will miss her dearly.

"The void in the camper van was another masterstroke, don't you think? I knew that the absence of such a hiding place had been Ramsey's downfall. That's about it, really. I confess.

Now, is there any chance of a cup of coffee; Columbian dark roast, if you have some?"

Thornton paused for a moment.

"Very enlightening James. The photographs of Elliot's activities will be most useful. Thank you for that."

He switched off the recorder.

"Tara, can you send out for some of Mr Oran's particular fancy? There is a point I wish to clarify in private. Please do not feel offended."

Tara left the room without a word.

"The person who told you of the sighting, James. I am sure I know who it is. But his account was less than accurate.

"Given how thorough your plan was, I am disappointed you did not check up on his story. You seem to have covered almost everything else, James, but perhaps you needed someone to be angry with? Someone to blame for your terrible loss?

"The sighting was one of sixty-three which we received within eight hours of the press release. The release gave a detailed description of the suspect, though maybe you already know that? We received calls from all over Ireland. At the time, we had no direction of travel or reliable intelligence to guide the enquiry. It was simply impossible to follow up on the calls. We narrowed the catchment, starting with those received within a fifty-mile radius and working out. Even that proved fruitless.

"The source you mentioned was discounted early, true, but he had not been used by the department for some time. In fact he had been removed from the source register some months before. His information had become wholly unreliable. I cannot go into details, but needless to say he was itching to get back on the payroll. His liking for crack cocaine far outstripped his unemployment benefits. Given what happened next, it seems the source may have been telling the truth in this instance. However, he had fed false intelligence to his handlers before, information that led them into dangerous scenarios, all so he could score some crack. It is true that Mr McCluskey brought it to my attention, but as one of many possible credible sightings.

"Did your source tell you any of this, James, or was it conveniently left out? Mistakes were made, they always are, but the case underwent a review. I was exonerated, though I assure you it is no comfort when faced with three dead children, even after seven years. I will never forget Holly.

"I have a copy of the report with me. I think you should read it."

Oran had become uncomfortable. Any indication of smugness had disappeared, leaving only uncertainty. Suddenly the coffee did not taste so good.

He read quickly, settling on the salient points, reading them again and again. Three sentences told him everything:

'We must balance the benefits of national press releases with the practicality of following up on the public's response. In terms of this enquiry it would have been impossible to investigate every sighting in the race against time. The sighting in Newcastle from former informant 'F' could not have been given credibility, bearing in mind his previous unreliability and drug addiction.'

He slid the folder across the table and sat thinking in silence. The hush was almost unbearable. Thornton resisted the temptation to speak. Two minutes passed and then,

"Mr Thornton this puts a very different light on matters."

Oran paused briefly again, considering the consequences of what he was about to say. Thornton indicated the tape recorder, and Oran nodded in agreement to begin the recording again.

"It appears that I have been rather cruelly manipulated, with terrible consequences. That does not rest easily with me at all. I had planned to take the secret of my accomplice's involvement to my grave, but I have reconsidered. Too many people have suffered because of his lies.

"I imagine Jimmy McCluskey is rather smug at the moment, expecting to be released without charge in a couple of hours. You have lots of circumstantial evidence, but not enough to indict him. I suspect the PPS has already confirmed this?"

Thornton nodded as Oran continued.

"McCluskey got in touch with me shortly after his release from prison. He knew about my wife's suicide and my admittance to a care facility following a severe bout of depression. I was in recovery when he called. He blamed you for Holly's death. He said that you failed to react to reliable intelligence. He said that he argued with you about it. He told me the informant was dependable, a man on the headquarters' register. He brought me proof of the reported sighting and told me it had been covered up; the police didn't want to admit the fault of one of their own, it would have been an embarrassment. And saving embarrassment was more important to the department than the truth, he said.

"I mulled over the information for a week or two. My pain was lessened as I came to focus on my hunger for justice. Punishing you gave me a reason to live. I contacted him. Over the next few months I put the plan together. I told McCluskey only what was required of him at any particular time. Mostly he just sat and listened, poor analytical skills and limited imagination in my opinion. I could see why he had been overlooked for promotion. He rattled on about it incessantly. I imagine you had him under surveillance shortly after I instructed him to drive through Newcastle early that morning.

"The Kingdom of Mourne is a tightly knit community. I presumed his presence on Moneyscalp Road was quickly noted.

"He received two calls from me. The first was on the night before he arrived, directing him through Newcastle. The second, when he left forty-one Moneyscalp Road, directing him to the Smyth's holiday let. It was only then that I told him his final destination – the cottage on Tullybrannigan Road. You should remember it from the original enquiry, Mr Thornton, the place where I spent so many happy times as a child with Bob and Sally and later with Gemma and Holly.

"By now you must know the contents of the SIM, two incoming calls but only one number, my number 07985669748. It was my pay-as-you-go, the one your search team will have found at Newtown Road. I suspect he will deny this and there will be no prints or DNA on the SIM.

"However, I taped the conversations. In fact, I taped all our encounters. I also kept a diary of our meetings. I can be a bit OCD. I find it difficult trusting people.

"You will find them in a hide at the rear of the cottage on Newtown Road. It is in the woodland just behind the fourth post from the left edge of the fence. I placed them there just in case. I never really liked him. He had a chip on each shoulder, a loathing of you and a repulsive desire for young girls. He denied it in the beginning, said it was an excuse to fire him because he wouldn't drop the reported sighting of Ramsey, but I knew. I just wish I had seen through all of his lies."

He turned off the tape.

Thornton sent for Tara Ritchie to scramble a search team. They would be at the house in an hour.

The two men sat in silence. There was little more to be said. For the first time Thornton felt empathy for Oran, sorrow even. A few hours ago he too had been on the brink of intolerable grief. Heaven only knows how he would have responded, or how it would have affected his relationship with Jayne. Would it have provoked another bout of depression in her? One from which she may never have recovered?

"James, there is one thing left that I have to know, did you know that we were onto you?" Thornton asked.

Oran lifted his head. He bore a self-satisfied expression. One reserved for that rare breed of perfectionists.

"Police magazines are so revealing these days, Mr Thornton; Police Beat, particularly so. Good work should always be recognised and publicised. Tara Ritchie looked so well the day she received an award from the chief constable. It must be six months ago now. She had dismantled a Hate Crime ring in South Belfast as I recall, a gang of fringe paramilitaries not worth a shit. I was tempted to take her when she arrived with the towels. But her capture could have been difficult. I can't imagine she would not have fought back. That was a calculated risk on your part. I liked your thinking. Anyway, it was not part of the plan.

"Nor was your daughter's seizure, Mr Thornton."

Oran became a little agitated.

"There would have been no symmetry, no satisfaction in her dying like that. I had intended an unforgettable finish to it all. The specifics I will take to my grave. For Rachel's sake, I am glad we never got there. I trust what I told you just now will remain between us, Mike. I am sure DI Ritchie would hate to think she nearly put everything at risk. Now, if you don't mind, I will have a lie down before I make my statement. Inform McCluskey that he will pay heavily for his lies, and please tell Rachel and Jayne I am sorry."

"I will, James."

Thornton left the room and came face to face with Eileen Parks. Together they walked along the corridor.

"You did well, Mike."

Thornton stopped, "I still don't think I understand, why he tried to revive her, I mean. Did he want to resuscitate her just to prolong her torture?"

Parks looked at him sympathetically and considered her answer for a moment.

"I was watching the interview; you heard what he said about the 'symmetry'? He wanted you to experience precisely what he had. He was a mathematician once upon a time, remember? There is logic to all of this, however twisted. It is like an attempt to balance the scales, to complete an equation in which you finally experienced what he did seven years ago."

"Logic?" Thornton raised his eyebrows in surprise and stepped in front of Parks, blocking her path.

"As much as someone driven mad can be said to be logical, Mike. He is sick, what he did was inexcusable, but it made sense to him.

"Rachel's seizure on the other hand, was unplanned, an anomaly. I think the way he saw it, if he left her, intact and alive in that cylinder, he wouldn't be to blame. If you were too late, if you didn't find her in time, it would all be your fault. You would have to live or die with the knowledge that you could have saved her, if only you had unravelled the clues in time. If she died whilst in his care, if he let her die of that seizure, it would have been his fault. That's why he revived her, Mike.

"You have to understand that he never planned to kill Rachel himself; he didn't consider leaving her in that canister to be equivalent to murdering her. By recreating Holly's death, using Ramsey's methods, he made it about you letting her die, you failing her, like you failed Holly.

"Like he failed Holly.

"You must remember from the original enquiry that he had missed the description of Ramsey released in the press conference before Holly was taken? Can you imagine the guilt; the incredible pain of knowing that if only he had recognised Ramsey, he could have protected his family? It would be unbearable.

"McCluskey changed things for him; he gave Oran purpose, a wrong to be righted, a truth to be revealed, justice to be served. Mike, don't underestimate the relief Oran would have felt, finally having someone else to blame. All that loathing and anger that had been directed inward could finally be deflected, the burden of his guilt shared.

"McCluskey made him believe you were to blame for Holly's death, and that you had escaped the blame, shrugged off the guilt, and he wanted to make it impossible for you to do that this time around.

"It wasn't ever really Rachel that he wanted to hurt, it was you."

Chapter 102

Tara Ritchie chose Detective Constables Brian Black and Kate Daly to record Oran's statement, a fitting thank you for two officers approaching retirement.

The mood in interview room two had changed. No longer was McCluskey reclined with his feet crossed and hands clasped behind his head like a holiday maker; instead his eyes were trained on the recorder and diary which had been strategically placed in front of him. As the tape played, each incriminating utterance sent another bead of sweat ambling down his furrowing brow. He tapped the table nervously.

For the most part it was a 'no comment' interview. No words were needed. The tapes said it all.

It was 6:10 p.m. when Brian Black and Kate Daly entered with joyful vigour. They held the tape in the air triumphantly, and the team knew the significance of the gesture. There was cheering and whooping. Tara Ritchie called John Allen.

"We got them, John! We got them both."

In Lisnasharragh, cans of lager hissed as their vacuum seals were broken. Allen saluted his guys and girls. They cheered their boss and showered him with a fair amount of beer.

Thornton arrived at seven thirty p.m. The box clinked as he set it on the table. Tony Rogers did the honours, popping the first cork indelicately, letting the froth erupt. ACC Barnett was last to arrive. The applause could not have been warmer or more richly deserved. He blushed and thanked them.

"Here you are, Charles," Thornton urged, offering a glass.

"Glad you remembered my name, Mike."

"Only when off-duty, Charles." Thornton winked.

The room quietened as Barnett tapped his glass.

"Ladies and gentleman, this has been an outstanding investigation. I thank all of you for your determined effort. You must excuse me as I single out one officer on whom the pressure must have been intense. Let us all raise a glass to your wonderful leader Detective Chief Superintendent Mike Thornton." The room erupted and Thornton accepted the congratulations bashfully.

He spoke for a couple of minutes, thanking each of them individually. Then he joked about the pending retirements, advising Brian Black to join Tony Rogers and take the bad look off him at Pilates classes. He encouraged Kate Daly to keep an eye on each of them. He thanked Barry Mulligan for toasting him in bubbly, reassuring him of the presence of a bottle of 'Bush' in the bottom drawer. He hailed Beth Chapman's sense of dress and pleaded with her to offer Steve Buckley some badly needed advice. He jibed Shauna McCrea and Tom Donnelly about their attention to detail and noted they were spending more off-duty time together. This raised a tongue-in-cheek whoop. He praised Tara Ritchie's tenacity, emphasising how well he had done to recruit her. Then ridiculed her insipid coffee, made palatable only by the presence of McVitie's chocolate digestives. He insisted that Columbian dark roast was to be the order of the day from now.

Then his sentiments changed.

"Tonight my daughter will be cuddled up beside her mother. She will be safe and she will be happy. Words can simply not describe how grateful I feel."

He thanked them and excused himself. Tonight he was on bedtime story duty, *The Little Mermaid*, as he recalled. He looked forward to it as never before.

Chapter 103

The next ten days rushed in like a spring tide. The defendants appeared in front of a district judge in Londonderry. McCluskey's bail application was rejected. Oran had not sought to waste the court's time with such a submission.

The team worked earnestly, chasing up statements and exhibits. Cross-border investigations added complications. The hearing would be in Belfast, but that was some way off. The men would be tried together.

Eamon Lynch was making sure that the Garda side of the enquiry was swift and accurate. Nothing was going to stop him from retiring on a high: all statements and exhibits were to be inspected personally on the twenty-fourth, the day of his retirement – no 'ifs' or 'buts' or 'maybes'. He was not disappointed.

In Belfast, Tara Ritchie was left to get on with it. Tony Rogers was superb, bringing every element together and helping to refocus those who let their concentration wander, reminding them all of the Turnbull Guidelines on identification, essential when operating in restricted light.

Lunch at Stormont was full of joy. The first and deputy-first ministers met the families at one p.m. The table overlooked the impressive stretch of lawns and trees. Edward Carson's statue stood, still urging people on. Perhaps soon, both sides of the community could respond to his appeal, seeking a pathway to a brighter future under a new regime.

The MacParlands spoke excitedly about their eagerly awaited holiday in Ibiza in August. The Reillys were equally enthused talking about their trip to Menorca around the same time. Portsalon had been placed on the backburner for now.

Thornton had booked adjoining rooms in San Sebastian, overlooking the beach. There was now an extra consideration however. An addition to the family's canine collection: a three-year-old black Lab called Sheba for Bella to play with.

Oran had asked for a loving home for her. Thornton felt obliged. He knew that in his daughter's hour of greatest need, regardless of what he had planned to do with her after, Oran had saved her. Whether what Oran had done was for himself, to evade guilt, or for Rachel, out of empathy for a frightened child, or for Thornton, to enable the plan to unfold as intended, Thornton could never be sure. But he was grateful nonetheless. As far as Rachel was concerned Sheba was just another rescue dog like Bella, who needed a good home. She settled in immediately, her tail wagged delightedly as she and Bella played endlessly with Rachel in the garden. At night they lay by Rachel's bedside, each raising a quizzical eyebrow when the door creaked open. Checking out the caller, eyes closing only when both were happy all was well.

Tommy McConville was taking a cottage in Connemara in August. Three generations would share the splendour of a comfortable retreat looking out towards the twelve 'Bens'. He, Nancy and the twins would climb Ben Corr and post 'selfies' from the summit overlooking Lough Inagh. Three days would be spent at the Connemara Pony Festival, another fishing from Cleggan harbour. The rest of the week would be spent doing very little.

By the range in the kitchen at night, his father would play the fiddle. Mother would accompany on the boron. The twins would sing 'Let it go', an anthem it seemed for the present generation, whilst Nancy would tackle 'The Sally Gardens'. He would bring tears to every eye with Phil Coulter's 'The Old Man' and wipe them away with 'The Irish Rover.' In that final song they would all join him.

The two ministers were coy about their holiday arrangements, but good fun nonetheless. Except for the little girls' shaven heads it was just like any other celebration.

Chapter 104

James Elliott lived in a quiet cul-de-sac in Whiteabbey, six miles from Belfast. Unbeknownst to him, his house was visited two nights previously. At the time he was in a country cottage near Castlewellan with three other well-known sex offenders. Their every move was followed and every conversation recorded.

At his home, devices were placed discreetly. He never spotted the minute difference in the Sky control nor did he sense his Dire Straits CD was anything other the recordings of his favourite band. Both provided exceptional tone and quality for the scientific support officers, listening in. It was clear he had never changed his ways, possibly he had gotten a little smarter, but not smart enough. His arrest was planned for the end of the week. The evidence was compelling. He was out on licence. This time the judge would not be so lenient.

Chapter 105

Eamon Lynch gathered up the remnants of his illustrious career. There was no fuss on the day he left the station, just as he had wanted. The calls from the Commissioner and Assistant Commissioner Larkin had been most welcome.

The cardboard box bulged under the weight of long gathered trinkets. He placed his Scott Gold Medal on top. Then he reached for the burnished metal box, wherein lay the reminders of his darkest times. He did not need to lift the lid. He knew precisely what it contained, the scribbled letter from the mother of a dead junkie, the photograph of his hanging nephew, Ramsey's taunting note and the photographs of little Emma Baillie.

He called for Brenda Hughes.

"Brenda, please take this box and burn the contents. I would prefer if they remained private."

As he headed out of the door for the last time, Eamon Lynch was looking to a future enriched by the past, not saddened by it. The memories in that box were to be left behind. His duty now over, Lynch wanted only the memories to be treasured: the marvellous times spent with wonderful colleagues throughout the length and breadth of his great country.

He hugged Brenda and wished her well.

"Look after the new boss just as well. Rosie Trainer will be a breath of fresh air. She is going places, tipped for top job someday. You will enjoy working with her, I'm sure of it.

"And don't forget the party is at eight p.m., Brenda. Kate is longing to see you again. I trust you will be showing off the handsome solicitor from O'Hara and Sons."

She smiled, "I will, sir."

"Brenda, as of twenty minutes ago I became just a plain civilian citizen of Letterkenny, County Donegal. It really is quite liberating. Please call me Eamon."

"All in good time, Mr Lynch, all in good time."

He backed out of his parking space for the last time and headed for the open road. A new chapter in his life was just around the next corner.

Chapter 106

Senior Prison Officer Stephen Yates had a gambling problem, a fact not commonly known within the service. He was fond of a drink as well, a fact more commonly known. James Oran had met him at the Dirty Duck alehouse in Holywood some years ago, just before Gemma died. He worked in Magilligan Prison, looking after the paedophiles and the perverts. He had been on watch when Ramsey committed suicide. The enquiry had his arsehole puckering for weeks.

He was a vulnerable man. Gamblers with a drink problem generally are. The loans at first were trifling amounts. Paid back within a week or two. But Oran was not his only creditor. The infamous Davy Rock was much less patient. An intolerant being who charged huge rates of interest and despised overdue advances. Outstanding debts were regularly met with broken bones and trips to the hospital. Yates was in the shit, twelve thousand pounds of it. The following night was the deadline Oran agreed to pay.

He had taped the transaction as he handed over the money. At a more convenient time, he played it back to Yates. The thought of redundancy turned him pale. In the service, deals with loan sharks were not tolerated. It left one susceptible to bribery and blackmail. He knew he would be out. The threat of exposure had hung over him ever since, the pressure of its existence reducing with time, until ten days ago, when Oran had walked onto the landing.

In the prison cell, the conversation had been short and to the point. A timed phone message was all that Oran requested. Set up the day before it was sent. By the time the message went down the phone, he would be well beyond the Governor's reach.

Yates would be off the hook for good, the recording to be disposed of as he wished and twenty thousand pounds waiting for collection in a railway station locker. The phone destroyed as soon as its message was sent.

With Davy Rock breathing down his neck again, Yates had little choice.

Chapter 107

Eamon and Kate Lynch were wonderful hosts. The theme was Hawaiian Nights. Men in extreme Hawaiian shirts over calf-length gabardine pants, finished off with flip-flops, were rivalled by women in brightly printed dresses or grass skirts with headscarves. Each guest was presented with a garland of plumerias, carnations and orchids as they arrived.

The music was truly Hawaiian, a medley of The Beamer Brothers, Keali Reichel and a female duo called Keahiwai. The punch was laced with Koloa Rum. A splash of pineapple juice masked its potency. The guests' overindulgence would make the limbo dancing interesting just before midnight.

"Thank you for coming, Mike, Jayne, it means a lot. I love the grass skirt, Jayne."

"We wouldn't have missed it for the world, Eamon," she said, kissing his cheek.

Frank Keenan looked just as ridiculous as everyone else as he strode smiling towards them.

Grainne Burrows was dressed to kill as usual. The new diamond ring sparkled on her finger. It seemed that Brian O'Grady was to do the decent thing.

She and Jayne were just feet away. An encounter was inevitable.

"Hi, Jayne, I am so pleased Rachel is back with you."

Grainne smiled tentatively. She knew the hurt that she had caused and that Jayne had no reason to forgive her. But it was nine years since Jayne had accepted Mike's humble plea and she felt it was time to leave the indiscretion in the past. She returned her smile and shook hands with Grainne graciously.

In the kitchen, the guys argued about both forces' finest rugby players.

In the garden the girls wiped the floor with the guys at limbo dancing. The guys tried to make up lost ground with songs. O'Grady gave them 'Gentle Annie', preceded by Kavanagh's poem 'Raglan Road'. He returned Grainne's smile as they both recalled that Sunday in South Dublin last autumn.

Thornton responded with 'Carrickfergus' and Lynch followed with 'Spancil Hill'. The party mood would take them until dawn at least.

Chapter 108

The cell was bleak and barren. Oran signed the last of the three letters and sealed the envelopes. He anticipated their delivery; it was his only way of saying sorry. He picked at the stitching on the waistband of his boxer shorts. It was time consuming, but then he had plenty to spare.

Finally, he plucked the scarlet ribbon from the cotton lining. He was tired and lonely. As he had told Thornton, he would spare the family the strain of a trial.

He thought of Gemma and Holly. He had loved them to distraction. The pain of their departures was no longer bearable.

He propped the bed frame against the door and fastened an anchor hitch, fashioned from the red ribbon, to a leg. The constriction was uncomfortable at first but he got used to it. The images of his loving family were growing stronger as his message caused Thornton's phone to twitch.

The ten-figure grid reference appeared first. Thornton did not have to ask the place to which it referred. He understood now the way that Oran's mind worked. He excused himself from the party momentarily and retired to the garden to be alone with the message. It contained expressions of deepening sorrow and regret. He wished Thornton's family well, and thanked him for adopting Sheba.

Thornton toyed with calling the prison immediately, sending officers scampering to Oran's rescue. But was this really what he wanted? Had James Oran not suffered long enough? It was 4:22 a.m. precisely.

Thornton would wait ten minutes or so. It was his bequest to a contrite and broken man. The phone settled in his pocket as he rejoined the party. He rushed towards Jayne and exchanged a loving embrace.

Chapter 109

Darkness was settling on Oran's fleeting life. His breathing was waning, his consciousness weakening. He thought of Mrs Crombie's kindness at the home, of Bob and Sally who changed his life. Then of Gemma, on the beach that day in July, of the trip to the Copeland Island, of their wedding day and finally Holly's arrival into their lives. Suddenly they were with him, blurred images at first but sharpening with every fleeting second. They were smiling, getting closer as his life ebbed away. Gemma and Holly were reaching out to rescue him.

The illusory strains of 'Gabriel's Oboe' were playing. Bob and Sally were beside them now, ageless and smiling as they had been at the children's home thirty years ago. As he breathed his last he felt the sum of their collective embrace. In his final moments he wondered if this was merely the cruel fancy of a dying man. But he had hope; hope that they were waiting patiently for him on the other side, ready to be reunited. This was his abiding wish. He prayed that God would be forgiving.

Thornton made the call.